RIVERSNOW

TESS THOMPSON

United States, 2017

This book is dedicated to my clever and courageous mother-in-law, Joci Kerr, who made and raised an amazing man.

PROLOGUE

1996

THE HALLWAY OF SAINT ANN CATHOLIC SCHOOL smelled of floor polish and hair spray. Clusters of girls in white shirts and plaid skirts huddled together near lockers, their chatter a collective rumble marked with an occasional high-pitched shriek. Outside the windows, the first snowfall of the year shed fat flakes. Genevieve Banks checked her appearance in her compact mirror. Big eyes, the color of dark tea and fringed with dark lashes, stared back at her. Her mother didn't allow her to wear makeup, other than a little mascara and lip gloss. Her small bust seemed completely disinclined to grow. Her unfortunate figure, described by tactless adults as a string bean, made her look like a little girl, whereas some of her schoolmates looked like young women. Apparently, prayers about waking to a bigger chest weren't heeded by God.

The bell for sixth period buzzed. She hated to be late to anything, especially Sister Maria's class. The tiny nun scared her. Gennie grabbed her books and zigzagged through girls on her way to Sister Maria's class. She slid into her usual seat in the front row, gaze directed at the door. *Where is Margaret?* If she didn't show soon, she'd be late, and Sister Maria would send her to the office after school for punishment, which, if the rumors were true, involved a ruler and the palm of one's hand. Gennie wouldn't know. She'd never gotten into trouble. The girls who had didn't speak of it.

Around her, girls opened books and settled into creaking chairs, the scent of their hairspray mingling with the particles of chalk floating from Sister Maria's furious writing on the board. As the final bell rang, a breathless Margaret slid into the seat next to her, crossed her feet at the ankles, and grinned at Gennie. Margaret had a secret. A boy. After school for the past week, she'd kissed him behind the statue of Colonel Murphy in the park. Yesterday she'd let him feel under her bra.

Gennie had shivered when Margaret had told her. They were only fifteen. Kissing a smelly boy was the last thing Gennie wanted. Margaret, though? She ran wild. *This Catholic stuff's for idiots,* she'd said.

"Good afternoon, girls," Sister Maria said.

"Good afternoon, Sister Maria," chimed the girls in unison.

Gennie tugged on her long socks to cover a patch of dry skin just under her knee. They all hated the scratchy wool socks that made their feet perspire inside their black loafers.

"First, some announcements." Sister Maria stood behind her desk, hands folded in front of her round middle, plump cheeks blazing pink. "Congratulations to Gennie Banks for winning the Wisconsin state essay contest."

What did she say? I won? She'd known the odds were against her going into the contest, but she'd decided to write what she knew and felt strongly about—her mother.

The assignment had been to write about leadership. *What qualities make a leader? What person in your life has demonstrated admirable leadership?*

She'd gone against the advice of Sister Maria to profile Sister Isabel, the school's principal, and had written about her mother instead. Widowed when Gennie was ten, her mother had the responsibilities of single parenthood and a full-time managerial position at their local bank. Having sat under her mother's desk while she worked, Gennie had observed how fair she was to her team, treating all as if they had a worthy contribution, no matter their position, from the janitors to the tellers to the loan officers.

"Yes, Gennie, I just got the news. Isn't that something, girls?"

"Yes, Sister Maria," they chimed in unison.

"The prize is spending an afternoon with Senator Rick Murphy." Sister Maria smiled, deep dimples appearing on both sides of her mouth, which made her seem less like a nun and more like a peer.

When she'd arrived last year to teach English and history, the rumor had gone around that she'd been married before becoming a nun. "We'll expect an article about him for the school paper, Gennie."

"Sure. I'd love to," Gennie said.

Margaret rolled her eyes and pretended to shudder. She hated writing.

"Did you have something to share with the class, Margaret?" Sister Maria asked.

"No, Sister," Margaret said.

"Now, open your books, so we can discuss your reading assignment from last night," Sister Maria said.

Gennie opened her English book to the Hemingway story *Hills Like White Elephants*. She'd read it last night but hadn't understood how the precise sentences unfolded into a plot of any kind. There was no story. Two people waited for a train. They drank beer. They disagreed about a decision, but for the life of her, she couldn't fathom what.

"Who knows the origin of the expression 'elephant in the room?'" Sister Maria asked.

Gennie had no idea. She should have looked it up last night. *Why didn't I think of that?* Sister Maria always asked questions that Gennie was incapable of discerning before class.

"Yes, Rosemary?" Sister Maria asked.

"Elephant in the room: that which is there, but not acknowledged," Rosemary said.

"Correct," Sister Maria said.

"And *white elephant* means something no one wants," Rosemary said.

Rosemary. She always knows the answers to everything. Rosemary the know-it-all. She probably knows what this silly story was about too.

Sister Maria crossed the room, her heels clicking on the wood floor, and closed the door. The room fell quieter as if the girls were all holding their breaths. She perched on the edge of the desk, smoothing her skirt. The Sisters wore regular clothes at St. Ann. No habits or robes like in the movies. Sister Maria wore long skirts and turtleneck sweaters. "I'm going to tell you something that cannot go out of this room."

The girls leaned forward in their seats. All but Margaret. She pretended not to care, doodling in her notebook.

"I'm not supposed to teach this story," Sister Maria said.

In her peripheral vision, Gennie saw Margaret's head jerk up. The clandestine had interested Margaret since her father had left her mother for a local barmaid. Since then, she'd been suspicious of everyone. *Everyone has a secret, Gennie.*

"Why?" Margaret asked. "Because it's about abortion?"

Several of the girls gasped. All thoughts of the contest evaporated from Gennie's mind. *Abortion? That's what the story is about?* Her heart beat fast in her chest, and her hands went numb as she waited for Sister Maria to continue.

"That's correct, Margaret. I take it you actually read this story?"

"It was short." Margaret shrugged. "Plus, the dude uses the shortest sentences ever. What's up with that?"

In a voice just above a whisper, Sister Maria said, "Girls, I struggle with certain sins. My love of Hemingway is one of them. God gave him a great gift."

"Not really," Margaret said under her breath.

If she'd heard, Sister Maria ignored Margaret. "His writing is *from* God, but not *of* God." Gennie smiled behind her hand, amused. This was surely a subtle difference. It was as if Hemingway were a forbidden fruit Sister Maria could not resist, even though she believed it would poison her. "I admire him. He created art, but we mustn't forget his ways—the drinking and suicide, the disregard for tradition." Sister Maria's eyes shone brightly in the dim room. "All that said, even though it's forbidden to teach this story, I'm compelled to do so."

"Why?" Margaret asked without raising her hand.

"It's a conversation we must have, and this story is a way for me to have it with you. The woman in the story does not want to do it. Do you all agree with that statement?"

No one, not even Rosemary, answered. Gennie had no idea, still reeling from the knowledge the story was about an abortion.

"It's a sin to kill a human life, no matter how small. This, girls, you must remember. Outside of these walls, you will hear differing opinions, but I want you to think about your own life. What if someone had decided to dispose of you? Think of it. No *you* in this world."

Gennie glanced over at Margaret. She stared down at the desk, a lone teardrop rolling down her cheek. *What is wrong?*

"That's all I'm going to say about this subject, but I hope in the years to come you will all remember this lesson. Do not put yourself in a position where you ever have to make a choice like this one. Do you understand?"

"Yes, Sister Maria."

"Excellent. Then we will talk no more of this distasteful subject."

* *

Later, Gennie walked home from school with her backpack slung over her shoulders, warm in her long, down jacket, thick gloves, and snow boots. She never walked to and from home in her loafers this time of year; they were left behind in lockers, their duty done for the day. A white powdering covered the sidewalks, but the snow had stopped, leaving a dense cloud layer swollen with unshed flakes. Margaret sidled up beside her.

"Hey," Margaret said.

"Hey."

Both their mothers worked and didn't arrive home until dinnertime. When Gennie had turned thirteen, her mom had decided she was old enough to stay home alone. Gennie liked the freedom and not having to ride the bus to her mother's work, but sometimes she missed the time with her mom, especially the drive home when they would listen to music or chat about their day.

Since then, she and Margaret had often spent the afternoon together doing homework. That is, until lately. *The boy* had ruined their homework schedule. "No park?"

"Not today."

Margaret had been quiet since English class. Gennie knew better than to press. Her best friend shut up tight if you asked too many questions. Since her parents' divorce, Margaret hadn't shared her feelings. Gennie wanted the old Margaret back. This new Margaret was hard and almost cold. Regardless, Gennie would never desert her. They'd been friends since they were first graders at St. Ann.

They passed the hardware store and waited on the corner for the light to change.

"Do you ever think the world would be better if you were never born?" Margaret asked.

Gennie glanced over at her, a flutter of shock in her chest. "I've never thought about it."

The light changed. They crossed the street.

Stopping in front of the candy store, they peered at the display of truffles in the window. Mrs. Wilson, the shopkeeper, waved to them but did not invite them inside to try samples as she was helping a customer. "No samples for us today," Margaret said.

"Maybe tomorrow," Gennie said.

With reluctance, they walked away from the window and continued down the street. "My parents got married because they were pregnant with me." Margaret spoke in a soft voice instead of the sassy tone she'd used so often lately. "I heard them arguing about it when he left. He said he would never have married her if it hadn't been for me."

Gennie wriggled her fingers inside her gloves, unsure what to say, as anger on Margaret's behalf surged through her. It was bad enough that he had left without explanation, but to add cruel words on his way out the door? There was no way to explain his words away or make them better than they were. Margaret's mother was kind but deflated, like a balloon a week after a birthday party, whereas her father remained buoyant. Underneath his charisma lurked a streak of cruelty.

Margaret slowed her pace. "Today, in class, I thought about how much better it would be if they'd had an abortion." Gennie strained to hear Margaret over the roar of a passing car in need of a muffler. The driver shifted gears and sped up, spraying muddy water on the sidewalk a hundred yards in front of them. "Then, my mother could have married someone else. Someone who loved her."

A wave of sadness swept over Gennie as she imagined her world without Margaret.

"Margaret Louisa, I would be lost if you weren't here. Think if I was alone at St. Ann without you. I'd probably be best friends with Rosemary." They giggled.

Gennie halted and grabbed her friend into an embrace. "Don't think these awful thoughts ever again. I need you here with me."

Margaret rested her head upon Gennie's shoulder. "It's hard to be a person sometimes."

"I know."

They walked in silence past the coffee shop where some of their classmates were standing in line for hot chocolates. Neither Gennie nor Margaret had money for two-dollar hot chocolates. They kept on walking.

"I don't think about what it would be like if I weren't here," Gennie said, "but I think about how different our lives would be if my dad hadn't died. I can't stop thinking about it." Five years ago, while on his way home from work, her father had been killed when a drunk driver swerved into his lane. "My mom's still sad all the time. She doesn't think I know, but I hear her crying at night."

Margaret switched her backpack to her other shoulder and linked her arm through Gennie's. "Yeah, my mom cries too." They headed down the street in silence, avoiding the crack in the sidewalk outside the butcher shop. Bad luck to step on it.

A snowflake landed on Gennie's nose. "Hey, it's snowing again." They were at the end of town. The road to Gennie's house was to the right, Margaret's to the left. "You want to come over?" Gennie asked. "You could help me think of some interview questions for Senator Murphy. My mom made some banana bread last night."

Margaret drew a line in the snow with her foot. "Yeah. Sure. My mom's going to freak when she hears you get to meet Senator Murphy. She always says you're destined for something great."

"That's nice of her." Gennie wasn't sure what Margaret's mother meant. Other than finding school easy, she was as ordinary as they came. She liked it that way. There was no reason to be anything but ordinary. They linked arms again and headed down the dirt road to Gennie's home. Snow fell steadily now, fluffy flakes landing in their hair and eyelashes.

"I think I'm going to stop seeing Eugene," Margaret said.

"Why?"

"He's pressuring me to go all the way, and I don't want to."

"I think it would be best if you gave him the boot," Gennie said.

"The boot? You sound like my mother."

They laughed, their warm breath white in the cold air. When their laughter trailed off, Gennie heard the faint sound of a high-pitched cry. It sounded like a kitten. Gennie tugged at Margaret's sleeve. "Do you hear that?"

Margaret's eyes widened. "Is it a meow?"

"It's kittens. Has to be." Gennie scanned the area, searching for the source of the mews. Near a tree, a small box perched on top of an exposed trunk, like a teeter-totter. "There, by the tree." She ran toward the box with Margaret at her heels.

Inside, two black kittens were curled together, their fur exactly alike, and their bodies squished together so they looked like one cat with two heads.

"Someone just left them here?" Gennie asked. "How could you leave a living creature in the snow?"

"What do we do?" Margaret asked.

"We have to take them home with us."

"My mother will never allow it."

"I'll take them to my house. My mom won't be able to resist them. She can't turn away any animal, especially not a baby one. If she doesn't want to keep them, we can find them homes. They can be adopted."

Gennie leaned over the box, picking up one of the kittens. Its green eyes stared into Gennie's. It mewed and mewed. Gennie stroked its soft fur and kissed the top of its head. "Don't worry, kitty. We'll make sure you have a good home." She smiled at Margaret, feeling mischievous. "Hopefully it'll be my home."

* *

To her surprise, Rick Murphy asked that Gennie come to his mansion for the interview. Over the phone, his secretary, Mrs.

Woods, told Gennie that the senator worked from home on Tuesdays. They would send a car to fetch her after school. Nothing had ever sounded more exciting or glamorous.

Margaret and a few other students stood at the curb, waving to Gennie as the car drove away from campus. The driver, an older man wearing a black suit, said nothing after his initial greeting, other than to tell her it would be about an hour's drive. It began to snow on the way. By the time they reached their destination, several inches had covered the ground. Flakes the size of nickels continued to fall. Gennie pulled her coat tighter around her middle as she slipped from the back seat of the town car and followed the driver up the slippery walkway. "Careful not to fall," he said. At the front door, he rang the bell. "Mrs. Woods will take care of you from here. That's the senator's secretary."

Mrs. Woods, tall and narrow, with eyes that snapped with intelligence, opened the door and introduced herself as the driver headed back to his car. Gennie struggled to remain composed as she followed Mrs. Woods across the foyer and through a grand living room to the back of the house. It was the biggest home she'd ever seen, with high ceilings, white pillars, and thick tapestries hung over the windows. Every surface shone under a crystal chandelier. The air smelled of lavender.

At a set of closed double doors, Mrs. Woods asked Gennie to sit in a hardback chair. "This is the senator's office. He should be with you shortly. I'm just down the hall if you need anything." Her heels clicked on the hardwood floor as she walked away, disappearing inside another door.

Gennie took off her coat and hung it over the back of the chair. She waited, fidgeting. The chair was hard and cold. There were no windows in the hallway. Was it still snowing? Her Mom would worry if she were too late getting home. What were the kittens doing? Probably asleep near the heater, all curled up together. So sweet and cuddly, and she'd been right. Her mom hadn't been able to resist them either. They'd named them Midnight and Moon. Given their jet-black fur, only one name made sense, but she didn't care. The names belonged together.

Gennie doodled in her notebook, drawing cats and wishing she'd brought a book to read.

Thirty minutes later, Mrs. Woods brought her a glass of water and a cookie, setting it on the side table. "The senator shouldn't be too much longer. He's on the phone with Washington. He'll spend a few minutes with you, and then send you home with his driver. The rest of the staff has gone home because of the snowstorm, and I'm afraid I must go as well."

"Snowstorm?"

"Yes. We've had ten inches in the last hour, but don't worry, the driver's car is a four-wheel-drive, so he won't have any trouble getting you home."

Gennie thanked her. Adults always exaggerated about the severities of snowstorms. They lived in Wisconsin, after all. Weren't they used to it by now? Anyway, it didn't matter how she got home, just that she was here.

She shivered with excitement. The senator was talking to Washington. He was probably on the phone with the president. What an amazing life the senator must have. She wouldn't take too much of his time. He had important matters to attend to. She would ask just three questions and be out of his way.

Gennie reached for the glass of water and took a sip to quench her dry mouth. The icy water made her teeth hurt. She picked up the cookie, then set it back on the plate, feeling too nervous to eat. Next to the plate, a purple orchid drooped in a graceful curtsy and tickled her hand. A painting of a seascape hung on the wall across from her. She stared at it, imagining what it would feel like to stand at the edge of the sea. Wisconsin had lakes, but no oceans. Someday she would visit the ocean. When she was grown and making money, she would take her mother there. They would have a picnic and swim, the sun warming their cold bones.

Finally, the double doors to his office opened, and Rick Murphy appeared in front of her. "Miss Banks?"

"Yes, that's me." She stood, her legs shaking. He was taller than she expected, with a barrel chest and wide shoulders. On television, he appeared handsome and charismatic, but he was even more so in person. There was an ease and self-assurance to his movements. This was a powerful man, and he knew it. He smiled, flashing white teeth, and held out his hand. She stared at it for a moment, unsure of what to do. Was she to shake his hand? She had so little experience interacting with men, she wasn't sure. "Thank you for this opportunity." She held out her hand, and he seized it in a tight grip, her entire hand disappearing in his large one. His nails, trimmed short and neat, were shiny like they had clear polish on them.

"Come on in. We can talk in my office. I'm sorry to have kept you waiting. When the president calls, one has to answer."

The president! She knew it. Her stomach did a flip as she looked around his office. It was just as she'd imagined, masculine and conservatively decorated in greens and tans. A mahogany desk, the centerpiece of the room, was set in front of the large picture window with a view of the rolling yard, now covered with snow. Four cozy chairs were arranged around a round coffee table. A bouquet of red roses decorated the table. Fresh flowers in November? She couldn't guess how much they'd cost.

"Please sit. I'm all yours. However, it's after five, Miss Banks, which means I'm allowed a cocktail." He crossed to the bar in the corner of the room and poured an amber liquid from a crystal, pitcher-type thing into a short glass. Was it whiskey? She didn't know anything about alcohol. Her mom didn't drink. After her dad had been killed, her mother had thrown away the few bottles of liquor he'd kept in the cabinet above the refrigerator. She never said why, but Gennie figured it was because a drunk had killed her dad.

There was Sister Maria, too, always going on about the evils of drinking. *Teetotalers, girls, is the right choice to make. Booze leads to nothing but bad decisions.*

Now, Senator Murphy sat across from her, lifting the material of his slacks as he crossed his legs. A hint of a tan sock showed above his black loafer. He wore a tan sweater that draped over his wide shoulders. The material was cashmere. She recognized it from the times she and her mother had window-shopped in the city.

She looked at her notepad; her were notes blurry and her were hands damp with perspiration. *Do not drop your pen. Think of a question to ask.*

"Were you really talking to the president?" she asked. This was not one of the questions she had on her list, but it was out of her mouth before she could stop it.

He smiled and sipped his drink, eyeing her over the rim of the glass. "Yes, I was talking to the president."

"I can't imagine."

"It's like talking to anyone else, except that he's the most powerful person in the free world." He smiled again, downing the rest of his drink. Rising from the chair, he pulled the sleeves of his sweater up to his elbows. "I think I'll have another. My wife frowns on whiskey before dinner, but she isn't here to nag me this evening."

It *was* whiskey. She shivered, again. This was beyond exciting. It was so much more than she'd hoped for, seeing this hidden side of the senator who drank whiskey and lied to his wife. There was something almost intimate about their exchange thus far. Familiar and insightful, like she was his biographer. Yes, that was it. She felt like a real writer, privy to the inside story of this powerful man's life. She sat up straighter, imagining herself as a reporter for one of the big magazines her mother sometimes read, the ones that gave detailed accounts of interviews with celebrities. She crossed her legs to seem more dignified, older. In her mind, she transformed into a sophisticated New Yorker. She wore a designer suit, high heel pumps, and her hair bobbed in the latest style. Sister Maria had told her to study him carefully, to take note of his every move and detail so that she could accurately portray him in her article.

"Where is your wife?" Real reporters probably asked questions not on their lists, depending on what their subjects revealed. She would do this too.

He poured another glass, larger than the previous. "She has a charity function tonight. A senator's wife has many duties. A lot of them unpleasant." His voice seemed gruffer than it had the moment before. Did alcohol make one's voice lower?

She felt lost suddenly and glanced down at her notebook as he took the seat across from her once more. She would ask one of the questions on her list. When she looked up, he was staring at her. His nose and chin were sharp, like a fox. The hairs on the back of her neck rose. What had changed in the room? Something sinister had entered, like smoke from under a door. She uncrossed her legs, intertwining her ankles instead, and squeezed her thighs together under her plaid skirt. A man shouldn't look at a girl like he wanted to eat her for dinner. Fear crept up the back of her spine.

"How old are you, Miss Banks?"

"Fifteen." She averted her eyes, focusing them on the roses.

He'd finished his drink and set it on the table. No coaster. Her mother always made her use a coaster. "You like roses?" he asked.

"Sure."

"I bet a lot of boys send you roses."

"No, sir. My mother wouldn't allow that."

Senator Murphy stood, fiddling with his belt. *Oh, my God, what's he doing?* With a swift movement, he tugged his belt from his waist. It slid off his body like a snake. A silent scream started in her head. This wasn't right.

She stood, ready to run, but she was too slow. He lunged at her and pushed her to the ground, covering her with his body, forcing her arms above her head. He tied them together with his belt. His breath, hard and fast, was hot on her neck and smelled sickly sweet, like cough syrup. Something pushed into her hip. Something hard. She screamed. He covered her mouth. "Be quiet, little one. I know what you want."

* *

When he was finished, he held her down as he tied her hands behind her back and gagged her with his tie, then blindfolded her with a scarf that he'd pulled from his pocket. She stumbled and almost fell as he dragged her out of the office and down the hallway. Seconds later, they were outside, the cold pressing against her bare legs. "I'm going to take you home myself. I sent my driver home." He spoke in a soft, calm voice, as if they'd finished the interview and he was offering her a lift home out of the kindness of his heart. She heard the sound of a car door opening before he thrust her inside. It smelled of new leather and his cologne.

She sobbed silently as they drove. The spot between her legs throbbed. How long would it take to get to her house? Would her mother be there? What would he tell her? The car lurched to a stop but remained running. She had no concept of time. Cold air prickled her face. He was out of the car. Where were they? He wouldn't let her out in front of her house. Of course he wouldn't. He knew her mother might be there. She would see how Gennie looked and know that he'd done something to her. She held her breath, trying to stop crying, straining to see through the blindfold until she felt as if her eyes might pop out of their sockets. Nothing but blackness. Should she run? He yanked her door open. Frigid air rushed up her skirt. He grabbed her, forcing her out of the car, and then loosened the tie from her wrists. "You be a good girl and don't tell anyone about this, you understand?"

She cried, unable to answer.

He shoved her against the car, pinning her to the cold metal with his hips. He ripped the blindfold and the gag off her. They were on a country road. It was dark. Snow continued to fall. Under her feet, there was at least a foot of fresh snow. He held her still by placing his hands on her hips. "I will kill your mother, your best friend, anyone and everyone you love if you ever utter a word to anyone." His mouth was near her ear. "Tell me you understand, or I'll kill you right now."

"I understand."

He yanked the collar of her coat and thrust her away from him. She landed on the cold snow.

She sobbed, crawling away from the car, but it didn't matter. He was done with her. He was in the car already, tires spinning as the car lurched forward and sped down the road. His tail lights faded from sight. Darkness enveloped her. She could see nothing, not even the hand in front of her face. Cold assaulted her weary body. She wrapped her arms around her middle, shuddering.

I'm going to die out here alone. I want to see my mom. Just one more time, God, please.

Her mother would be home soon, wondering where she was. Panic would set in. Police would be called. A search would ensue, like it had for the missing girl last year. They'd never found her, that missing girl. She'd died alone, like this. They would not look for Gennie here, down a deserted back road.

She curled into a fetal position and wept without sound, waiting to die. Something poked her side. She reached inside her jacket pocket, curling her fingers over cold metal. Her flashlight. Her father had given it to her the Christmas before he'd died. She carried it everywhere with her. *In case you ever get stuck in the dark*, he'd said when he'd presented it to her, his brown eyes soft as she pulled it from the package.

She sat up, wincing from pain, and pressed the button to turn it on, pointing it in front of her, then moved the light in a circle around her. There was a forest on one side of the road and a flat field on the other. A scarecrow stood in the field, weary from the weather, with only a frayed shirt to cover his straw body. She knew this scarecrow. Yes, she *knew* him. She was near her home. Just down the road, her house waited, warm and familiar. She was close. He'd dumped her near her own home, but she was so disoriented, she hadn't realized where she was. *I will kill your mother*. Her teeth chattered with cold and fear. Her mom must never know what had happened. How would she keep it from her? If she walked in the door looking this way, her mom would know.

Panic rose in her. She vomited into the snow, her head swirling. What time was it? Her mom didn't get home until almost seven, so she wouldn't be home yet. If she hurried, Gennie could make it home and clean up before her mom returned. She rose to her feet. *Hurry. Hurry. Run if you have to.*

She jumped, startled by a rustling in the trees. Holding her breath, she pointed the light in the direction of the noise and gasped. An elk stood between two trees, hooves buried in the deep snow. Giant antlers tipped as he bowed his head; his breath billowed like clouds in the frigid air. She wiped her nose with the back of her arm.

The elk snorted, tossing his head.

"What? What is it?" she whispered. "What do I do?"

Be brave, sweetheart. It was the voice of her father. *Point your flashlight in front of you, and follow the light home.*

* *

By mid-March, the temperatures had risen to the forties for several weeks, and the snow was slushy and dirty, making everything feel desolate and depressed. Gennie and Margaret walked home from school in silence. They stopped in front of the candy shop. It was closed, but they sat on the bench under the awning anyway.

"What's going on with you, Gennie?" Margaret asked. "Something happened. You have to tell me what it is."

Gennie started to cry painful sobs that rocked her body. Margaret put her skinny arms around Gennie and held her.

"I think I'm pregnant," Gennie said.

Margaret's hands clamped her shoulders. "What? How is that possible?"

"I'm scared to tell you, but I have to tell someone because I don't know what to do."

"You can trust me."

"You cannot tell anyone." She prepared herself to lie, to tell the story like she'd rehearsed in her head many times.

"I promise."

"One day after school, I was walking home without you and a van pulled up beside me. The door opened and a man dragged me inside so fast I didn't know what happened. He tied me up." She started to cry again. "He forced himself on me. He said he'd kill my mom if I ever told anyone."

All color drained from Margaret's face. "Oh my God."

"I'm scared."

"Gennie, I'm-I don't know what to say." She shook her head hard enough that her barrette fell out of her hair and onto the sidewalk. Neither girl reached to get it. Margaret squeezed her hands together and took in a deep breath, like she did when she was trying to understand a hard math problem. "No period since then?"

"Right. Not since early November."

Margaret counted on her fingers. "So, like four months along."

"I guess so."

"Do you want to get rid of it?" Before Gennie could answer, Margaret continued, "It may be too late. I don't know if they would do it this far along. I think three months might be the limit."

Gennie cried harder. "The thing is, I felt something yesterday. A flutter, like butterfly wings. I went to the bookstore and looked inside one of those pregnancy books. That's what the baby feels like when you first feel them kick. There's a baby inside me. A person. I can't kill it."

"You'll have to give it up. You can't raise a baby. Right? Isn't that the only option if you don't want to do the other thing?"

"Yes. But I don't know what my mom will say. She might want me to have an abortion if it was still possible, and I don't want to."

"Shit, Gennie, I don't know." Margaret buried her face in her hands. "You have to tell her. There's no way around it."

"She'll make me go to the police. I'm afraid he'll come after her."

"Okay, let me think for a second," Margaret said, pressing her fingers into her eyes. After a moment, she looked up, squinting against the bright clouds. "If she makes you go to the police, just tell them what you told me. You can't identify him."

"Yeah, maybe. I don't want anyone at school to know about the baby."

"Do you remember that girl Cassandra? Two years above us?" Margaret asked.

"I think so. Didn't she move?"

"The rumor is that she was pregnant and her family sent her somewhere to have the baby. Like a place with nuns. Someone told me Sister Maria helped her arrange it."

"Sister Maria?"

"Yeah. Maybe you could go there. Your mom will have to let you if you're this far along. You can go there and have the baby, and then come back here like nothing happened. I'll tell everyone at school that you're going to some fancy overseas school or something."

"How am I going to tell my mother? I feel so ashamed."

"This is not your fault, Gennie." Margaret reached for her and held her close, Gennie's tears soaking the collar of her jacket. "You must remember that, always."

*   *

That evening, Gennie fell asleep on the couch while waiting for her mother to come home. She woke to the sound of keys in the back door. Sitting up, she rubbed her eyes, which were sore and swollen.

Her mom, Joan Banks, clicked across the kitchen floor, calling to Gennie. Once in the living room, her mother kicked off her of two-inch black pumps, shabby and in need of polishing, and sank into the green plaid recliner. It was an ugly chair, they both agreed, but they couldn't dispose of it. The chair was her dad's favorite place to sit. His indentation remained in the cushions.

"Sweetheart, are you sick? Were you sleeping?"

"Not sick. Just really tired."

"Poor baby. It's been a long week, hasn't it?" Her mom wore a black skirt with a yellow blouse and nude stockings. She rubbed her left foot with her thumbs. "I'm beat too. Should we order pizza for dinner?"

"Mom, I have something I have to tell you." Gennie's voice shook, but she continued onward, afraid to stop and lose courage altogether.

Her mom sat forward, dropping both feet to the floor. The recliner squeaked. "What's the matter?"

Gennie started to cry, despite her efforts to remain strong. Seeing her mom's concerned expression was too much.

"You're scaring me, Gennie. Tell me what's happened."

She wiped her eyes and took in a shaky breath. "A couple months ago, I walking home from school and a man grabbed me." She told her the same story she'd told Margaret, finishing with her desire to have the baby and give it up for adoption. Her mom looked stunned for a moment before bursting into tears.

She crossed the room and sat next to Gennie, taking her in her arms. Gennie collapsed against her mother's skinny frame, crying. "My poor baby," her mother murmured.

"I don't want anyone to know. Margaret says Sister Maria knows of a place I could go and have the baby. Nuns run it, and they would help us find a good home for the baby."

Her mom furrowed her brow and clasped her hands in her lap. "Are you sure this is what you want to do? Have the baby? There are other ways to take care of it."

"I don't want to do any of those things. I felt it move inside me, Mommy."

"You did? Like butterflies?"

"Yes. Just like that." Her mom snuggled her close, kissing the top of her head like she had when Gennie was a small girl. "When did this happen?"

"The last week of November."

"What about the police?" her mom asked in a voice laced with confusion and anger. This had undone her, bewildered her, so that she didn't even sound like herself. It was like after Gennie's father died, when she'd walked around in a daze for months. "We should go to the police." She'd gone completely white and her hands shook. "This man, do you think you could identify him?"

"No. It was dark in the van, and he wore a mask."

"We have to go to the police anyway."

"Mommy, please don't make me. It's been too many months, and they'll think I'm lying."

Her eyes were suddenly sharp. "What makes you think that?"

"Because we have no proof. I'm just another pregnant teen to them," Gennie said. "And this town is so small. It'll get out, and I don't want anyone to know."

"What about school?"

"I'll have to make it up somehow."

Her mom smelled of Dial soap and a floral perfume. Every year of their marriage, her father had given her mother the perfume as a Christmas gift. Gennie bought it for her mother now, every December, with her babysitting money. "Mommy, I love you so much." The tears came again, choking her.

Her mom drew back to peer at Gennie's face. "I love you, baby. We're going to get through this. No matter what, you have me. Nothing will ever change that."

Relief flooded Gennie. She was safe now. Her mom would take care of everything. Gennie could go back to being a kid, maybe, after this was over.

A few minutes went by. Gennie could almost hear her mom's brain churning, working out what to do. When her mother spoke again, her voice was back to normal, serene and determined. "I'll call Sister Maria tonight and see about the adoption procedures. Regardless, I want you here with me, in our house, in your room. *I'll* take care of you, not some strangers. They can help us place the baby, but I'll take care of the rest. You understand? You're my baby, and I won't let you go through this alone."

"Yes, I understand."

"Afterward, we'll see about moving away."

"Moving?"

"Maybe somewhere warm. Someplace to make a fresh start."

"Like California?"

"Yes, maybe Los Angeles. Near the beach."

"I'm sorry, Mommy."

"This isn't your fault, sweetie. That's the main thing you must understand. I'll find someone for you to talk with about everything. A therapist or a support group or something. Anything that will help you heal. And sunshine. We need sunshine. I hate this godforsaken snow."

"Okay, Mommy." Like a baby bird, she nestled against her mother's neck and let the tears flow once more.

CHAPTER ONE

2016

A COLD FRONT moved into River Valley two days before Thanksgiving. The Oregon sky lowered and turned the color of smoke. As Gennie and Stefan Spencer filmed their final take of their final scene, Gennie knew snow would fall before the hour turned. She could smell it in the air. It would be heavy and dense, like the snow in Wisconsin. She shivered, pulling her sweater tighter as she and Stefan walked to their trailers. It was all done. *A wrap.* Tomorrow she would go home to Los Angeles. That fact made her want to fall on her knees and weep.

"I'm freezing," she said.

"Here. Take my jacket." Stefan shrugged out of his leather jacket and wrapped it around her shoulders.

"I hate snow." The collar of his jacket smelled of his cologne: bourbon with a hint of vanilla. The scent made her ache with longing. *Don't cry. Don't let him see how much it hurts to let him go.*

Stefan wrapped his arm around her shoulders. "What kind of talk is that for a Wisconsin girl?" Around them, crew members shouted to one another over the sounds of drills and hammers as they dismantled the imaginary world. If only the world they'd created with the set and the actors and the well-written script were real. She wished she were more like the heroine she played in the film, brave and ready to fight for love no matter the cost.

"I haven't lived there since I was sixteen. California's my home now." An edge crept into her voice. She couldn't stop it. "I never have to worry about snow in Malibu."'

"Malibu at Christmas? Blasphemy."

"I know. You want to get back to your forest."

"I do. Being here has only made me realize how much I miss home." Stefan's primary home was on a large piece of land in British Columbia, Canada. It was beautiful there, he'd told her, like River Valley, with its mountains and rivers and a billion stars.

"Come home with me for the holiday weekend," he said. "It's only four days. We can fly your mother up too. My mother would love to meet you both."

She shook her head. "I thought you understood. I just can't."

"I *don't* understand. I won't ever understand." He stuck his hands into the pockets of his jeans, pulling the fabric tighter over his muscular thighs. Dressed in a flannel shirt and work boots, he could have been part of the crew instead of the lead actor. Except for his sensitive ice-blue eyes and soft, full lips, the man exuded testosterone. *A man's man*, she had thought the first time she'd met him.

"Stefan, please, let it go." She brushed a flake from the end of her nose. *Stupid snow.*

"I don't get it." They reached the steps of her trailer and stopped. His jaw was set, and his eyes were darker under the gray sky. "It's just a few days, Gennie. An invitation from your good buddy Stefan." She suspected he meant his words to sound light and teasing, but a bitter edge crept into his tone. She frustrated him. *Join the club.* She frustrated herself.

"Don't. Not today. Not on our last day together," she said. "Please, can't we just have fun tonight?"

His features softened. He thrust his shoulders forward and rubbed his hands together. Looking up at the sky, he let out a deep sigh. In that breath, she felt him letting go, distancing himself and accepting the inevitable. His defeat made her sad. Was she forever doomed to hurt the people who loved her? "Yes," he said, "we can just have fun tonight. I'll pick you up in a few minutes for the party. Ben just texted that everyone's already there."

"Bella's probably three shots in by now," Gennie said, trying to be funny. It fell flat. Their usual banter felt unnatural with their departure looming.

"I'll change clothes and clean up a little. Is thirty minutes enough time?"

"Yes." She reached for his hand. "I'm sorry, Stefan."

"As am I." He pulled his hand away and stuffed it into the pocket of his jeans.

"There are things, Stefan. Things in my past that hurt me…that I can't seem to move past. I know it's impossible to understand, but it's the way it is. I'm not available, emotionally or otherwise. You deserve better." Large, soft flakes fell, catching in Stefan's brown hair, creating a frozen doily over his head. Gennie tilted her face to the sky. A flake landed in her eyelashes.

"It doesn't change how I feel about you. It doesn't mean that it's not killing me to let you go."

She flinched, knocked momentarily senseless by his stark honesty. "It's better this way. For you. You should trust me on that."

"I got it, Gennie." He tucked a strand of hair behind one ear and flashed a false smile. "Get inside and change into something warm. I'll buy you a hot toddy when we get there."

"Okay, yeah. See you in a few." She went inside, closing the door behind her. Despite the warmth of the trailer, she kept Stefan's jacket on, wrapping it close to her body. These last months had been the happiest of her career, but it wasn't just because of the work. It was Stefan. She loved him. Who was she kidding? She was *in* love with him. Stefan had climbed the tower she'd encased herself in and gotten to her.

They must part now—before either of them fell deeper. In the end, it would cause them less pain. *Do not think about it. Keep moving, like you always do.* She would leave tomorrow for the next stop in her nomadic life. *Keep running as fast as you can. Don't look back.* She did one film after another, without time off in between. There was always a new place to see, new people to meet, and a new story to fall into, so her own story faded from consciousness. She buried herself in the work, in the character's life. This was the only way to outsmart the pain.

She must get ready for the party. All this brooding could wait until tomorrow. She shrugged out of the jacket and moved to toss it onto the table.

She gasped. A vase with a dozen red roses sat on the dining table. *Oh no. What was the date today?* Her stomach lurched as she realized it was two days before Thanksgiving. Every year, Murphy sent roses on the anniversary of the day he attacked her. They were a reminder to remain silent because he was still out there. No matter how famous she'd become, he could still get to her if he wanted. He could still hurt her mother. She rushed to the door and yanked it open and called out to Stefan. "Stefan, wait."

Almost to his trailer, he turned around and sprinted back toward her. When he reached her, he put his hands on her upper arms, searching her face. "What is it?"

She pointed toward the interior of her trailer. "Flowers. On the table." Her teeth chattered. "Destroy them."

He let her go and stepped inside the trailer. She stumbled down the steps to wait for him in the open air. She tilted her face to the sky, letting the snow fall upon her, into her lashes and her hair and the bare skin of her face and hands. The flakes, each different from the one before, did not melt when they reached her skin. *Ice cannot melt on ice.*

Stefan exited the trailer carrying the bouquet, then called out to one of the crew members. "Can you get rid of these, please?"

She walked back up the stairs. Stefan's footprints were on the steps, indentions in the snow.

Stefan returned. "They're gone."

"I can still smell them."

He went to the cupboard and rifled through the contents. Blair, her assistant, always stocked it with the items Gennie liked: rice cakes, bottled water, raw almonds, Vanity Fair magazines. It surprised her when Stefan pulled out a bottle of air freshener. "Says it smells like a pine forest. Will that do?"

She nodded and sat at the table, wiping away the condensation from where the vase had left a watermark. Who had delivered the flowers? Probably some production assistant because Blair was on a plane to see her mother for the holiday. Blair knew to intercept them, so Gennie didn't have to see them. She'd never asked Gennie why. She probably figured Gennie had a phobia about roses. Many celebrities had strange quirks that were indulged by the people who worked for them. Money and fame had a way of making the ridiculous seem normal. It was all a matter of perspective.

On the first day they had worked together, Gennie instructed Blair not accept any bouquets of flowers, especially not roses.

"Throw them out or send them home with someone," she'd said. Blair, pushing her glasses further up the bridge of her nose, had simply nodded and scratched the instruction into her notepad.

Stefan sat across from Gennie, cocking his head to the side. "Who sent those?"

"A crazy stalker, I guess."

"The card said happy anniversary. Has this happened before?"

"I don't know."

"You don't know?"

"I mean, yes, it's happened before. It's probably harmless."

"You wouldn't have reacted the way you did if this was nothing but a harmless fan sending flowers. Dammit, Gennie. After all these months, you still can't trust me? All these secrets of yours—don't you ever get sick of them? Jesus, it's me, not some acquaintance. We've spend almost every waking hour together for the past three months!" His hands were clenched at his side, veins bulging in his muscular arms. An image of a lion floated before her, roaring and shaking his mane. Stefan was like a lion, majestic and pretty, but dangerous too. She suspected that in a split second if someone or something threatened her, he could become violent.

She rose from the table, stepping backward toward the dressing area, the pulse at her neck fluttering fast. "I don't want to talk about this any longer," she said.

He put up his hands. "Fine. I know my place." He stood. "I'll pick you up in a few minutes."

"Fine."

His brow wrinkled. An awkward silence hung between them for a few seconds. *Please, let it go.*

"Wear your dancing shoes," Stefan said. "Tommy's band has something special planned for us tonight."

After he left, her throat ached from trying to keep the tears at bay. She didn't want him to know he made her want to cry. He'd never been angry with her before, and she felt shaken. She sat for a moment, taking in deep breaths, like her therapist had taught her, to control the panic attacks.

Her phone buzzed with a call. It was her mother. They talked every day without fail. It would be good to hear her voice and to remember that she waited for Gennie in Malibu, their refuge. It was all she needed. Her mother and their view of the ocean. Everything would be fine.

* *

They drove toward town without speaking. Stefan seemed at ease driving in the heavy snowfall, despite the way it covered the windshield as fast as the wipers could clear it. The XM radio, set to the '90s station, played Celine Dion's "Because You Loved Me." On the screen, the year 1996 was in parenthesis next to the name of the song. "Will you turn it to something else?" she said, tugging on the shoulder strap of her seat belt.

"No nineties music?" He raised his eyebrows, teasing, as he moved the dial to a contemporary music blend. "But it's a representation of our youth."

"Exactly."

"How old were we in 1996? Fifteen?"

"That's right." She pretended to be interested in something outside the window.

He fell silent. She could almost hear the questions he wanted to ask, even though he knew the unspoken rule. *Do not ask Gennie about her childhood.* If he asked too many questions about her past, she went mute.

They crossed the valley. The hay fields, yellow when she had first arrived in River Valley, were now white with the dusting of snow, as were the surrounding mountains. They passed the road where Annie and Drake Webber lived; their huge house sat perched on the side of the mountain, hidden in the trees. She and Stefan had spent countless nights there, most recently to celebrate the marriage of her best friend, Bella, to Ben Fleck.

As they entered town, River Valley's welcome sign informed them of the population—still 1425. Stefan gestured toward the sign. "You think they'll change the sign when Annie has her baby?"

Gennie smiled. "Maybe. We should ask Mike."

Stefan chuckled, slowing the car as they entered the city limits. "As the town's self-appointed mayor, Mike would change the sign using White-Out if he had to." They both smiled. Mike Huller and the group of new friends they'd made were on a crusade to reinvent the town from a dying timber community to a thriving tourist destination. Thus far, they'd managed to add a gourmet restaurant, Riversong, the River Valley Lodge, and the Second Chance Inn, where some cast and crew had stayed. All of this in addition to a high-tech call center, formerly run by Ben. According to Annie, the chef at Riversong, the town was a completely different place than it had been three years ago when Lee Tucker and Mike first opened Riversong. Happy to leave corporate life, Ben was in the process of opening a fly-fishing shop. Bella was launching a makeup and skin care line, which would be headquartered in River Valley. Gennie had agreed to help finance it and be the "face" of Bella's dream.

It had snowed at least two inches in the thirty minutes since the first flake had fallen. Main Street had not yet been cleared of snow and looked quaint and pretty under the blanket of white. There were few cars on the road, with several abandoned curbside. "These Oregon folks don't know how to drive in the snow," Stefan said. "Good thing you have a Canuck to get you around." He slowed the car to under ten miles an hour as they inched their way to the inn.

Gennie barely heard him. Children peppered the sidewalks of Main Street, throwing snowballs, building snowmen, and pushing one another on sleds. She averted her eyes, fussing with the radio, but the familiar pang came. The baby would be twenty now, no longer a child. Gennie pushed the thoughts away.

Stefan drew her hand away from the dashboard and held it in his. "You want me to put on one of your country stations?"

"Never mind. Everything's agitating me." She shrugged, searching for a way to explain her odd behavior. "I need a drink."

"Almost there." He squeezed her hand and then let it go to twist the knob on the radio. "Here, how about one of the news stations? I have no idea what's happened in the world in the past several days."

The voice of the newscaster came through the speakers. "Wisconsin Senator Rick Murphy was interviewed today on the CBS morning talk show about his bid for the presidency."

"Well, that's not a surprise," Stefan said.

"Turn it off, please," she said.

He obeyed, but not before shooting her a questioning glance.

Stefan was correct. Murphy's announcement wasn't a surprise. He'd hinted about the presidency for years. *The man's everywhere. I can't get away from him.* It would only get worse if he won. She might have to move to Europe.

As Stefan pulled into their parking spot behind the inn, he looked at her, alarm in his eyes but his voice soft. "You all right?"

"I don't want to hear anything about the Murphy family."

"Really? Aren't they considered American royalty? And Wisconsin? Your home state? I thought you'd be proud."

"Not everyone from Wisconsin likes them. Can we just go inside?"

"Hang tight. I'll come around and get you." He got out, letting a gust of cold air inside the car. When he reached her door, he opened it and offered his hand. She stepped down, feeling apprehensive, like a hooved animal on ice.

"Don't worry, I'll make sure you don't slip," Stefan said.

She didn't answer as they crossed the parking lot toward Riversong. "I should've grabbed a hat." She meant to say it lightly, but it came out sounding like a petulant child.

"You hungry?" he said this in the same teasing, gentle voice as earlier. It was their joke. He'd taken to silently handing her protein bars when they were on set if her blood sugar plummeted and she seemed tired or cranky.

"Kind of. This weather." The awful snow was in her nose and on her skin and in front of her eyes. She was empty, depleted. Desolate.

As they entered the warm and cozy restaurant, packed with all their new friends and the cast and crew, including their lovely costar Cleo Tanner and her husband, Seattle police detective Peter Ball, the emptiness decreased. Bella was at the bar, wearing a tight red dress that barely covered her round, firm bottom, with a line of tequila shots in front of her. She screamed and waved them over.

"Finally. We thought you two would never get here." Bella grabbed Gennie and forced her into a hug. She caught a whiff of lime and tequila on Bella's breath. "We started in on the drinking without you two." Bella wore her dark, wavy hair in a stylish, short bob. She was chic and cool—the type of woman other women secretly took their cues from about what to wear or read or see. Gennie knew the makeup line would be a huge success because of it.

Ben, his dark blond hair wet from either the shower or the snow, slapped Stefan on the shoulder. "How does it feel, old man, to be done with the film?"

"Honestly? I wish my time here didn't have to end." Stefan took a shot glass of tequila and raised it toward Ben and Bella. "Cheers. I'm going to miss the heck out of you guys." He tossed back the shot. "Gennie, you want one?"

"No, thank you." She smiled at Stefan. "I leave the hard stuff to Bella."

"Well, somebody has to do it for heaven's sake." Bella was trying to stop cursing and had recently started using *heaven* in place of its more offensive counterparts. It sounded stilted and strange coming from her sassy mouth.

Cindi, Riversong's bartender, poured Gennie a glass of chilled white wine. "Here you go, Miss Genevieve. I made sure to have it nice and cold like you prefer." Cindi was one of the only people who called her by her formal name, which seemed counterintuitive given Cindi's plain way of speaking. Regardless, Gennie found it endearing.

She thanked her and took a dainty sip as she watched Cindi fluff her hair with her fingertips. Recently, Bella had convinced her to shorten it to a layered bob and color it a dark blond instead of various shades of yellow that did not exist in nature. Bella had changed her makeup, too, replacing Cindi's predisposition for blue eye shadow and purple eyeliner with attractive shades of browns. All of which resulted in a transformation from the persona of a zany, small-town bartender to a sophisticated socialite. Regardless of appearance, Cindi was still a gun-toting, foul-mouthed, small-town woman who men feared and women secretly admired. No one messed with Cindi, especially after the news of her taking down a madman with a single bullet from her shotgun had circulated through River Valley. "Well, shoot, I'm gonna to miss the socks off you, Genevieve Banks. You'll come visit us, won't you?"

Gennie smiled. "Every chance I get. Plus, with Bella and Ben here along with the *Bellalicious* headquarters, I'll want to come and see how business is going."

Cindi raised her eyebrows and slapped the counter. "Oh, it's going to be something to have our own cosmetic company right here in River Valley. Never thought I'd see the day."

Bella downed another shot and slammed it on the counter, grinning at Ben. "Come on, baby. I want to say hi to Annie in the kitchen."

Ben put out his arm. "Come on, then." He grinned at Stefan. "Happy wife, happy life, right?"

"Not sure how that silly girl's going to run a business." Cindi grabbed the empty shot glass and tucked it under the bar.

Gennie chuckled. "She's smarter than she seems. I've known her a long time. I'd trust her with my life, tequila shots or not."

"Well, that's the kind of friend you need, for sure." Cindi fixed her gaze on Stefan. "And for you, young man? IPA?"

"You know how to make a man happy, Cindi. You sure you won't marry me?"

Cindi flushed and reached for a pint glass. "Oh, hush now, you know I'm spoken for. Anyway, you two drink up, especially since all you have to do is stumble next door to the inn." She started to fill the beer glass with an IPA from the tap, holding it at an angle so the foam ran off the side. "And Lee's got it fixed so no paparazzi can get to you tonight. This is a private party for just the cast and crew. Here you go, handsome." After sliding the glass of beer toward Stefan, she excused herself to take care of a patron at the other end of the bar. Glancing that way, Gennie gave a small wave. It was one of the young production assistants who always had a cigarette tucked behind her left ear and chewed gum as if punishing it for being too minty.

Stefan raised his glass of beer. "To my favorite leading lady."

"To my favorite leading man." They clinked glasses.

* *

The evening passed quickly. Too quickly. By twilight, eight inches of snow had covered River Valley and the surrounding mountains. Quite unusual, Lee and Tommy told them, for this time of year. While the unfortunate snowplow driver worked to clear the streets, Gennie and Stefan dined inside the warm restaurant on Annie's succulent dinner: rack of lamb with mint sauce, a medley of vegetables, rosemary potatoes, and blackberry cheesecake for dessert. Gennie permitted herself full portions and ate as if she were not scheduled to begin filming a new project right after the Thanksgiving holiday. She drank two glasses of wine and felt loose and warm. If only this moment could last forever.

After dinner, several couples rose to dance to Tommy's band. She stayed in her seat, enjoying his beautiful voice.

Stefan reached across the table, tapping her hand. "Would you like to dance?"

"Dance? Do you dance?" she asked, teasing, knowing full well that he danced. They'd spent many Friday nights on this very dance floor, cutting a rug to Tommy's music.

"I'll dance with you, Genevieve Banks, anytime."

Stefan held her loosely, with only inches between their bodies, as they swayed to the music. She inhaled his spicy scent and wrapped her fingers in his hair. Song after song, they danced together in the far corner of the floor, the world nothing but the two of them. Her heart beat the seconds away until Tommy announced last call and last song.

Stefan's eyes were soft as he covered her hand with his. "We've officially closed the place down. You have to go to bed before you turn into a pumpkin."

They said their goodbyes to their new friends, promising to visit soon. Gennie managed to keep from crying. She would do that later, in the privacy of her room.

CHAPTER TWO

THE HALLWAY OF Linus's Second Chance Inn smelled of new carpet. They walked down the hallway to their rooms, holding hands, fingers intertwined. They stayed next door to each other in the largest rooms at the inn, located on the top floor. Other than her gated home in Malibu, she'd never felt safer.

We have to say goodbye in less than a minute. Stefan has to leave me here and walk away. I have to go inside and take off my makeup and crawl into a cold bed and try to sleep knowing that in the morning, he will not come with coffee and drive me to the set.

Instead, in the morning, the car would come to take her to the airport. By mid-afternoon tomorrow, she'd be with her mother in Malibu.

They were at the door. Number 7. Lucky number 7. She dropped his hand and pulled her key card from her purse, then gave it to him. Stefan took the card, turning it over three times. "Guess this is it." He smiled.

"My car comes at eight a.m. tomorrow," she said.

"And the princess needs her sleep." He turned away, inserted the card into the lock, and went inside the room. She watched him from the doorway. He opened the closet first and peered inside, then looked in the bathroom and finally the bedroom. "All clear." He flipped on the gas fireplace. "Come. Get warm." As the flames caught, she moved to stand next to him, warming the back of her legs. He grasped a lock of her hair, twisting it around his finger. "The time went too fast."

"It did."

"We just need to talk Richard into directing another film with us, eh?" Stefan said "eh" and pronounced sorry with a long *o*, except when he was on script. He smiled, the corners of his eyes crinkling.

"It has to be in the next five years, or it'll be too late for me." She made a cutting gesture at her neck. "Five years until I turn forty. I'll be dead to Hollywood."

"You'll work as long as you want, Gennie."

"I hope so. It's all I have." *Why did I say that out loud?* Confessions like that could give Stefan ammunition. If work was all she had, then why not allow for their relationship? Surprisingly, he didn't say anything. The late hour and the wine had made her vision dimmer than usual, as if minuscule gray matter covered everything. *Make sure you say everything you want to say before he walks out this door.* "I've never worked with anyone better."

All pretense had left his face. He gazed at her with stark vulnerability. "I appreciate that."

"You're not just an action hero star. You're the real thing. An artist. You're going to be nominated for *Vice*, just you wait and see." His performance as a gritty cop addicted to painkillers was already getting Oscar buzz.

Grimacing, he shrugged his shoulders. "My team's lobbying for a nomination, which makes me feel ridiculous and hopeful at the same time. It's terrible to want something so much. I'm not proud of it—this desire for outside affirmation, eh?"

"As an artist, it's impossible not to feel that way. Anyway, I was intimidated to work with you." *Stop stalling and let him go. You've tortured him enough.*

He grinned. "That's only because you heard I do my own stunts."

She laughed. "Well, yes, that was part of it. That and your propensity for brawls with the paparazzi."

"You know they deserve it."

"I do." She tugged the collar of her sweater. "I *am* jealous of how the crew liked you better than me. That's never happened before." After two days on set, he knew everyone's name, how many kids they had, if they preferred wine or beer. His trailer door was always open and the retrigerator stocked with drinks. "Not to mention that you can switch from shouting at a football game in your trailer to filming an intensely emotional scene without missing a beat."

"I've never grown out of my schoolboy ways."

When he leaves this room, he will start the rest of his life. He'll meet someone and marry her and have a family. I'll be nothing but a distant memory. "I'm sorry I can't be what you need." Her voice caught. "You're such a good man. This is all me. Please know that." Eyes stinging with unshed tears, she looked down at her hands to avoid his gaze. *Do not cry.*

"Thank you, sweet Gennie." He took her hands, kissing each one in turn, before letting go. "I'm going to miss you."

She brushed his crow's feet with the tip of her fingers. Her hand drifted down his cheek. "Me too."

"One more day with you only leaves me wanting one more. I'm in love with you. Head over heels."

She searched for the words that would help him understand. "I wish I could give you what you want."

"Do you know what that is?"

"It's what every man wants. A woman who can give herself emotionally and physically. I can't do either." *I might break into hundreds of pieces, like a snowball thrown against a tree.*

"I'd do anything to make you happy. Anything. Love is about compromise."

"You think that, but after time you'd see it's not enough." Moody, her ex-husband, had tried. For an entire year, he'd sacrificed his own needs to make their marriage work. As much as he'd loved her, he could not remain married to a woman incapable of physical intimacy. He'd cheated on her while he was on tour with his band. Who could blame him? He was a rock star. Women threw themselves at him every night. Finally, he could no longer resist. The same would happen to Stefan. And like Moody, it would devastate him.

"What happened to you?" Stefan asked

She turned away. "I don't talk about it."

He grabbed her hand. "You're not the only one with a secret."

Whatever your secrets, they are not like mine. "Please, don't make this harder."

"Yeah, okay. I'll let you get some sleep now." His tone was gentle but sad. "No matter what, I'll be here for you. Remember that, okay? If you ever need me, I'm only a phone call away." He kissed her on the cheek.

A moment later he was gone.

The scent of his cologne on her hands the only proof he'd been there at all.

She stared at the fireplace for several minutes before moving to the window. The snow fell again, illuminated by the lampposts on the street. *Bed. Just go to sleep. The pain's gone during sleep.* In a daze, she changed into soft flannel pajamas, washed her face, and brushed her teeth. Crawling under the blankets, she let the tears tumble down her hot cheeks. Like so many nights before, she cried herself to sleep.

CHAPTER THREE

THE LIGHT OF DAY had not yet come when the vibration of her mobile phone woke Gennie from a deep sleep. It was her manager, Trix Traggert.

"Hey." She fell back into the bed, pulling the feather comforter around her. "What's up?"

"Gennie, I'm sorry to wake you, but we need to get on top of something right away." Trix sounded breathless, like she was walking fast. This wasn't unusual. The woman lived on overpriced cappuccinos.

"Is it the rumors about Stefan and me? I told you yesterday, we're just friends. But there's nothing we can do to keep the press from making things up." She yawned and resisted the urge to scratch her tired eyes. Was it a photo of the two of them dancing last night? Maybe someone had taken a photograph and leaked it to the press? No, it was impossible. The cast and crew were all people she trusted. The staff at Riversong were her friends. They protected their own here in River Valley. Turning to her side, she rested her cheek in the crook of her arm.

"No, it's nothing about you and Stefan. If only." Trix paused, and Gennie heard the sound of high heels click-clacking over a hard surface in the background. Trix was at her office already. Did the woman ever stop working? "Listen, you better sit down for this."

"It's six a.m., Trix. I'm in bed."

"Oh, yeah, right. A story is all over the internet and the news. They're saying you had a baby twenty years ago. And that you abandoned her."

Blood rushed to her head, pulsating with the rhythm of her pounding heart. She sat up and brought her hand to her mouth, afraid she might be sick. "It can't be."

She was transported back to the day, almost twenty years ago, when she'd given birth to a healthy baby girl. Throughout labor, she'd focused on the small wooden cross hanging on the wall. When the baby had finally come, after nearly fourteen hours of excruciating labor, she'd fallen back on the pillows, exhausted.

The baby in the nurse's arms started to cry.

"She sounds like a baby kitten," Gennie whispered.

"Do you want to see her?" the nurse asked.

"Yes, please."

The nurse set her in Gennie's arms. The baby, wrapped in a pink blanket and wearing a little cap of the same color, stopped crying for a second as she looked up at Gennie. Gennie pulled the blanket apart and took hold of one of the baby's hands. Tiny fingers wrapped around Gennie's index finger. She removed the pink cap and kissed the baby's forehead. The baby had a thicket of black hair. "Have a good life, baby girl. I love you." She wrapped her back in her blanket and handed her to the nurse. "Take her. Please." The baby started to cry. Gennie turned away, facing the wall so she didn't have to see them walk out of the room. The cries faded until there was nothing but silence.

After all these years, the cries still haunted her.

"I didn't abandon her. I gave her up for adoption," Gennie said.

"Oh, crap, so it's true?" Trix's voice squeaked an octave higher.

"How did they find out?" It was a closed adoption. Secret. Sister Maria had promised. *You've chosen a lovely couple for this baby. They want a child more than anything. She'll be loved. No one ever needs to know. You've made their dream come true. And you can move forward now. Build a life despite what's happened.*

Trix cleared her throat. "Apparently, the baby's adoptive mother died of cancer two years ago. The father and daughter are estranged. He sold a story to one of the rags that you abandoned the baby at some Catholic church, and he and his late wife took her in, even though they were struggling financially. Later, after you became rich, they approached you for money and you said no, threatening to ruin them if they ever contacted you again. A photo of the girl is plastered all over the internet and television."

Her daughter's photograph. Plastered everywhere.

"Gennie, she looks just like you."

"What?"

"It's eerie, in fact," Trix said.

"He gave them her photos?"

"Yeah. And her address. The press is camped out in front of her campus apartment."

George Bentley had sold out his own daughter? The mild-mannered man she'd agreed to give the baby to? He'd told their secrets to the press? And his wife, Sally? Dead so young? Sister Maria had assured her they were a happy couple. George was a big man, with rippling muscles, who worked in a warehouse moving boxes onto trucks. Sally was a secretary at an elementary school. They'd told her they'd wanted nothing more than to have a child but were having trouble adopting because they were working-class people. When Sally had explained their situation, Gennie had cried, thinking of her own parents. Money didn't make a childhood happy or sad. It was love. Sally had asked her what she knew about the baby's father. Gennie had told them the same story she'd told her mother. "I was raped by a stranger."

She'd been frightened that Sally and George Bentley wouldn't want a child born from rape, that perhaps they would think the baby was flawed because of the origin of conception, but they hadn't flinched. Sally was a strong Catholic who believed all children started out innocent and perfect. "We will love her no matter what," Sally had said, glancing at her husband.

"Always," George said. What had happened to George Bentley to change him?

"They never contacted me for money," Gennie said. "I didn't abandon her. It was a closed adoption arranged through the church, all on the up and up, Trix. I swear. The records will prove that."

"You know how this goes, Gennie. We've been through this crap before. Public perception outweighs the truth."

"You mean with Moody?"

"Yeah. Listen, we've got to get on this. We can't just put out a statement this time. I'm pulling a team together. We need a strategy to deal with this, like yesterday."

The groupie Moody had slept with in a hotel room in Nashville had talked, revealing every sordid detail in countless interviews. It had all made Moody look terrible, especially since the fairy-tale story of the bad-boy rocker and America's Hollywood princess had caught the collective imagination. The press and public opinion had torn Moody to shreds. Only Gennie knew he wasn't to blame. He'd been loyal to her, but even good men had their limits. These people who sold information for cash and a moment of fame were the ones without moral redemption.

Despite Trix's urging, Gennie had never spoken publicly about Moody's affair and their subsequent divorce. She'd released a brief statement asking for privacy, along with a sentence or two about marriage being difficult and that nothing was ever black and white. She'd ended it by saying Moody was a good man for whom she had undying respect and love. She'd been attacked by some of the women's groups for that one; they wanted a concrete statement condemning Moody for infidelity. However, as everyone who's ever been married knows, things are never that simple.

"Did you hear what I said?" Without waiting for an answer, Trix plowed forward, speaking louder as if Gennie had a hearing problem. "Listen, I called Reid Wilson. He's prepared to meet this morning, even though it's a holiday weekend. I told him we'd conference call you on your way to the airport." Reid Wilson, the Scandal Whisperer. He worked at her publicity firm, specializing in celebrity damage control. One only called Reid for a "code red" scandal.

"I put a baby up for adoption when I was a teenager. Who cares?"

"Babe, this is on every news channel and all over the web. They're making you out to be the type of girl who leaves her baby in a dumpster to die. You've been without reproach for your entire career, and the vultures have patiently waited for you to fall. You stand back from this and your reputation and career will spiral downward in a matter of weeks. Trust me. We've seen it too many times before."

Trix continued, this time with a greater tone of impatience, "You've got to get in front of this. There's no way this is going to blow over anytime soon. Reid can set our strategy, and we'll have you booked on the morning talk shows by tomorrow." Trix sounded breathless, like she was walking up a hill. *Get in front of this? How would they do that?* "One other thing. The girl contacted me. Her name's Sarah. Seems like a great kid. She said she has no intention of asking for money or anything, but she wants to meet you. She has a lot of questions. She's been looking for you since her mother died."

Sarah. They had named her Sarah. "She has?"

"She could start talking to the press. It's best to keep her close."

"Jeez, Trix, how thoughtful of you."

"Listen, this is no time for you or me to go all sentimental. You pay me to keep scandal from touching you. I'm just doing my job."

"I need to call my mother. I'll call you back in an hour."

"Fine. One hour. That's all you have, though. I mean it, Gennie. This is serious. You can't just pull your ostrich move. And I'm texting you Sarah's number. You can decide if you want to call her."

After Gennie hung up, she sat for a moment, shaking and staring at the text with Sarah's number. *My baby is all grown up. She wants to meet me.* All this echoed in her mind in a mess of jumbled thoughts. *Looking for me? She was looking for me. What would I tell her about her father?* Was it best for Gennie to stay away and let the poor girl live her life without knowing the truth? Yes, of course it was. Learning she came from a rape could devastate her. It was up to Gennie to protect her, just as it had always been.

A text showed up on her screen from the driver who was supposed to pick her up at eight, saying the roads were closed until the afternoon.

She went to the window. Sure enough, they were snowed in by at least two feet of snow. *Great.* Now what was she supposed to do? She needed to talk to her mom. No decisions until they talked it through. Her mom would know what to do.

She answered after several rings. "Genevieve?" She sounded sleepy. "Is everything all right?"

"Mom, George Bentley went to the press. It's all over the news."

"What? It can't be."

"Yes, Mom. It is." Without taking a breath, she filled her mother in on everything she knew.

"How could he do such a thing? They seemed like such a nice couple."

"He must have money problems," Gennie said. "Everything's always about money."

"Are you coming home today? We can figure out what to do together."

"I'm snowed in here for the morning at least." She explained what the driver had said. "But, Mom, I'm thinking I should just stay here until we figure out what to do. The press thinks I'm in Hawaii. I don't think I can face the paparazzi right now."

"My poor baby. Do you want me to come there? I can be on a plane this afternoon."

Gennie thought for a moment. "Yes, Mom." Her voice shook. "I need you."

"Consider it done."

"I'll call Blair and have her send a car and arrange a flight for you. Can you be ready?"

"Of course, honey. I'll have to dig out my winter jacket and boots."

"Thanks, Mom."

"I'll see you this afternoon."

She dialed Blair next. Most of Gennie's colleagues had their assistants travel with them, but she felt more comfortable taking care of many things on her own. Having an assistant with her made her feel trapped and like nothing in her life was private. So Blair worked from Los Angeles most of the time, only occasionally coming to the locations where Gennie filmed. She'd been in Oregon just last week, helping Gennie sort through some details of her upcoming projects. This past Monday, Gennie had insisted Blair fly home to Georgia to be with her family for the holidays.

Blair answered right away. "Oh, Gennie. I just saw the news. Why are they saying all these things about you?" Blair was twenty-nine and, having grown up in a small town in Northern Georgia, still had a thick southern accent. Even though she'd lived in Los Angeles for half a decade, the sweet little sundresses and cardigans she wore always made her look like she'd just stepped out of a Baptist church service.

"I didn't abandon her. I gave her up for adoption."

"Because you were so young?"

"Yes, mostly." Gennie played with the trim on the bed sheet. "It's complicated. But I want you to know it isn't how it looks."

"Gennie, I know you'd never just toss a baby out in the snow."

"Jesus, is that what they're saying?"

"The father's insinuating as much," Blair said.

She asked Blair to make travel arrangements for her mother. After they disconnected, Gennie grabbed the throw blanket from the end of the bed and wrapped it around her shoulders.

Two seconds later, Stefan called.

"You saw the news," she said.

"No, I was asleep. Richard saw it on the news and called me."

"Trix says they're making it out like I'm a baby killer. Is it that bad?"

"They've named it 'Babybanks-gate.'"

"Oh God."

"Do you want me to come to your room?"

Her instinct was to say no, but of everyone in the world, he was the person she most wanted to see. "Yeah, that would be good. Thanks."

They hung up just as the phone buzzed again. This time it was Bella.

"Is the story true?"

Gennie repeated what she'd just said to Blair.

"I can't believe you never told me. We're supposed to be best friends. You know everything about me. Don't you trust me?"

"Bella, it's nothing to do with trust. I made a decision a long time ago never to tell anyone about the baby."

"What really happened?"

Her right eye twitched. Should she tell Bella she'd been raped? Gennie had no doubt she could trust Bella, but did she want to say the words out loud to anyone? What good would it do for Bella to know? "I got pregnant at fifteen, and I gave the baby up for adoption. Legal and closed adoption. I chose the adoptive parents from a large pool of candidates. I thought they would be great parents for her. The Buckleys were not supposed to talk about it." She walked to the window, moving the shade an inch to look outside. More snow had fallen while they'd slept. At least twelve inches lined the railing of the balcony.

"What a dick," Bella said.

"Seems I didn't choose the right couple after all."

"I'm so sorry, Gennie. Is there anything I can do?"

"No, I'm fine. You have your hands full with Bellalicious. I don't want you to worry over this."

In the past few weeks, Bella had spent much of her time flying back and forth to and from Los Angeles, working with chemists to make the beta products. *Good God, the business.* What would this do the business? She hadn't thought about Bellalicious until now. Bella had worked like the devil to make it successful. What would a scandal like this do their business plans? Would it hurt the marketing campaign to have Gennie as the face of the company? The scandal might put the whole project in jeopardy. It would certainly distract the consumer from their products or messaging. "I don't have my head around any of this yet, but you may need to find another celebrity to be the face of our company. I don't want this to jeopardize all of your hard work." The launch of the products was a year away. There was time to change course if needed. The most important thing was Bella's success. She'd worked too hard to have Gennie ruin it.

"Don't be ridiculous," Bella said. "Once you explain everything, all will be forgiven. You did the right thing. A fifteen-year-old can't raise a baby. Everyone will see that. And, don't worry about what this means for our company. You decide how you want to handle this and we'll figure it out. Together."

"We'll see." A knock on the door drew her attention away from Bella. *Stefan.* She fought tears of relief. She needed to see him, to talk all this through with him. "I'll call you later when my phone isn't blowing up."

After hanging up with Bella, she pulled a sweatshirt over her head to cover her filmy pajama top and went to the door. As soon as it opened, Stefan stepped inside and pulled her into his arms. "Are you okay?" The door swung closed behind them.

Resting her cheek against his shoulder, she wrapped her arms around his neck, clinging to his warmth. "I'm so cold."

"You're probably in shock. Let's turn on the fire." With his arm around her, he led her over to the chairs in front of the fireplace. "Sit. I'll make us some coffee." He flipped the fireplace switch, and the flames sputtered to life. "I talked to Tommy before I came over. It'll take until the afternoon to clear the roads. Let's just hope your location doesn't leak to the press. All we need is a million reporters outside the inn."

"No one knows where I am."

"Let's hope it stays that way," Stefan said.

"Trix put out false reports yesterday that we'd finished filming and I'd flown immediately to Hawaii for the Thanksgiving holiday. Sky's staying at some hotel in Maui with instructions to sit poolside in big sunglasses and a hat and order drinks under my name." Sky was a former model of the same height and build as Gennie. Not only did Sky stand in as a body double during filming, but they also often hired her to throw the paparazzi off of Gennie's true whereabouts. "There's probably a hundred members of the press on a plane to Hawaii as we speak." Had Trix warned Sky of the impending trouble? Most likely, she had. Trix never left one detail unattended. "Trix wants Reid to help us with public perception."

Stefan, at the bar, pushed a button on the Keurig. "The Scandal Whisperer guy?" The aroma of coffee filled the room.

"That's right."

He handed her a cup. "Drink this. It'll warm you."

She thanked him, holding the cup between her cold hands. He'd made it just as she liked it. A teaspoon of cream, no sugar.

After he'd made another cup, he joined her by the fire. Facial stubble and bloodshot eyes made him look older than when she'd last seen him.

"Did you sleep?" she asked.

"Not much." He sipped from his mug. They were both silent for a moment, sipping their coffee.

She decided she would tell Stefan exactly what she'd just told Bella. No more, no less. Except, the words wouldn't come.

Before she could think of a way to start, Stefan spoke. "Do you want to tell me about it?"

"I didn't want to tell anyone about it. It happened a long time ago."

His expression darkened. He turned toward the fire. "I understand. The past should remain the past."

"I was practically a child when it happened. I didn't abandon her." She told him the same story she'd told Bella. "It was all done properly. That was important to my mother. The church helped us pick the parents. We thought the Bentleys were good people. Good Catholics. It was a closed adoption. Records sealed."

Had she imagined it, or had he flinched when she'd said the last part?

The air had gone from the room. She couldn't breathe. Black dots appeared before her eyes. Her hand shook as she set her coffee cup on the side table. "I can't do this again. I can't relive this nightmare." She wasn't strong enough to continue lying, and yet it was her only option. She must do everything she could to protect the people she loved.

Stefan set his mug aside and knelt on the floor. He wrapped his fingers around her upper arms. "Sweetheart, just breathe. Here, breathe with me. Just in and out, that's right."

She followed his directions until the black dots disappeared.

"It's going to be all right," he said. "You have nothing to be ashamed of. Reid can fix the public perception. You can do an interview or whatever. You were a teenager who did the right thing."

"I thought I did." Hot tears scalded her cheeks. "She wants to meet me. She knows who I am now. She's been looking for me."

He reached across her and pulled several tissues from the box on the side table. "Do you want to meet her?" He placed the tissues in her hand.

She wiped under her eyes and nose. "I want to. But I shouldn't. She'll have questions I'm not prepared to answer."

"What kind of questions?"

"She'll want to know why I gave her up. Who is her father? Were we in love? How did she come to be? And, no matter what, I can't tell her the truth." She blew into the tissues. "All I've ever wanted was for her to have a normal life. A safe life."

"Safe?" His eyes went wide, then searching. "Because of your fame? The paparazzi? What do you mean?"

She reached for more tissues and pressed them into her stinging eyes. "No. It's not that. I could protect her from all of this. It's so much bigger than the paparazzi." She shuddered, remembering how Murphy had repeated the same phrase over and over as he thrust inside her. *You want this, little girl, you want this.*

"Gennie, what is it? What happened?" Stefan wrapped his hands around her knees.

She met his searching gaze without the energy to hide her pain. Yet, she could not bring herself to tell him the truth. To utter the words out loud felt impossible. "It wasn't just that I was fifteen with a baby out of wedlock."

His eyes narrowed. He blinked and cocked his head to the right. His gaze shifted to the ceiling and back to her face. His face flushed and heat radiated from his skin. He opened his mouth, then closed it. He wrapped both his hands in his messy hair, holding his head for a moment like it hurt. "Oh, Gennie, no." She'd said too much. He understood it all now. Her arms fell to her lap, hands clenched like claws, grasping at the fabric of her pajamas. He pried them loose and held them like baby birds he didn't want to crush in his damp palms. His classically trained voice wavered. "You were raped."

The back of her throat ached. "Yes," she whispered.

"Sweetheart, I'm so sorry." He sat back on his haunches, tears in his eyes, his hands limp in his lap. "I see now." The muscle in his left cheek twitched. "I understand everything now."

"I didn't want the baby to ever know the truth. That's why it was so important to me that it was a closed adoption."

"Was it someone you knew?"

She flinched like he'd slapped her. "I can't tell you." Reality faded, and memory yanked her back to the worst moments of her life. Those moments invaded her mind and hijacked her senses. A purple vein protruded from his forehead and spittle formed on the sides of his mouth. He smelled of booze and sweat as he ripped her in two. She screamed from the burning pain until he put his hand over her mouth and nose. When he ejaculated, he bleated like a goat and shuddered. When he took his hand from her face, the scent of blood and metal gagged her. She was so young; she didn't know the scent of a man's semen. It wasn't until later, when she sat on the toilet in her own bathroom, howling and wishing she were dead, that she realized the smell of metal was from his ejaculation. It had made its way into her nose, lingering long after she had showered and scrubbed her skin raw. She had no idea that it had also impregnated her.

Now, she wept into her hands, thinking of the little girl he killed that day. She was never again innocent, never again truly at peace. He stole her youth in the five minutes it took him to have what he wanted.

Stefan pulled her into his lap like she was a rag doll and held her while she cried, smoothing her hair and murmuring reassurances. After a few moments, she'd managed to stop crying, but she couldn't stop shaking.

"You need to get warm. Let's get you under covers," he said.

He arranged pillows so she could sit upright and helped her into bed, tucking the covers around her legs and brushing her hair from where it had stuck to her damp cheeks.

Stefan didn't press her for details like she thought he would. Instead, he walked over to the bar and made her a cup of tea. Without a word, he handed it to her and sat back on the side of the bed.

She took a sip and set it on the bedside table. Sitting back on the pillows, she stared at the ceiling. "I've never told anyone the truth about who it was. I made up a story about a stranger and a van because he threatened to kill my mother or anyone else I loved. He's a powerful man, with resources to do whatever he wants to whomever he wants. It was true then, and it's true now."

He spoke softly. "Who is he?" Another level of understanding crossed his face. "He's a public figure."

"He's powerful, with more money than God." Her voice shook, but she continued anyway. She must say it all to Stefan. Right now. She had to, or she would die. "Those roses yesterday? He sends them every year on the anniversary of that day to remind me he can do it again, or he can hurt the people I love at any time. He's everywhere, Stefan."

"Jesus, Gennie. Who is this guy?" He'd kept his face stoic during her diatribe, but now the muscle of his left cheek pulsated once again in a steady rhythm. "President of the United States?"

"Not yet."

Stefan stared at her. "Are you talking about Rick Murphy?"

She nodded, letting out a deep breath. "Rick Murphy was in his first term as a Wisconsin state senator when I was fifteen." There was no further explanation needed. Everyone knew the Murphy story. They were old money, as rich as the Rockefellers or the Gettys. "Twenty years ago, Rick Murphy was thirty-four. I was fifteen. I won an essay contest and was granted an interview with him for my school's paper." Her voice cracked as bile rose in her throat. "It was in his office." She stopped talking. It was enough. Stefan could fill in the rest. "When he was done, he blindfolded me and left me on a dirt road not far from my house. It was dark. Snow so high I could barely walk. I didn't know where I was. I thought I was going to die."

Tears trickled down the sides of his face. "Oh, baby, I'm sorry."

"It took me months to understand what had happened—that I was pregnant. That's when I told my mother the partial truth about what had happened. She'd made me go to the police, but they had no leads since I'd lied, and the man I'd described didn't exist. Honestly, I think they thought I was lying about the rape to make an excuse for the pregnancy. It didn't matter by then. My mom helped me get through it. She was by my side the entire time. When it was over, we sold the house in Wisconsin and came to Los Angeles. She wanted me to have a fresh start. I took an acting class, and I figured out that escaping into someone else's skin was the only way to bear the pain of what had happened. I've been using it ever since."

"What made you decide to have the baby?" he asked gently.

"I was four months along before I realized I was pregnant. That's about the time most women feel the baby's first movements. That's what happened to me. I felt her fluttering inside me, and I knew I could never make the choice to end her life."

He wiped under his eyes and took her hand. "You're a brave girl, Gennie Banks."

"There's not a day I haven't thought of her. I've been curious, of course, about how she turned out, what she looks like. But, given everything, I've always felt it was best for her if her origin was kept a secret. Now, I don't know what to do. I don't want her to suffer."

"They showed her photograph on television. And they have footage of her going into her apartment. They keep playing it over and over." He opened his mouth as if to say something further but seemed to think better of it.

"You were going to say she looks like me, weren't you?" she asked. "Trix already told me."

He nodded. "From what I can tell, she's taller than you and athletic rather than slender, but yes, she looks like you."

"Athletic?"

"She swims for her college team."

"Does she seem happy? Could you tell? Of course you couldn't. That's a ridiculous question." She cringed at how desperate she sounded.

"They said she was at UCLA on a scholarship and that she's a good student. She wants to be a teacher."

"She's going to be under scrutiny the rest of her life. I hate that. It's one thing for you and me, but she didn't ask to be famous."

"What are you going to do about her request to meet you?"

"Now that she knows who I am, I don't think I have much choice but to meet her. It would hurt her further if I rejected her. I just can't tell her the truth about the rape or her father. She must never know how she came to be if she's to have any semblance of a normal life. I will keep it a secret from her. It's the only way to protect her."

"Gennie, can I ask you something?"

"Of course."

"Do you think it's cost you to carry around a secret for so long?"

"You mean about Murphy?"

"Yes."

She played with the sheet, rubbing it between her fingers. "The toll is too high to calculate." Looking up, she met his gaze. "It's cost me you."

"Would it surprise you to know that I understand the toll, that I might even be able to calculate the relationships lost because I've calculated my own losses?"

"It would," she said.

"I have a secret too. As big as yours. Maybe bigger." His voice broke. He brushed tears from the corners of his eyes. Clearing his throat, he reached for her tea and took a sip. "I think about that question a lot. What's it cost me to keep a secret this big for so long? Would I be a better man if it had never happened? Would I be a better man if I'd ever told the truth?"

She took his hand. "I don't know. It depends on the secret, I guess."

"I've never told anyone and didn't think I ever would. Until I met you. You're the only person I've ever felt I could trust. The only person I thought would understand and not judge me or blame me. I didn't know why I felt this when you were so obviously unavailable.

But now, I know why. We've both been to hell and released back into the world with a secret attached to our souls. I saw it in you, without knowing what it was."

She stared at him. "What's your hell?"

He took another sip of tea before setting it back on the table. "When I was twelve years old, I killed my father."

Gennie stifled a gasp. Surely, she had heard him wrong. Her mind tumbled over the possibilities. Was it an accident? Or had it been on purpose?

He continued, staring into his lap while he spoke, "My father was a mean man, especially when he drank. He'd come home drunk from the bars and beat the crap out of my mom at least once a week. My mom made me promise I would never come into their bedroom or the kitchen or any room when they were fighting—she called it fighting, but it wasn't a fight. It was spousal abuse, plain and simple. When I was small, I obeyed her wishes, but when I was about nine, I started trying to rescue her. He would turn on me. He was big and strong, and I was a kid, so you can imagine how that went."

Stefan rubbed his chin and looked up at the ceiling. "My best friend's dad was a gun guy. Most men where I'm from keep guns around for protection and hunting. The summer I turned eleven, I asked him if he'd teach me to shoot. I was good at it. Pretty soon I hit the target easily. My friend's dad said I was a natural.

"One night, I woke up to the sound of my mom screaming from their bedroom. I'd never heard her scream that way."

Gennie's heart beat faster. *What was it? What was the bastard doing to her?*

"I was terrified. It sounded like she was being cut in half. Without thinking, I was out of bed and kicked open their bedroom door. He was on top of her on the floor, his pants around his ankles. Her nightgown was around her waist. He had his hunting knife in his hand, about to plunge it into her chest. I could see that he'd already done it at least once because there was blood all over her nightgown. It was all clear to me. He'd raped her and then stabbed her."

How had he known what was happening? He was so young.

"His shotgun was on the nightstand. I grabbed it and unlocked the safety just like I'd been taught, and I aimed it at him."

"Oh no," she whispered. Her limbs tingled with fear, knowing what came next. *He killed his father. Stefan killed him.*

"I knew it was loaded. He always kept it loaded. And I shot him in the head."

"Oh my God, Stefan." Her hands flew to her mouth. *The poor little boy. Had he seen his father's brain splattered all over everything? How could Stefan ever recover from that?*

"I don't remember anything after that. The police came and they questioned me, but I can't recall anything I said. No one locked doors in those parts, so my mother told the police an intruder had come into the house and shot him using my dad's gun. The police chief and my mom grew up together, and he knew the truth of what was going on in our house. Everyone in town did. Bruises weren't so easy to disguise, and everyone knew what kind of man he was. If the chief believed her, I don't know, but the investigation was cut short and nothing ever came of it."

"Except you've lived with the guilt and shame." Gennie pulled his hand into her lap, stroking his wrist. *He's like me. Tortured with a secret. Full of shame and regret. He understands me.*

"The only time I can forget is when I'm acting. Or, lately, when I'm with you."

Just like me.

"What I saw that night burned into my consciousness in a way I can never escape. The brutality of monsters like my dad and Murphy is unforgivable. I hope they both burn in hell for it." His eyes shone like a child with a high fever. "So, Gennie, I get it. I get it all. And I'm sorry. My understanding of why you're the way you are is deeper than you can imagine. I love you. I would always love you, no matter what. Do you understand what I'm saying?"

"I think I do. I had no idea what you've been through, or your poor mother. Is she all right?"

"Like you, she will never be the same."

"As much as she'd like to, she can't ever be fully whole," Gennie said. *She wants to be, but she can't. No matter how she tries, she can't ever forget.*

"Right."

"It's not like a wound on the outside that will eventually heal." *It's way down deep where no one can see. The darkness wants to take you down with it. The demons shout to surrender to them.* "Do you and your mom ever talk about it?"

"Not really. I think she likes to pretend it never happened. She has a lot of guilt, as you can imagine."

His mother's guilt and shame must be unbearable. Gennie had felt shame too. *What had I done to make him choose me?* "When he was done, he called me a slut and said that I'd provoked him. I was a little girl. I had no idea what it meant to provoke someone." She squeezed his wrist. "You were a little boy. Your instinct to protect your mother was good, not bad."

"Then how come I feel like a criminal?"

Her heart twisted, feeling his pain course through her own body. *It's not your fault. It was never your fault.* "Because human beings are complicated." She stared into his eyes. *Sensitive eyes. Searching eyes. I want to make his pain go away. Do something. Take his pain away. Say something that will make him better.* "You're not to blame. Not for any of it."

He caressed the side of her face with his fingertips. "About two years after my father's death, my mom came home from church on a Sunday morning. I was in the other room when she came in, but I could tell she was angry by the way she stomped around the kitchen and slammed pots and pans. I figured she was mad at me because I wouldn't get up for church. I didn't want to, but I went in there and asked her what was wrong. She told me the preacher had given a sermon that morning about thankfulness. He said that if you approach your life from a position of thankfulness, it's more likely a miracle will come."

"Why did it make her mad? Did she think it was a lie?"

He nodded. "She said it was all good and well for a person like fat Preacher Robinson to talk about miracles with his perfect wife and perfect daughters sitting in the front pew, but where was our miracle? We'd been given nothing but hard times, she said. Nothing but hard men who hurt us. She sat down at the kitchen table and cried. I stood there, just watching her, wishing I were dead. Finally, she looked up at me and said, 'Why has God forsaken us?'"

Why indeed? Where were you, God? Then and that day in Murphy's office?

"It ripped at my heart to see how broken she was. I vowed in that moment to never let her feel forsaken by God or me ever again. That desire has driven every moment of my life since. It drove me during the early years when I could barely pay my rent. I worked harder than anyone in class, on my body, on my craft, all so I could give her a few miracles. After I had made it, I bought her the house she'd always wanted and a fancy car and a full-time housekeeper. Anything she wants, I give her. I take her places she could only dream of when I was young. The drive I have? It's all for her."

"Has it changed her? Does she believe in miracles now?"

"Maybe. I don't know. She's like you. There's a sadness in her eyes that I can't seem to remedy."

She's sad, like me.

"But I *am* thankful, every day, for everything. I'm thankful I'm the guy who gets to be here for you."

"Oh, Stefan. I'm glad it's you. It couldn't be anyone else." Tears leaked from the corners of her eyes. *I don't deserve you, but I am so thankful.* "I do believe in miracles, Stefan. In spite of everything."

"Tell me why," he said, gently.

"That night, afterward, when I was blindfolded and tied, he shoved me into his car and we drove for what seemed like hours." She stopped, suddenly remembering a detail she'd forgotten. "He played the radio. Pop songs. Loud, like a teenager. I'd forgotten that part."

Stefan took her hand. "No wonder you hate nineties music."

"He dumped me on the side of the road. I had no idea where I was. It had snowed at least a foot that afternoon and was so dark I couldn't see my hand in front of me. No stars. No moon. I thought I'd die out there, alone. Then, three things happened. Three miracles. I remembered I had a flashlight in my coat pocket. My father had given it to me the Christmas before he died. I shone it all around me, and I saw a scarecrow across the street. I knew where I was; my house was just up the road. My best friend and I passed that scarecrow on the way home every day."

His gaze remained steady. "What was the third miracle?"

"I heard this rustling in the woods. It was an elk with enormous antlers. He just stood there, looking at me. I called out to him—asked him what to do. That's when I heard the voice of my father in my head. He said to follow the light home. Which I did."

"That's incredible, Gennie."

"It was my father. I'm sure of it. God sent him to me."

"Have you ever seen the elk again?" he asked.

"No. Not since that night. But I feel him with me sometimes. This sense of peace washes over me, and I know he's there, not far away, and someday I'll see him again." She smiled. "In human form."

"That feeling of peace? I feel that way every time I'm with you. Like you're where I belong."

Last night, when you left, the pain was so bad I thought I was dying. Like the time in the snow. "I feel safe with you. Safer than I've ever felt."

"Gennie, could our meeting be a miracle? Maybe God brought us together, knowing we needed one another, knowing we belong together."

She shivered. Goose bumps dotted her arms. Had God brought this remarkable man to her? Was it time to forgive God for what had happened? *I was an innocent child, just like Stefan was. God was nowhere that day.* An image of her classmates, all sitting primly in English class with their white socks and plaid skirts and hair ties flashed before her mind. The warmth of Margaret as they walked arm-in-arm home from school. The sweet scent of the candy shop. She was innocent then. All had been well. She had trusted that God would always be there, but He wasn't. Had He returned to her now?

Belong together? Did they belong together? "Maybe." *I want him beside me. I want his warmth against me.* It was the most important thing. She must have him next to her, as close as possible. She scooted to the middle of the bed and lifted the covers. "Get in here."

He raised his eyebrows. "Are you sure?"

She smiled and patted the spot she'd just vacated. "Please. I'm so cold."

He got into bed and lay on his back. She pulled the covers over them. When she snuggled next to him, he wrapped his arms around her waist, holding her against his chest. His body, solid and warm, calmed her. She was safe here. She was safe with Stefan. *You're the light I must follow home.*

"You're the best man I know," she said.

"And I adore every part of you." He kissed the top of her head.

"Even all the parts no one else can see?" *All the invisible demons lurking in my heart, wanting to extinguish the light?*

"Especially those." His arms tightened around her.

"Yours too.

"Can you try and sleep awhile?"

"I think so." She closed her eyes, utterly exhausted. "Stay with me, please. Don't leave."

"I won't leave until you tell me to."

"What if I never tell you to leave?"

"Then I'll stay forever."

A few moments later, she was asleep. Gennie dreamt of the elk. She rode on his strong back, with a billion stars overhead.

CHAPTER FOUR

SHE WOKE SEVERAL HOURS LATER curled next to Stefan. He slept on his stomach, with one arm under the pillow. His eyelashes splayed against his cheekbones; she could easily imagine him as a little boy. She watched him for a few moments, contemplating all they had shared that morning. Everything was different. Revealing their secrets had moved their connection to a deeper place, one as intimate as sex itself. They knew each other in a way no one else, except their mothers, knew them.

She slipped from the bed, careful not to shake it. He needed to sleep, even if she couldn't. It was only nine o'clock. The early morning phone call from Trix felt like it had happened a lifetime ago. In her socks, she went to the window and lifted one slat of the wooden shutter. The sky was a brilliant blue, and the snow sparkled silver in the sunlight.

A memory came to her. She was six years old, holding her father's hand. They looked out the window into their yard. A fresh blizzard had come the night before, but now the sun shone, making the snow sparkle and dance. "Fairy dust, Daddy. I see fairy dust." He dropped to his knees and wrapped his arms around her, holding her close. "We could use some magic about now," he said.

"It's right there, Daddy. All the magic we need."

She touched the cold glass where ice made an etching like a snowflake. *Daddy, I miss you.*

What had Stefan said? *Do you think it's cost you to carry around a secret for so long?* What had it cost her to keep the complete truth from her mother? She had done it to protect her, but had it robbed them of a more intimate relationship? They were close. The tragedy of the past had not torn them apart but had brought them closer. Would they be even more so if she'd told her about Murphy? What did our secrets and half-truths cost us? What had they cost her?

She turned away from the window. Stefan had awakened and was sitting up, watching her. "Hi."

"Did I wake you?" she asked.

"Maybe, but it doesn't matter. I'm feeling much better."

"Me too." She glanced at the clock. "I have to have a video conference call with Trix and Reid in a half hour."

He was out of bed, stretching his arms over his head. His t-shirt rose a few inches, and she caught a glimpse of his taut stomach. How did the man make a baggy pair of sweatpants and a t-shirt look that good? Her hands twitched at her sides. *I want to touch him. Know his every part of his body with my fingertips like a blind person reading braille.*

"You should eat something," he said. "I'll check and see if Linus left our goodies." At the Second Chance Inn scones were left outside each guest's room in an attractive basket that included marionberry jam and whipped butter. Gennie had requested her basket be given to someone else, explaining that she had to watch her weight carefully. Instead, without her asking for it, Linus had started leaving her two pieces of dry wheat toast and a boiled egg. She loved Linus for it and the many other small kindnesses he'd shown her during her stay.

Stefan went out to the hallway for a moment and returned with their baskets. "Linus never lets us down," he said.

After arranging the food on the small table and making fresh cups of coffee, they sat down to eat. Gennie was surprised to find she was hungry, even using some of Stefan's jam for her toast.

"Do you think there have been others?" Stefan asked.

"Others?"

"Other victims."

"I don't know." Taken aback by the abrupt question, she set aside her toast, feeling suddenly nauseous. "I've not allowed myself to think about it." *I didn't want to know. I was too scared to even ask myself the question.* "If he threatened them like he did me, they could all be in hiding too."

"If there are others and you came forward, it might encourage them to come forward as well. There's power in numbers."

She stared at him, shocked. "You think I should come forward?" *I can't come forward. Don't ask me to.*

He ran his hand through his messy hair. "I'm not sure, Gennie. It's just that, well, when I woke up, I started thinking he might be a serial rapist. What if you could save other women from being hurt? You're rich and you're famous. You have a power that others might not."

"What about Sarah? I don't want her to know the truth."

He picked up the cap from the tiny jar of jam, turning it over in his hand. "Our secrets have hurt us. I wonder if it wouldn't be better that she knew the truth. The whole truth."

She stared at the floor. *Don't panic. Just breathe. I don't have to do anything but keep my mother and Sarah safe.* "He'll say I'm lying. He could wreck my career, or worse, hurt someone I love."

"If you accuse him he'll be forced to take a DNA test, proving his guilt," Stefan said. "My best friend, Grant Perry, is an attorney who represents victims like you all the time. He's the best there is. He can help you figure out the best approach."

"Murphy will spin the truth. Say I was a little tart and seduced him."

"You were fifteen years old. Whether it was consensual or not, it's still rape."

"He'll say he had no idea I was so young. Then he'll apologize to his wife, but the scandal will ruin his chances for the presidency. That will enrage him. I won't ever be safe. One day you'll get a call that I've overdosed in my hotel room, or driven my car off a cliff, and you'll be the only one who knows it was arranged by him. You'll be powerless to prove it, and if you try, you'll be next." Her voice had risen an octave. *Just stop talking. I don't have to defend my decisions, not even to Stefan.*

"This monster could become president. We'd have a rapist in the White House."

"There's Sarah to consider," she said.

"Are you going to meet her?" he asked.

She hesitated, unsure of the answer. "I don't know what to do. I need more time to think."

He reached across the table and took her hand. "Whatever you decide, I'm here for you."

"No matter what I decide?" *Even if I stay hidden under my lies?*

"No matter what." He squeezed her hand. "Whatever you want, I will support you. If you want to fight him, though, I'm ready."

I need time to think. It's all too fast. "I should take a shower before my video conference."

After letting go of her hand, he crumpled his napkin and left it on the table. "I'll pop over to my room and get cleaned up too. I need to call my mom and tell her I won't be home for the weekend after all."

"What? No, you have to go. She'll be so disappointed." *Please stay with me. Say you'll stay.*

"It's best that you remain here in town until all this gets sorted out. You're safer here than anywhere, especially since everyone thinks you're in Hawaii. And wherever you are, I will be."

"But, Stefan…" She trailed off, not knowing what to say.

"If you want me to stay, that is," he said.

"I want you to stay."

"Then I will."

* *

Later, Gennie dialed into a video call with Reid and Trix. The quality of the feed was so good it felt almost as if she were there with them in Reid's Beverly Hills home office. They sat in twin chairs next to a large window, a swimming pool and manicured garden in the background. Reid, tanned, with salt and pepper hair, was casually dressed in khakis and a loose t-shirt. Trix wore a designer suit. Petite and so thin she looked almost ill, her bleached blond hair was perfectly fixed into loose curls. No matter the time of day or night, she sipped from a large Starbucks coffee.

Reid took the lead, his voice and demeanor soothing, unflappable, no matter the situation. One could not do this kind of work and be the nervous type. "If it's all right with you, Genevieve, let's talk through how we should approach this with the public."

"Fine," Gennie said. "Where do we start?"

She looked over at Stefan. He sat in the chair by the window, out of the camera's view, with a pad and pencil in his lap, doodling.

"Why don't you tell us your version of the story," said Reid.

She launched into the story of the rape, leaving out the part about Murphy. "So, the long and short of it is, I did not abandon my baby. On the contrary, I made a very careful decision for her."

"Yes, I see. It must have been a hard decision," Reid said.

"I never thought of doing anything else," Gennie said.

"Was it because you were raised Catholic?"

"It influenced me some, sure. Mostly, though, it was just me. The baby was a person to me, no matter how she came to be."

"Are you comfortable talking about whether your faith factored into the decision?"

"Not really. It's a personal decision, and I'm not interested in telling anyone what they should do. It was the right choice for me. For others, especially in cases of rape, it might not be. I don't want to get pulled into the national debate over abortion."

"Are you prepared to discuss the rape?" Reid asked.

"I'm not sure. There's Sarah to think of. She doesn't know about any of this, other than her biological mother was an unwed teen."

"Yes, her well-being complicates things. I'm not saying I agree with this strategy, but you could simply leave out the detail about the rape," said Reid. "Giving up a baby at fifteen was a respectable choice. This isn't the Victorian Era. That said, if you talk about the rape and that you decided to have the baby anyway, well, it adds a very human element to it—especially if you emphasize that your decision was personal, as you believe everyone's should be. You'll be perceived as selfless, thinking of the baby's well-being before anything else. Both sides of the argument will be appeased."

Beside him, Trix sighed. The bangles on her skinny arms clinked.

"What're you thinking, Trix?" Reid asked.

"I want you to tell the truth about the rape, Gennie. It's hot right now, this sexual abuse thing. Everyone and their mother's coming forward lately."

"For heaven's sake, Trix, this is a real thing that happens to real women. It's not a fad to be exploited," Gennie said.

"All I'm saying is that the timing of this might be perfect for you to become the sexual abuse ambassador. You could do a lot of good with it, and the publicity would be tremendous."

"The sexual abuse ambassador?" Gennie asked. "Honestly, Trix."

"All right, ladies. Let's get back on track here," Reid said.

"Listen, guys, I want to meet Sarah first and talk this over with her," Gennie said. "I must respect her wishes on something that will affect her for the rest of her life."

"Gennie, who do you want to give the interview to? All the big guys will want it."

"Raquel Birdwell," Gennie said.

"Raquel? Not Matt or George?" Trix asked.

"I want Raquel. We go back. She'll handle it with sensitivity." And she was a woman. It had to be a woman.

Trix waved her hands in a gesture of impatience. "Well, it's the day before Thanksgiving. I don't know if we can get her to fly from New York to River Woods or wherever the hell you are," Trix said.

"River Valley," Gennie said. "She'll fly out here if I ask her to."

"Fine. I'll arrange it. We'll put it out to the media that you'll be doing a tell-all interview airing the day after Thanksgiving," Trix said. "The ratings will be amazing."

"I'll call Raquel myself," Gennie said. "I want to explain things to her."

"Sure. Fine. Whatever. As long as you get her there," Trix said.

"Gennie, let us know what you decide to do, and we'll help however we can. Good luck meeting Sarah," Reid said.

"Thanks. I need a little luck." She looked away from the computer screen. An icicle hung from the window, melting under the sunlight. She focused her gaze back on the screen. "Regardless of what exactly I'll say, I'll do the interview with Raquel the day after tomorrow. We'll go from there."

Reid nodded, giving her a slight smile. "Sounds good. Happy Thanksgiving."

Trix was staring into the computer camera with a glazed expression. It was best to hang up before she went into fighter mode.

"Thanks for your time. Trix, I'll call you later." Gennie closed the screen and shut the lid of her laptop. She stared at the ceiling for a moment, then called Raquel to ask if they could arrange an interview.

Raquel answered on the first ring. "Gennie, I saw the story. Are you all right?"

"I've been better. I need to talk publicly about what happened. Would you like the interview? I know it's a bad time with the holiday, and I'm in the middle of Oregon. It's pretty here. There's snow. Very festive, actually."

"I don't have much going on. The kids are with their dad for a ski weekend, so I'm all alone. I was going to take a few days off, but what the heck. I've never been to Oregon before. Do I need a flannel shirt?"

Gennie smiled. "No, but it's a small town. Very small."

"Did you finish filming?"

"We wrapped yesterday. Just in time for my world to blow up."

"Can you tell me the real story?" asked Raquel.

She took a deep breath and repeated her story. Each time it was more succinct, like rewriting an essay. "But I'm not sure how much I want to tell. I need to talk with Sarah first."

"You're going to meet her?"

"Yes. If she wants to meet me, I'll make sure it happens."

"Gennie, this must be incredibly difficult. I'm sorry you have to go through all this."

"Thanks. I'm appreciative that you'll come out here on a holiday weekend."

"You can repay me by taking me to that restaurant you were raving about the last time we talked. What's it called? Something to do with a song."

"Riversong. Yes, I will take you." Raquel was famous for her love of food.

"They're closed the day after Thanksgiving, though," Gennie said.

"Really? You *are* in a Podunk town."

"Just wait until you see it. If you don't fall in love, I'll be surprised," Gennie said. "And the people are nice. No one bothers me here, and they've succeeded more than once in running off the paparazzi for Stefan and me."

"Stefan Spencer?" Raquel asked. "Is he still there? I'd love to interview him one of these days. Put in a good word for me?"

"I'll let him know you're interested."

"Are the rumors true about you two?" Raquel asked.

"Not exactly." She flushed. "It's complicated."

"Ah, I see," Raquel said.

They spoke for a few more minutes, agreeing that their assistants would work out any further details. "I'll see you tomorrow."

After she hung up, Gennie put aside her phone, not wanting to see further messages from anyone, Stefan murmured an expletive under his breath. He looked over at her, waving his phone. "Richard just texted. We need to turn on the news. George Bentley's on the ABC morning show." He crossed the room and used the remote to turn on the television and find the correct local channel. "This is it."

A young, female talk show host, with glossy blond hair, sat across from a man with the face of an English bulldog.

"I can't believe that's George," Gennie said. He looked nothing like the young man she'd met during their interview. A paunch and a receding hairline, plus deep bags under his eyes, had replaced the boy-next-door good looks.

"Twenty years ago, you adopted a baby from a teenaged girl?"

"That's correct. From Genevieve Banks. She was just a kid then, of course, but we recognized her right away when we saw the publicity for her first film about ten years ago. We had no idea she wanted to be an actress when we adopted Sarah."

"Was it a closed adoption?"

"Sure, yeah."

"If that's the case, aren't you violating that agreement by going public with this?"

"This isn't about me. This is about a woman the world worships who abandoned her baby. I think people deserve to know what kind of person she truly is. We're not fancy people. We've struggled. I've had trouble finding work. My wife left a lot of medical bills after the cancer took her. We went to Ms. Banks and asked her for help, and she ridiculed us—told us it was nothing to do with her. I just want her to take responsibility for what she did."

What a liar. He'd never come to her. She'd assumed all this time that Sarah was in a good home, safe and loved. Instead, she had been raised by a morally bankrupt man. What had happened to him to change him, or had her judgment of character been flawed? Her reasoning skills had not fully formed; she'd been naïve and ridiculously innocent. Her mother, however, had been in complete agreement that they were the right couple. She turned to Stefan. "He never came to me. I would've given them money if they had."

"I know," Stefan said.

The reporter continued. "Mr. Bentley, with all due respect, there are holes in your story. If Ms. Banks abandoned her baby, how did you know she was the birth mother?"

He flinched and turned red. "Because Sarah looks just like her. We put the pieces together."

"How long have you been estranged from your daughter?"

"We're not estranged."

"That's not what she said when we called her for a comment. She indicated that she hasn't talked to you since your wife passed away two years ago. What caused the estrangement?"

"It has nothing to do with this. It's no one's business anyway," George said.

"Sarah said you argued over money. In this case, her college fund. She says you depleted it because of a gambling problem."

"Simply untrue," George said. "I needed that money to pay for my late wife's medical bills."

"She also said that she'd been looking for her birth mother for several years, but the adoption papers were closed. Why didn't you share with her that you knew who her birth mother was?"

George's blinked several times in a row, almost like he had a nervous tick. Beads of sweat were evident on his forehead. "Sarah never told me she'd been looking. That's news to me."

"Thank you, Mr. Bentley, for coming on to share your story with us," the reporter said.

"Thank you," George said. The show went to commercial.

Stefan muted the sound. "He needs money, that much is clear. If it's true he has a gambling problem, then he could owe scary guys big cash. It happens all the time. In desperation, he went this route."

"Do you think it's true he used her college fund?" Gennie asked.

"Probably," Stefan said.

"I wonder why he didn't just come to me? Ask me for money in exchange for his silence?"

"I suspect he wants the limelight and publicity. He's enjoying making you look bad because he's a failure. You're rich while he sees himself as the victim of a hard life."

She stared at him, marveling at his insight. "No wonder you're such a good actor."

He cocked his head to the side. "How so?"

"That was an insightful observation."

A knock sounded on the door. "Who could that be?" Stefan crossed the room and peered through the peephole. "It's Linus," he said, opening the door.

Linus stood in the hallway, holding fresh towels and a large basket. "Good morning. I brought you some goodies and news from the outside world."

Stefan opened the door wider. "Come on in."

Linus set the towels and basket on the desk. "This is a little something I put together for you, Gennie. It has the most delicious smelling bath bubbles, a bottle of white wine, dark chocolate, and one of Ellen White's marionberry pies. I know you don't eat bad things like pie, but under the circumstances, you might make an exception." He held up an envelope. "This is a little card from the Riversong gang. Annie told me to tell you to call the restaurant if you want anything, and I'll bring it over to you."

"Linus, this is so thoughtful of you," Gennie said. "All of this isn't necessary. We just finished the breakfast you left."

"It's obvious what this Bentley character's after. I don't want you to worry about a thing. While you're here with us, I'll make sure to keep you safe from paparazzi. You two can stay in these rooms for however long you need to."

"Do you have a room for my mother?" Gennie asked. "She'll be here this afternoon."

"I have one room left, thank goodness," Linus said.

"Raquel Birdwell's flying in tomorrow," Gennie said. "To interview me. I had Blair book her at the lodge. She's a suite kind of a girl."

"Raquel Birdwell?" Linus put his hand on his forehead like he might faint. "She's fabulous. Love her. I'll call my buddy who runs the lodge and make sure they pull out all the stops." He continued without taking a breath, his eyes alight with excitement, "Where will you conduct the interview? We could do it in my lobby, but it's not private. The room here seems too small." He snapped his fingers. "I know. You should use Annie and Drake's house. It's perfect for an interview."

"Would they mind?" Stefan asked. "Because you're right. It's the perfect location."

"They'll be happy to help," Linus said. "I'll call them right away. Leave everything to me. Now, I should run and leave you two alone." `

"Linus, before you go," Gennie said.

He halted at the door. "Yes?"

"I didn't abandon the baby. I put her up for a very legal adoption. I thought she was with good people all this time."

"Sweetie, you've been part of our community for months now. We consider you a friend, not a movie star. We know you here. And anyone who knows you, knows you would never do such a thing."

She smiled, fighting tears. "Thank you for the treats and for your support. Will you tell the others thank you for the card?"

"Absolutely. You get some rest before your mother arrives. If she's anything like mine, you'll need it."

CHAPTER FIVE

GENNIE'S MOM ARRIVED AROUND THREE, having been fetched from the airport by a brave Tommy who said a few snowy roads didn't scare him. When they appeared at her door, Gennie almost wept with joy to see them. Her mom wore a white ski jacket with a faux fur collar. Tommy, dressed in a bomber jacket and ski cap, held her small suitcase. It always amazed Gennie how economically her mother could pack for a trip. She ushered them both into the room, thanking Tommy for driving in this dreadful weather.

"It was my pleasure," Tommy said, giving her mom a wink. "We had a good talk. Plus, I go crazy if I'm indoors for too long." Tommy plucked his knit hat from his head and brushed his fingers through his hair.

"The streets are slick, but Tommy drove without any trouble." Cheeks flushed and eyes bright, her mom looked well, despite the reasons for being here. Her hair, cut into flattering layers that flipped out at her jawline, made her appear youthful and sassy. All traces of gray were hidden with a perfect color job. Five years ago, she'd surprised Gennie by asking for a facelift. Gennie had found a doctor in Beverly Hills with an impeccable reputation, and he'd done a marvelous job, taking years away without stretching the skin to give her that "stuck in a wind tunnel" look.

"Did you know Tommy wrote the number one country song on the charts this week?" her mother asked. "We heard it on the radio just now."

"Joan, you're going to give me a big head, which my wife will not appreciate," Tommy said with a self-deprecating grin.

"Phooey. I bet she's enormously proud of you." Her mom set her purse on the desk next to the basket of goodies. "It's so exciting.

You'd think I'd get used to all these famous people around me all time, Tommy, but with Gennie, I still think of her as just my little girl, not some big movie star."

"We were all star-struck when she and Stefan first arrived, but now we just think of them as part of our gang," Tommy said.

"She's told me over the phone how much fun she's had, and it's gorgeous here." Her mom smiled as she walked over to the window and peered out at the scenery. "I should've come up sooner."

"I told you, Mom."

"Yes, you did. I should've listened."

It would be dark soon, but for now, the sun fought hard against its impending retirement. Hanging just above the mountains, its orange light cast shadows across the snow.

"What a sight." Her mother turned to look back at Gennie. "Truth be told, Tommy, I love the weather in Malibu and hardly ever want to leave. The beach is my special place. I love walking and smelling that beachy smell."

"I understand perfectly. The first time I came here to River Valley and jumped into the river on a hot August day, I never wanted to leave," Tommy said.

While they chatted for a few more moments about their love of water, Gennie pondered Tommy's choice to live in River Valley over someplace like Nashville or Los Angeles. Although he had the talent to be a star like Moody, he was happier in River Valley with his wife and daughter, writing songs for other people to sing rather than pursuing that life for himself. If he had any regrets, it wasn't obvious. He appeared to be undeniably comfortable in his own skin and at peace with his decisions. *If only I felt the same.*

Tommy scrunched his knit hat back on his head, arranging it over his ears. "I'll be on my way and let you two talk. Lee wanted me to tell you to keep your chin up. She says everything will work itself out."

Gennie knew from Bella that Lee's first husband had committed suicide over a failed business decision. Lee was left to sort out his debt to a dangerous loan shark. She'd found a second chance for happiness in River Valley. Bella said there was magic in the river, believing the water restored and healed. Given Lee's and Bella's happy endings, perhaps there was something to the theory.

"Before I go, Lee and Annie wondered if you would like to come for Thanksgiving tomorrow? The whole gang will be there. And it sounds like Stefan's sticking around as well. We're hoping all three of you will join us."

Gennie glanced at her mom. "It sounds nice. We'll talk about it and let you know. Thanks for the invite."

"Yes, so thoughtful of you," her Mom said.

"I'm out of here. Bye, ladies," Tommy said.

They said goodbye and she thanked him again for the ride. After he was gone, Gennie hugged her mom. "I'm so glad you're here."

Her mom held the sides of Gennie's face, peering into her eyes. "My Gennie girl. Are you all right?"

"It's brought up so much."

"For me too." She gestured toward the small sitting area in front of the fire. "Come, let's sit. We'll talk it all out and come up with a plan."

The unopened basket of goodies caught her attention. *I want a glass of wine for this conversation. No, too early. Tea. Have tea instead.* "Mom, I'm going to make tea. Would you like some?"

"No thank you, sweetie." She had settled into a chair and was untying her snow boots. "They gave us coffee on the plane."

Gennie made a cup of tea with the Keurig, then moved to the chair next to her mom. "Did you see the news stories?"

"I did. I saw her. Sarah. I'd always wondered what they'd chosen to name her. She looks so much like you and your father."

"Yes, it's undeniable whose she is."

"When I saw her photograph on television, I felt a connection to her right way. Perhaps because she looks like you."

"Sarah called Trix. She wants to meet me," Gennie said.

Her mother raised an eyebrow. "I figured as much. How do you feel about it? Do you want to meet her, or will it be too painful?"

"I want to, but I'm worried."

"Are you afraid she'll ask about her father?"

"Yes. I don't want to hurt her with the truth." *Speaking of the truth, I have to break your heart now.* She took a deep breath. "Mom, there's something I have to tell you. Something I haven't been truthful about." *Get control of yourself. You can do this.* She cleared her throat and stalled further by taking a sip of tea.

"Honey, what is it? You're scaring me."

"I lied to you about the rape. It wasn't a stranger. It was Senator Murphy. He attacked me at his home the afternoon I went there for the interview." She told her the rest of the story, stopping at points to blow her nose.

All color had drained from her mom's face. "Why didn't you tell me?"

"He said if I told anyone he would kill you."

Her mom wiped her eyes. "And he's powerful enough to do it and get away with it."

"Yes," Gennie said. She told her of the annual delivery of roses. "He made sure I didn't forget."

"My poor baby."

Unable to bear the look of pain on her mother's face, she sipped her tea. "I'm sorry I lied, Mom, but I was so afraid. I didn't want to jeopardize your safety, and I thought if you knew you would try to go after him. I couldn't lose you. I *can't* lose you."

"Why are you telling me now?"

"Because I realized I don't want to have any secrets from you. I need you to help me figure out what to do."

"Rick Murphy. I can't believe it. That bastard." She spoke his name like she tasted something bitter. She stood.

Her hands are shaking. They shook the day I told her I was pregnant. She was always so calm, so level-headed, but this was too much. *I shouldn't have told her.*

"I think I will have a cup of tea after all," her mom said.

"I'll get it. You sit." At the Keurig, Gennie chose a peppermint pod. *Peppermint always makes her feel better.*

Gennie placed the mug on the side table between the chairs. "Here you are."

"Peppermint. Thank you, honey." She took a large sip, then coughed. Her hands continued to shake as she took another drink. "This is a lot to take in."

"Now you know why I'm hesitant to meet Sarah." Genie remained standing, letting the heat from the fire warm the back of her legs.

Her eyes, glassy with unshed tears, widened. "But you want to?"

"I do. What about you?" Gennie asked. "Do you want to meet her?"

"I would, but like you, I'm worried about her well-being. This is a complex situation we're bringing her into."

"She's already in it," Gennie said. "It's cruel to deny her a meeting. I can imagine how curious she must be. I've thought about it a lot over the years, wondering if she felt rejected because her mother gave her up. It's only natural to want answers."

"Yes, there's no doubt you have to meet her. I'd like to meet her too."

"Did you ever think about her, Mom?"

"All the time."

"Me too. How come we never talked about her?" Gennie asked.

"I never wanted to bring her up in case it hurt you to remember. I was there when you had to send her away. I saw what it did to you." Her mom's voice broke. She waved her hand in front of her eyes. "I'm sorry, sweetie. It was hard for me too. When they took her away, it took everything in me not to run down the hall and grab her back. I knew it wasn't right for you or for her, but damn if it didn't almost kill me."

Gennie reached over and took her mother's hand. "You're strong, Mom. You've always been so strong."

"I haven't felt that way, sweetie."

They sipped their tea in silence for a moment, both staring at the fire. *Talk to her about what to do.*

"Stefan thinks I should tell the truth about Murphy. He thinks there are probably others."

"I agree. We're not as vulnerable as we were twenty years ago. We have wealth now. You can hire the best attorney. You can hire people to protect us. We can't just stay silent and let him hurt more girls. Think of Bill Cosby. Once one woman had the courage to come forward, the others did too. Like with him, you can't be an isolated case. Murphy could become president." She shuddered. "It makes me sick."

"That's what Stefan said. But if I go public, there's no choice but to tell Sarah the whole truth."

Her mom didn't speak for a few seconds. *She's thinking it through. Trying to figure out what we should do.* After a moment, she looked over at Gennie. "I understand why you did it, but it feels terrible that you kept a secret that big from me for such a long time. I can't help but think this is all happening for a reason. That leads me to one conclusion: you should start with telling her the truth and go from there. It affects her life as much as it does yours. Once this goes public, she will be forever known as Rick Murphy's child from a rape. And, Gennie, let's face it, your fame will make things that much worse. The scrutiny will be difficult for her. But the truth is always the better choice."

"It's not just the public scrutiny. What if he goes after her? If I go public, he will do whatever it takes to destroy all of us."

"We'll hire bodyguards for all of us if it comes to that. Or something. We have the resources."

"I suppose we do. I'm sorry I lied to you all these years, Mom. Are you angry?"

"Sweetheart, of course not. Your decisions were made from love, and that bastard scared you. You were a little girl. And, the truth is, he's a dangerous person. We know money can buy a lot of things, including protection from the law. We've seen it over and over again. Look at the Kennedy's for heaven's sake. But honey, you have to do what's right. Stefan's correct. There are probably others. We can't stay silent and let others get hurt."

"He *will* come after me." She couldn't stop the quiver in her voice. "I'm scared."

Her mother sipped her tea, looking over her cup at Gennie. "Your father was the greatest man I ever knew."

She smiled. "I know, Mom. You've only told me that four thousand times." *What does this have to do with anything?*

"That's because it's true. He was a great man in an ordinary life. He always believed we should be the hero in our own stories."

"He was my hero," Gennie said. *He still is.*

"I know, sweetie. He was mine too. We had such a happy marriage. Even though it was cut short, I believe we loved one another so well that we had more joy in our fifteen years together than those lucky enough to have forty."

"I can remember you laughing together in the kitchen," Gennie said. "I associate the smell of dinner cooking with laughter." After he died, she would wake in the middle of the night hearing his laugh…until she remembered he was gone. *And my heart broke all over again.*

"He made me laugh like no one else ever could." Her mother took another sip of her tea, shaking her head, perhaps remembering a specific moment. *What moment did she think of most?*

"We were a wonderful team because we had different strengths. I was the practical one, but he was brave and compassionate and emotionally intelligent. He used his intuition to make decisions, while I used my reasoning skills. You know, always the accountant. We knew one another so well, and we made decisions together about everything. About you. About money. You name it, we discussed it and came up with a plan. When he died, I was lost. Without his intuition, I had no idea what to do, especially when it came to you. The two of you were so alike. He used to tell me sometimes he could actually hear your thoughts just by observing the expressions on your face. How he loved you. You were simply devastated when we lost him, and I had no earthly idea how to help you. My own grief was so consuming."

"Mom, you were perfect. The perfect mother."

"I can think of so many moments I could've been better. Anyway, I suppose you wonder where I'm going with all this."

"The thought had occurred to me," Gennie said, chuckling.

"Your father was a great man in an ordinary life. What would he tell you to do?"

Fight. Stand up to him. Take him down. "He would tell me to fight Murphy." *But I'm not a hero. I'm still a scared little girl.*

"I believe that's true."

"I don't know if I can, though. I don't know if I have it in me," Gennie said.

"You do. And, your life is not ordinary. You're rich and famous. You have power. You have the chance to do something extraordinary. Your compassion for others must outweigh your fear. Do you understand?"

"I think so." *But I don't know if I can do it.*

"Do you remember when we first moved out to L.A. and you asked if you could take acting classes?"

"Sure. The studio off Melrose." It had smelled of cabbage. She had never been able to figure out why.

"I was terrified for you, but I let you go. I thought you were too raw still, too fragile, but you marched into that class with your head held high. When I picked you up, your cheeks were pink—for the first time since it had all happened. I knew then you would survive. You're a survivor, my Gennie girl. You're my hero. I want you to know that. Your enormous talent and work ethic have given me so much to be proud of, but it's your courage that's always amazed me. Your decision to have the baby and then make a life for yourself, even with all the pain and loss, was extraordinary. For heaven's sake, you conquered Hollywood to become the highest paid actress on the planet. You did that. With your grit. So you look fear in the face and spit on it. We're taking Rick Murphy down."

"Mom, you think too much of me."

"A mother knows her child, sometimes better than they know themselves."

Was she brave? Could she do this? *The elk.* She remembered his breath in the cold air, the proud lift of his head. *Daddy, I wish you were here.* "I need a good lawyer."

Her mom patted her leg. "That's a good first step."

"Stefan's best friend is an attorney in Hollywood. He's represented rape victims before."

"I'm surprised you shared everything with him, Gennie girl. I take it you've grown close during filming?" The casual tone of her mother's question didn't match the intense questioning in her eyes. *She wants to know how I feel about him.* Could she admit the truth?

"Yes. Very close," Gennie said.

"Close friends?"

Can I say it out loud? Mommy, I'm in love with him. "He understands me the way no one ever has. He accepts me the way I am, even though I've nearly driven him crazy. I've fallen for him." She paused, gathering courage. *Just say it.* "I'm in love with him."

"Oh, honey, I'm glad."

"But you know it's not that simple. I'm so messed up, and I don't want to destroy him like I did Moody."

"Things are different, though, with Stefan. I can see it in your eyes. You told him about *everything*. You've never done that with anyone, even me. You trust him."

"He's different than other men. He's been through more than most people. Like me. This morning when all this came out, he came right over, even though last night we'd parted ways. He told me he wanted more, but I didn't think I could do it. I don't want to hurt him like I did Moody. Then, this morning, when I told him the real story about what happened all those years ago, he shared his own past. Our connection grew deeper."

"Can you share it with me?" asked Mom.

"I'm the only one he's ever told. I don't think he'd want me to."

"I understand." She smiled. "Maybe someday, after we know one another, he will share it with me."

"I can't wait for you to meet him. You're going to love him."

"If you love him, I will love him."

* *

After getting her mother settled into her own room, Gennie went back upstairs. It was time. She would call Sarah. With shaking hands, she punched in Sarah's number. It rang four times before a girl answered. "This is Sarah."

Gennie fought tears, swallowing the painful lump in the back of her throat. "Hi, Sarah. This is Gennie Banks."

"Oh, wow. Thanks for calling."

"Yes, sure. Of course. I'm sorry for all this." *I'm sorry your father's a monster. Both of your fathers.*

"Thanks. It's my dad. He's gone crazy. It's gambling. He has a bad problem. I know you never wanted me to know who you were, so I'm sorry if this is majorly screwing with your life."

She's hurt. She feels rejected. "I wanted you to have a good life with good people. I was only fifteen."

"My mom told me that part."

"Trix said you'd like to meet me."

"Yeah. Would you want to?" She had a husky voice and sounded very *west coast*. Californians claimed they had no accents, but that wasn't true.

"Yes, I would like to meet you. I'm in Oregon right now, and this situation with your father has made it necessary for me to stay here for a while, out of public view. I'd be willing to fly you up here if you wanted. We could meet and spend some time talking."

"Really? Like tomorrow?" Sarah asked.

Tomorrow? It's Thanksgiving. Why not tomorrow? The sooner the better.

Sarah continued, sounding breathless. "I know it's Thanksgiving, but since my mom died, I don't really have anywhere to go. I'm just hanging out here in my apartment. I can't really go out because there's like a million photographers outside my building."

Gennie explained that she'd have Trix help her get out of the apartment and to the airport. "Are you willing to be a little creative?" Gennie asked.

"I guess so."

"I'll have her call you in a few minutes. If I send a plane for you, can you be ready at eight tomorrow morning?"

"A plane? Like a private plane?"

"I think that's for the best," Gennie said. "Given all the paparazzi."

"Okay. Cool. Weird, but cool."

Gennie smiled. "Wait for Trix's call. She'll guide you through everything. Also, my mother's with me. She'd like to meet you as well."

"Really? That'd be sick."

"Sick?"

"Good. Like really good."

Gennie laughed. "All right then. I'll see you tomorrow."

"Awesome. Bye."

"Goodnight, Sarah."

*   *

It was nearly five o'clock when she knocked on Stefan's door. He answered, freshly shaven and wearing jeans and a flannel shirt. Her stomach flipped at the sight of him. *It's ridiculous how good looking he is.*

He held out his arms, and she went to him, letting him pull her close. "You smell good," she said.

"Did your mother arrive?"

"Yes. She's resting in her room. I'm going to take her next door for dinner at seven. Will you join us? She's dying to meet you."

He smiled, teasing her with his eyes. "You told her about me?"

"Your name came up a few times, yes."

"Should I take that as a good sign?" he asked.

"I think so." She wrapped her arms tighter around his neck, breathing in his scent. "I've decided something."

"Come sit and tell me what you've decided. I'm having a glass of wine. You want some?"

"Nothing has ever sounded better." She sat in one of the chairs by the fireplace. "Is this the first time I've ever been in your room?"

He shrugged. "I guess so. We usually hang at your place, so to speak."

His room was identical to hers except it was considerably messier. Clothes were strewn about the bed and several scripts lay open on the coffee table, along with a half dozen coffee mugs, a baseball cap, and a candy bar wrapper. A half-empty bottle of whiskey on the desk and an open laptop completed the picture of a reclusive artist. "Weren't you planning on leaving this morning?"

"Yeah, why do you ask?"

"You don't look packed," she said.

"I wasn't. I always pack last minute," he said. "Don't you?"

"Sort of. But all my stuff is neatly put in drawers and hung up in the closet, so it's easy to get out fast." Truth be told, she'd worn the same clothes often over the past few months, surprised about how little she needed. Several pairs of jeans, a couple of sun dresses, and some t-shirts had been her wardrobe since she arrived. *I love it here. I don't want to leave. I don't want to go back to my complicated life.*

He crossed the room with her wine. "It *is* a bit messy, I guess." Laughing, he handed her the glass and moved a pile of books from the other chair and sat, propping his feet up on the ottoman. *He makes everything look like home. Cozy and soft.*

She sank back into the chair and placed her legs next to his on the ottoman, letting the flames warm her feet. Why did his room feel so much warmer than her own?

He wore thick socks that bunched around his toes. She imagined him as a little boy. *Small and fierce with those sad, soulful eyes.*

"I told my mom the truth this afternoon."

"About Murphy."

She nodded. "She thinks I should go after him."

He swirled his wine. "I do too."

"I know." She sipped her wine. "And I talked to Sarah. She's coming tomorrow."

"Holy shit."

"Yeah. Holy shit," Gennie said.

"You want to call Grant now before it gets too late?"

"Let's do it."

* *

Grant was at home when Stefan called. After she told him the details of her case, he suggested she start with filing a civil suit against Murphy to prove paternity. Once it was proven that Sarah is Murphy's daughter, Grant would file criminal charges with the District Attorney's office. "If I hustle, I can get the motion filed today so we can get results sooner rather than later."

They chatted about a few other details, such as his fees and where to send paperwork. "Gennie, I'm sorry this happened to you," Grant said at the end of the call. "But this is open and shut for statutory rape if Sarah's his daughter. He *will* go to jail."

After she'd hung up phone, Gennie looked over at Stefan. "I guess I'd better buckle up."

"I believe so." He reached across the table, running his hands through her long hair. Outside, night had come. "You're so pretty in the firelight."

"You don't look so bad yourself." She sipped her wine, turning away for a moment, suddenly shy. *I can't look at him, or I might start to cry. He's gentle and kind. He's a good man, like my father was.*

"Do you ever wonder if people would like you as much if they knew who you really are?" he asked.

"Everyone does," she said, turning to him.

His eyes burned into her. "Do they? I always thought it was just me."

"It's not just you. I saw the real you this morning."

"And you still like me?" He smiled, his eyes soft.

"I still like you." *I want to kiss him. Really kiss him. I want to feel his body against mine. I want his hands on my skin.*

"Gennie, did you hear what I said?"

"What? Sorry, no."

"I said, let's take a walk downtown before we take your mom to dinner. There's something I want you to see."

I'd go with you anywhere, anytime.

*   *

Bundled in knit hats and heavy coats, they waved to Linus at the front desk, then walked outside to the street. A blast of frigid air stung her cheeks and nose. She pulled her hat over her ears and thrust her gloved hands into her jacket pockets. Sounds of laughter and voices spilled out from Riversong. As they passed the window of the restaurant, faces of happy diners glowed in the candlelight. Up and down Main Street, streetlamps cast a soft glow. Shopkeepers had shoveled snow from the sidewalks in front of their establishments. Christmas lights, strung around the streetlamps, trees, and storefronts, twinkled. "It's like a picture postcard," she said.

"Or a movie set." Stefan looped his arm through hers.

They stood for a moment. She gathered the images, folding them into the recesses of her mind. *If only I could stay forever in this moment.*

"Come on, let's walk," Stefan said. They strolled north toward the end of town. The sky had cleared and billions of stars as bright as the holiday lights blanketed the black night. A sliver of moon hung low, like a lone ornament on a tree. Various storefronts cast yellow light onto the sidewalks. "When I was a kid, one of the highlights of the season was the annual lighting of the tree in my little town," Stefan said. "My mom took me every year and afterward she made spaghetti and meatballs. My favorite."

"Spaghetti and meatballs. That happens to be one of the meals I can cook, as long as the meatballs are the frozen kind that comes in a plastic bag."

"I don't worship you because of your culinary skills."

She laughed. "I can rest easier now."

They passed the diner. It was closed for the night, the lights dimmed over the counter and tables. Next door, the toy store was also closed. Taking the lead from Riversong, the owner had named it Rivertoys, all one word. A giant dollhouse and a train set had equal property in the storefront window. Did children still yearn for these gifts or had technology taken their place?

Rivertoys had opened after Gennie and Stefan's arrival to River Valley, owned by a transplant from San Francisco named Willa Wilde. Bella, who made it her business to know everyone else's business, said it had been Willa's dream to own an old-fashioned toy store like the ones from years past. "Does the name Willa Wilde make you think of a porn star?" she asked.

He laughed. "Kind of."

"My dad loved Christmas." Gennie let out a long breath, remembering the way his eyes sparkled on Christmas morning. "He was the guy in the neighborhood with the over-the-top lights." *Until he died, and then the lights went out, in their yard and in her mother's eyes.*

"Multi-colored or white?" Stefan asked.

"The giant color lights. Remember those?"

"Sure."

She touched the window with her gloved fingers. "My dad built a dollhouse for me when I was six. I went crazy when I saw it under the tree. My mother made all these tiny clothes for the dolls. It was a family, like ours, only with two girls instead of one. What was your favorite gift ever?"

"I got a sled the year I was eight," he said. "I used it so much the bottom became completely slick. We'd get going upwards of twenty miles an hour."

"Twenty? How did you know how fast you were going?"

He grinned. "I'm not sure."

"This sounds like one of those fishing stories."

"No, this was legit," he said.

They walked a little further, then crossed the street, walking back toward the center of town. They stopped when they reached the town square. Located directly across the street from Riversong, it was a glorious centerpiece to the little town. Snowmen and snowwomen, decorated with hats and scarves, hung out in various corners of the park. The gazebo, adorned with the same white lights as the rest of the town, shone brightly in the middle of the square. Gennie sighed. *If only I could stay here and not have to face my real life. What if this were my real life instead of the one I'm currently living? What would it feel like to live here, to be part of this community?*

"I wanted you to see it all lit up," Stefan said, gesturing toward the lights. "Mike turned them on this morning. Don't you love them?"

"I do." *He's like a kid. He makes me feel like a kid.*

"It seemed like such a shame the town didn't have a town square. Now look at it."

"You did this?" Gennie marveled at the design. It was simple but elegant; traditional yet fresh. An old-fashioned gazebo was the star of the square. Brick paths, benches, and various types of foliage were the supporting characters. Images of weddings, picnics, and concerts in the summer flashed through her mind. *This is a symbol of community.* "It's almost too perfect to be real."

"I'm just showing off, but yeah. I bought the lot and had that ratty building torn down." They walked over to the small fir tree at the edge of the park. "It was Mike's idea to plant the fir tree. He said every town should have a tree to light the day after Thanksgiving." Only three feet tall now, someday it would be tall enough to string lights upon it.

How many years until the planted tree is big enough to enjoy? I will be an old lady by then. Where will I be? Will I be all alone?

A path to the gazebo had been cleared of snow. "While you were visiting with your mom earlier, Mike and I got some exercise clearing the walkway and the gazebo." He led her up the steps. "It might be slippery, though, so be careful."

"It makes me want to dance like Cinderella at the ball." She twirled in a circle until the lights blurred and she felt breathless.

"You want to dance, we shall dance." He took his phone from his pocket. "No nineties music. How about country?"

"That seems appropriate."

A country ballad started. He set his phone on the railing. After bowing, he offered his hand. "Would you care for a dance, Ms. Banks?"

She went into his arms, their thick jackets like marshmallows between them.

Neither of them said anything for a few minutes as they danced. "I couldn't dance a step when I got my first period-role," she said. "They had to bring a professional on set to train me for the one dance scene."

"Well, it must have worked. You're like a feather," he said.

"It's much easier without a corset squeezing the life out of you."

She rested her cheek against the soft material of his jacket. *What would it feel like to kiss him here, under a billion stars and the sliver of the moon and all these lights that sparkled? I'm not afraid here. This is what it feels like to be normal. An ordinary woman on a date with a man she loves.*

The song ended and another began. Out of the corner of her eye, she noticed that several people walking by had stopped to watch them.

"Hey, you two." It was Mike and his wife, Sharon. Gennie hadn't recognized them all bundled up in coats and hats. They traipsed through the snow until they reached the gazebo.

"We're dancing," Stefan said. "Care to join us?"

"We'd be delighted," Mike said. "As a matter of fact, we have a few others wanting to join the party." Lee often said Mike reminded her of one of the men in the old Marlboro cigarette ads. Gennie agreed. He was rugged with sinewy muscles and a face that could make a cowgirl swoon, even in his sixties. His piercing blue eyes hinted at his zest for life. His wife, Sharon, on the other hand, looked like she'd just walked out of a Beverly Hills salon. She was tall, slender, and graceful—the epitome of sophistication. Tonight, she wore a knit cap over her smooth, blond hair and a purple coat.

"Party?" Gennie asked.

No one answered her. Tommy and Lee spilled out of Riversong with Cindi behind them, carrying pitchers of beer and plastic cups.

Ben and Bella drove up and parked on the street. When they exited the car, Bella shouted to them, "Hey now, let's get this party started." She wore a hat lit with red lights and carried a bottle of booze. She started to run, but was no match for the deep snow and slowed to a trudge, then tripped and fell. "Don't worry, the bottle's fine." Like a flag, she raised her arm out of the snow, bottle intact.

Ben carried a card table under one arm. When he reached Bella, he offered his hand. "Come on, baby."

Grinning and back on her feet, Bella brushed snow from her jacket as she made her way to the gazebo. When she reached them, she grabbed Gennie in a bear hug. "I was going insane trapped inside the house, but Drake sent the snowplow guy over to clear our driveway."

"I'm glad to see you," Gennie said. *How did Drake order a snowplow to a private residence? She knew the answer, of course. This was River Valley. Things like that happened all the time.*

When Ben reached the bottom of the gazebo steps, he straightened the legs of the table, setting it in the snow. Lee and Bella covered it with a tablecloth. Suddenly, Linus was there, with her mother on his arm. "Mom, what're you doing here?" Gennie asked.

"Linus knocked on my door and said we were to meet you here. So here I am." Her mom's eyes sparkled in the lights. "Isn't it lovely, Gennie?"

"Yes, Mom, it is." She took Stefan's hand. "Mom, this is Stefan."

"It's a pleasure to meet you, Stefan. I'm Joan Banks." She smiled and held out her hand encased in a pink mitten.

Stefan kissed her hand. "The pleasure's all mine, Mrs. Banks. I've heard a lot about you."

"You may call me Joan. I've heard a bit about you too."

They grinned at each other and continued to chat, but Gennie's attention was drawn to John, Linus's partner, setting a bucket of beverages on the table. Annie and one of the servers from the restaurant arrived with warming trays, presumably full of food. Drake and Mike were setting up heating lamps in the gazebo.

"What's happening?" Gennie asked. "Why's everyone here?"

"We're having a party in your honor," Stefan said.

A party for me? "But it's not my birthday." *These wonderful people are too much. This is too much.*

No one answered. A swarm of activity happened all around her. Cindi was pouring drinks. Lee, Ben, and Bella delivered them. Stefan placed a glass of white wine in her hand. Tommy took his guitar out of the case and started tuning.

Once everyone had a drink, they all gathered around her. Mike clinked a knife against his glass. Everyone hushed as he began to speak. "Gennie, my father used to say that when hard times hit, you'd better hope you have real friends to lean on. False friends are everywhere when things are going well, when you're on the top, but when you stumble or fall, suddenly no one's there to pick you up. That's not how we roll here. Hard times show you who your friends are, and we want it to be loud and clear that we are just that—your friends. Not because of what you do, but because of who you are inside. We're here for you in good times or bad, no matter what. Home is where your tribe lives. We are your tribe." He reached behind him, lifting a square box. "This is a little something to remember that we have your back."

He handed her the box. She lifted the lid. Inside was a pair of red leather cowboy boots with steel toes. "Oh my gosh, I love them." She held one up for everyone to see.

"You wear those and remember you're a badass," Cindi said.

"I will. Maybe I'll never take them off." The lights blurred through Gennie's tears. "Thank you, Mike. Everyone, thank you. It's been an awful day, as you can imagine. This whole thing's a nightmare, but I'm glad I was still here when the news broke this morning. There's no place I feel safer or more loved."

"Them Hollywood folks know how to make a story out of nothing, that's what," Cindi said. "How you two can stand working with those idiots, I don't know."

"I didn't abandon the baby," Gennie said. "The adoption was legal and was supposed to be sealed."

"We understand," Lee said. "And we have nothing but respect for what you did."

"I'm happy and nervous to tell you all that Sarah, my daughter, contacted me. She's coming here to River Valley to meet me."

Annie, her pregnant belly obvious despite her thick jacket, spoke next. "Drake and I want you and Stefan to stay in our guest house for the remainder of the weekend. It's only a matter of time before the reporters figure out where you are, especially if Sarah comes here. We have room for your mom and Sarah, too, in our guest rooms inside the house."

"No one gets through my gate," Drake said. It was true. They lived behind an impenetrable gate and fence. No one could get in without the code.

"It *would* take a great burden from my mind," Gennie said. *They have no idea what they're offering. A place to stay safe from Murphy.*

"And now, we're going to have some fun." Tommy picked up his guitar and perched on the edge of the stool. "Any requests?"

"How about 'With a Little Help from My Friends,'" Stefan said.

*   *

After a few songs, Bella took Gennie aside. "Come on. I need to pee, and you have to come with me."

They crossed the street to the restaurant, slipping in the back door to the bar, giggling like they were truant schoolgirls. Cozy and warm, the bar was nearly empty, with just a few people sitting at the counter. With Cindi at the party, one of the young waiters tended bar. He waved as they passed by on the way to the bathroom. After they were done, Bella dragged her back out to the bar. "You're sitting right there"—she pointed to a table in the corner—"and you're telling me everything."

"God, you're bossy," Gennie said.

They sat. Bella cued the bartender to bring them a shot of tequila for her and a glass of wine for Gennie.

After he set the drinks down in front of them, Bella crossed her arms. "Spill it."

"When I was fifteen, Rick Murphy raped me."

"*Senator* Murphy?" Bella asked.

"Yes. And I got pregnant." She went on to tell her the details. *Each time I tell my story, it gets easier.*

Bella stared at her with her usual intensity until she finished the entire story.

"Holy crap. Gennie, what the hell? How did you live with this all these years? Knowing he was out there?"

"I've done as he asked. I've kept quiet. But I can't stay quiet any longer. My mom and Stefan are right. If it saves even one girl from the same fate, I have to do it."

"Listen, no matter what, I've got your back. You hear me?"

"I know you do." *Sweet, feisty Bella never backed down from a fight.*

"This really messed you up, didn't it? With Moody. Stefan. I get it now."

"Yeah. It's really messed me up."

"I'm sorry, babe. Fuck, sometimes I hate men," Bella said.

"I thought you were trying not to curse?"

"This is a cursing emergency."

* *

Hours later, after dancing, eating, and drinking, they were all cold and exhausted and had to admit that the party must end. Gennie thanked them all, giving hugs all around, before heading across the street with Stefan. "Let's get back to the room and warm up. You have a big day tomorrow, and I don't want you getting sick," he said.

"Will you stay with me tonight?" she asked. "I don't want to be alone." *I won't be able to sleep alone now that I know what it feels like to sleep next to you.*

"Do you mean…sleep in the same bed?"

She smiled. "Yes, like this morning."

"My room or yours?"

"Mine. It's neater."

"Marginally," he said.

"No. Not marginally."

They laughed as they walked into the lit lobby. A young girl sat at the reception desk, typing into the computer. She looked up and smiled, asking if they needed anything.

"No, we're good for the night," Stefan said. "Headed up to our rooms."

"Have a nice night," she said.

Stopping first in Stefan's room, he took off his jacket and hat, and grabbed a few items of clothing, along with his toothbrush. Once they were safely in her room, she took off her outer layer, surprised to see it was after eleven. *Where did the night go?* She stood at the window, watching their friends drive down the street. *How is it possible for some people to be so good when others are so bad?* In the reflection of the glass, she saw Stefan sit on the bed and pull his sweater over his head. *I can feel him from here.*

She closed the shade on both windows and turned to look at him. He wore just a t-shirt and jeans. A pair of flannel pajama bottoms and another t-shirt were folded neatly beside him. She shivered, aching to touch him.

"You okay?" he asked. "I can turn up the heat if you're cold."

She moved to the bed and wrapped her arms around his neck. "Will you kiss me?"

He blinked. "Kiss you?"

"Yes. I want you to kiss me."

He leaned close, brushing her messy hair away from her face, then kissed her softly on the mouth, lingering for a second or two, tasting of sweet whiskey.

She pressed into him. He tightened his arms around her waist as their kiss intensified. Her toes tingled. Her legs were lead. *Do not let fear ruin this. I am safe with Stefan. He will stop when I want him to.* After another moment, she drew away, and with her thumb, traced his bottom lip.

"Was it all right?"

"Yes," she whispered. "It was perfect." She slipped a finger under his shirt collar, her gaze on the pulse at his neck. "I love you."

"You do?" His arms loosened, and he placed his hands on her hips.

She met his glassy gaze. "I don't know what I'm capable of giving, only what I'm capable of stealing from you."

"Stealing?" He raised his eyebrows. "What do you mean?"

"You give me everything I need, but I don't know if I can do the same for you."

He cocked his head to the side. "How about you let me decide what I need and want? Maybe you don't have to take responsibility for everyone's well-being. I'm a big boy. I know you now in a way I didn't last night, and I'm still here. I'm stubborn, Gennie, and I'm not giving up on the idea of us."

She swallowed the lump in her throat and tried to smile. "Fine, then. If that's what you want."

"That's what I want."

CHAPTER SIX

THANKSGIVING MORNING, Gennie sat in Annie and Drake's living room, watching the second hand move around the antique clock on the mantel above the fireplace. The temperature had dropped into the twenties overnight. Icicles dangled outside the large windows, sparkling in the sunlight. A fire in the stone fireplace crackled, bringing heat to Gennie's cheeks. Across from her, Stefan fidgeted with tassels on one of Annie's soft blankets and pushed against the rug with his toes, lifting it an inch off the wood floor and then dropping it. Aromas of sage and onions wafted from the kitchen where Annie made stuffing for the turkey.

When they had arrived that morning, Annie had taken them out to the guesthouse. Knowing it was safe here eased Gennie's mind, but she would miss her cozy room at the inn. The guesthouse had a sitting room, a bedroom, a small kitchen, and a bathroom. Annie had made up a fold-out couch in the front room, clearly unsure if they were sharing a bed or not. Gennie blushed and avoided Stefan's gaze.

Whatever Trix had done had been successful because Sarah had escaped Los Angeles without alerting the press. The plane had landed an hour ago, and the driver had called Gennie to say they were on their way. Now, it was eight minutes after ten. *At any moment my daughter will walk in this door.* She wiped clammy hands on the thighs of her jeans. *I feel like Alice, upside down in a new world.*

The doorbell rang. She looked at Stefan, swallowing the bile that had risen in her throat. "I might be sick."

"It's going to be fine. Just keep breathing."

Gennie rose from the couch and headed to the foyer. Annie had beat her there. She stood in the doorway, shaking a young woman's hand. "I'm Annie. Gennie's friend. Welcome to my home."

This is my daughter. My baby, all grown up.
Sarah was tall, with wide shoulders and long legs. "Thank you for having me." Dark, waist-length hair fell in a shiny sheet down her back. *She looks just like me, only taller.*

"Hi, Sarah." Gennie stepped forward, shaking. Neither of them spoke for a split second, like deer startled by an unexpected noise in the woods, until Sarah made a small back and forth movement with her head, like she was watching the fastest tennis match in the world. *She as nervous as I am.*

"Hi." She flashed Gennie a tentative smile. "It's nice to meet you."

The lump in Gennie's throat made it hard to speak. "It's nice to meet *you*." *Do not cry. Stay calm. Stay poised. Don't scare her with your intensity.* "Did you have a good flight?"

"Yeah. It was a weird to fly on a private plane. I felt like the president or something."

"We wanted you to get out of there without the press knowing. Seems as though we were successful."

Sarah grinned, her eyes lighting up like a child watching a funny show. "They put a disguise on me. A white wig and a little old lady coat and a cane. It was hilarious. I felt invisible, which was a tremendous relief. This scrutiny's been kind of bizarre."

"I'm sorry. It's hard for me, and I've been in the public eye for a long time."

"Getting to meet you was worth it," Sarah said.

She isn't angry. She's not here to accuse me of anything. She wants to get to know me.

Annie, who had been hovering just outside their view, stepped forward, gesturing toward the living room. "Come into the sitting room. You guys can talk more comfortably there. Sarah, would you like something to eat?"

"No, thank you. I'm too nervous. I haven't had much of an appetite the past couple days." Sarah laughed softly, nothing more than a couple tufts of air in and out. "I don't even know how to describe the last forty-eight hours. Everything feels surreal."

This poor child. She shouldn't have to deal with this. Damn you, George Bentley. Gennie's legs trembled as she and Sarah walked back into the living room, both dizzy and breathless. Beads of sweat dripped down the small of her back.

When she had gone into the foyer to meet Sarah, Stefan had remained behind. Now, he stood by the couch with his hands in the back pockets of his jeans.

"Wow. Stefan Spencer. I can't believe you're just standing here in front of me." Sarah promptly put her hand over her mouth. "I'm sorry. You probably hate that."

"It's fine. Part of the job." Stefan held out his hand, grinning. "Nice to meet you, Sarah."

Annie stepped closer to Stefan. "Would you like to join me in the kitchen for some coffee cake?" she asked him.

"Coffee cake? You know I can't resist cake." He kissed Gennie's cheek. "Just holler if either of you needs anything."

After they left, Gennie and Sarah sat on opposite ends of the couch. Gennie found it hard not to stare.

"Is Stefan your boyfriend?" Sarah asked.

"What is it you kids say? It's complicated."

"He seems super nice. I love his movies."

"We just wrapped a film together here in River Valley and we became close."

"I know what you mean. There's a guy at school and we're friends. He wants more and I really like him, but this stuff with my dad has me all screwed up. I have trouble trusting men, I guess." She turned toward the window. "It's beautiful here. I've never seen such tall mountains. I grew up in Los Angeles. Everything's brown there."

How in the world had they both ended up in Los Angeles? What are the odds? "How did your parents end up in California?" Gennie asked. "When I met them they were in Wisconsin."

"My dad got a job there when I was a baby. I don't remember Wisconsin at all. My mother hated the weather there. She was from California originally. You probably didn't know that."

"It didn't come up, no," Gennie said. "I have a house in Malibu."

"A house or a home?"

Gennie blinked, surprised by the question. "More on the house side. I've never really felt at home there, but then again, who can beat the beach?"

"Malibu's pretty awesome."

"You can come over anytime. As soon as I get home, that is. I travel a lot." She hesitated, looking at her hands. "It's a little overwhelming to realize we were living in the same area all this time."

"Yeah. I thought the same thing when I first heard," Sarah said. "It's weird that I've been watching your movies all my life and had no idea you were my mother. But now that I know, it's obvious. We look alike."

"When you were born, they only let me hold you for a few minutes. Your face was all squished up and red. I couldn't tell what you would look like later." Fighting tears, she looked away, gathering her emotions. *Be brave. Be like Daddy.* "I've thought about you a lot, wondering what you looked like, what your interests were, what kind of girl you were."

"Yeah, me too. About you, that is. I know the adoption was closed, so I wasn't sure you'd agree to meet me. I had to try. I've wanted to meet you for such a long time." Sarah smiled the same tentative smile from earlier, her eyes glossy. "My mom always told me you must have loved me very much to make such a hard decision."

"She was right. I was fifteen and still a child. I couldn't have provided a good home for you."

"Was it hard, though? To let me go? I've wondered that a lot." Her voice broke.

"Oh, Sarah, it was the hardest thing I've ever done. Please don't ever think it was a decision I made lightly or that it didn't almost kill me when they took you away." Tears came fast and steady. "It was agonizing." Grabbing a tissue, she dabbed at her cheeks and blew her nose. "When you cried for the first time, it was like a dagger pierced my heart. I loved you instantly. I loved you enough to let you go, knowing it was the best thing for you, but there isn't a day I haven't thought about you. It's an ache that never goes away. That said, I knew you were with good people who would love you as their own. All I wanted was for you to have a good life."

"When you're adopted," Sarah said, "it's impossible not to wonder if there is something wrong with you—maybe there's a reason your mother didn't want you. Even though Mom told me that wasn't the case, it's a thought that creeps in sometimes, mostly at night when I can't sleep." She swiped at the corners of her eyes with the back of her index fingers.

Gennie took several tissues from the box on the coffee table and handed them to Sarah. "I remember very well when I met with your parents. I thought they would give you the very best kind of life. Love and security. They reminded me of my own parents, especially your mother."

"She was our girl scout troop leader and the room mom for all my classes. She made homemade meals every night and never missed one of my swim meets. But we didn't talk about things, really. I didn't feel I could share any of my feelings about being adopted. She felt fragile to me, even before she got sick. I would've died rather than hurt her."

Gennie nodded. "After my father died, I felt like I had to protect my mother, but she was much stronger than I ever realized."

"I'd like to meet her," Sarah said.

"She wants to meet you. Very much."

"What happened to your father?" Sarah asked.

"He was killed in a car accident when I was ten. A drunk driver. I have photos of him I can show you. We look like him. He was an incredible person. I miss him every day."

"I suppose you saw my father's interview yesterday?" Sarah asked.

"I did see it, yes."

"I'm sorry. It's awful, what he's done. I can't make any excuses for him, even if I wanted to. We haven't spoken since my mother died. When she got sick, my dad couldn't handle the stress. He started gambling more. It wasn't until her funeral, when we had to beg for money from friends to bury her, that I realized he'd lost everything. Even the house. I don't think my mother ever knew, which is a blessing. I'm rambling. I do that when I'm nervous." She took in a deep breath and continued before Gennie could say anything. "After I found out about his gambling, we had a big fight. He told me then that you were raped."

Gennie's heart beat faster; the palms of her hands were wet with perspiration.

Sarah's voice quivered. "My mother never told me that part."

"We didn't want you to know."

"Because you thought it would be too hard for me?"

"That's right. We didn't want you questioning your own character or thinking you were an awful accident because you weren't. You were a perfect, innocent baby that God wanted on this earth. I believe that to be true...I know that to be true."

"Most women would have aborted. And I wouldn't be here. It's weird to think about."

Gather the right words. Tell her the ugly truth. She has a right to know. "The circumstances of the rape." She stopped, her voice breaking. "It was as bad as you can imagine. I had no experience with boys, let alone a man. I was scared out of my mind when I figured out I was going to have a baby." She took in a shaky breath and grabbed tissues, wiping under her eyes. "I didn't figure out I was pregnant until I was about twenty weeks along. Days after I took a test and it was positive, I felt this fluttering in my stomach. It was you. A little person growing inside me. You became the most important thing in my life. My own needs had to come second, at least for the next few months. That's when I went to my mom, and she helped me come up with a plan for your adoption. I knew it was the right decision, even though it was hard to let you go. I wanted your well-being more than anything."

Sarah's wide eyes never left Gennie's face. "I don't know if I could ever be that brave."

"You never do until you have to." Gennie shifted on the sofa, scooting forward and placing her feet on the floor. *How do I tell her who her father is?*

In a small voice, Sarah asked the question Gennie knew she would. "Did you know him? The man who raped you?"

"He was...he *is* a public figure. A politician."

"He's someone powerful." Sarah stared at her, transfixed. "Someone I would know."

"I think so. Do you know who Rick Murphy is?"

"The guy running for president?" Her face had blanched of all color.

"Yes."

Gennie told Sarah about the essay contest and how she'd gone to his home office to meet with him. "After it happened, he threatened to kill my mother if I ever told anyone. All these years, I've kept quiet because I wanted to protect my family. I lied to my mother to protect her." She wiped under her nose with the tissues. "But given everything that's happened, it seems clear that I should come forward."

"Because he might do it to someone else?"

"Yes, exactly."

"Will you ever be able to look at me and think of anything besides him?" Sarah asked.

"Gosh, yes. I don't see him. I see you. You're beautiful and smart and kind. A sperm donor is not a father."

"My adopted dad isn't so great either." Sarah tucked her hair behind her ears, laughing softly. "Talk about daddy issues."

"I wish it were different for you." *It breaks my heart that it isn't. Damn you, George Bentley. Damn you to hell, Rick Murphy.*

Sarah looked down at her lap. "It's a lot to take in."

"I know it is. I'm sorry." *Tell her the rest.* "And there's more. I've set up an interview for tomorrow with Rachel Birdwell. I'm going to tell her about the rape and file a motion for a paternity test—unless you don't want me to. If you're uncomfortable with the world knowing who your father is and how you came to be, I'll pull the plug on the whole thing."

"No, you have to do it. The world should know he's a monster."

It's becoming real to her now. Soon she will feel sick.

"He can buy anyone off," Gennie said, "including police and judges. You name it, and he has access to it."

Sarah stared at the ceiling. "In one of my courses last year, my professor told us his theory about Senator Murphy's father. My professor believes that in 1967, he killed a girl and the family had it covered up."

Gennie nodded. "You mean Minnie Stevens."

Mike Murphy, Rick Murphy's father, was in his thirties—and married—when he drove his mistress home from a party while drunk. The car spun out of control and wrapped around a tree. He dragged her from the car, but according to the coroner, she'd died on impact. No charges were brought against him because Murphy claimed she was driving the car, even though eyewitnesses saw them leave the party together with *him* in the driver's seat. Although not prosecuted, the senior Murphy's chance at the White House was ruined. His son was the next Murphy hope.

"It was a huge scandal at the time, but yes, nothing was ever proven."

"But that girl wasn't famous or rich like you. You're America's favorite actress. You have power that Minnie Stevens didn't."

"I have more power than she did, but not enough to fight the Murphy family. I'm worried about your safety."

"Gennie, if there are others and you tell the truth, maybe it would give them the courage to do the same. He wouldn't be able to destroy all of you at once."

She hadn't thought of that. *If there are others, we can band together to fight him.*

"You could hire bodyguards for us," Sarah said.

"Bodyguards?"

"Yeah, like in that movie with Kevin Costner."

Gennie chuckled. "You mean *The Bodyguard*?"

"Right. I want a young, hot one that follows me around everywhere."

"How would you feel about moving in with me for a while? I could hire a driver/bodyguard for you."

"If that's what it takes to get him, then yes."

Sarah stared into the fire, tapping her fingers on the arms of her chair. After a few minutes, she turned to Gennie. "You have to do this. He needs to be stopped. I'm willing to sit for an interview, too, if you think that would help."

Gennie went to the window and pushed back the curtains. Right at that moment, an icicle fell from the roof and shattered on the hard snow. Could she share her brutal experience? She wasn't sure she was that brave. In fact, she knew that down deep she was a coward, hiding all these years behind her fear instead of exposing a monster. Gennie let go of the curtain. It fell back into place, dimming the room.

"Regardless of if we can prove it was nonconsensual, I was fifteen. He'll be charged with child rape."

"He'll go to prison, where he belongs," Sarah said.

"It will add a level of scrutiny to your life that will never go away. The press will go crazy. You'll forever be known as Rick Murphy's child. Are you prepared for that?"

"I'm not, but that doesn't mean we shouldn't do it."

Gennie chuckled. "I suppose."

"What about you? What will this do to your career?"

"I have no idea. I'm more worried about our immediate danger. This is going to be a long process before we can put him in jail."

"What is it they say? The truth will set you free?" Sarah asked.

"Something like that."

She didn't even hesitate. She immediately thought of others. This is a good girl.

Gennie sensed movement in the doorway. She turned to see her mother coming in from the foyer. "Hi, Mom."

"Hi, sweetie." Looking stylish in a red dress and black boots, her mother crossed the room to where they sat on the couch. Gennie and Sarah stood.

"I'm Joan Banks. Gennie's mother."

Sarah held out her hand, but her mother grabbed her into a hug. "You look so much like my late husband." Tears spilled from her eyes. "You're absolutely stunning." She turned to Gennie. "She's your spitting image except she has your father's height." Back to Sarah, she continued, "He was a wonderful athlete. I hear you are too."

"I *do* love sports. I swim for UCLA," Sarah said.

"So I've heard. Your grandfather loved the water too. Anything active, he was all over it."

"What about you, Gennie? Did you like sports?" Sarah asked.

"No, I was more the nerdy bookworm type," Gennie said. "More like my mom."

"She always made me proud. Still does, of course. You must have the same work ethic. UCLA is terribly impressive."

"I was lucky to get in," Sarah said. "I'm not very good at math. I'm majoring in English. I want to be an elementary school teacher. I love kids."

"You won't believe it, but my mother was a kindergarten teacher," her mom said.

"Really?" Sarah's face lit up. "Maybe I take after her." Color had returned to her cheeks. *The resilience of the young.*

They all sat back on the couch. *I can see her as a teacher, patiently teaching them to read and write. The children will all love her.*

"Can you tell me about Gennie when she was young?" Sarah asked.

"Gennie's my favorite subject, so that will be no problem."

They all laughed. *Sarah laughs like my mom. Both have husky laughs, suppressed inside their chests.*

Her mom continued, "I never thought she'd become an actress. She was shy as could be when she was little, always hiding behind her father in the grocery store. A twiggy little thing; she was always the smallest in class. She loved books. Always had her nose in a book."

Me too." Sarah looked over at Gennie and flashed a shy smile.

"She had a best friend named Margaret," said her mom. "They were thick as thieves. Do you have good friends at school?"

"I have a lot of cool friends from my team, and I'm super close with my roommate, Lily. We were roommates in the dorms my first year, and we bonded immediately. She's the greatest. We were freshman when my mom got sick, and Lily was a huge support. I didn't think I could go back to school after mom died. It happened right before Christmas, but Lily basically made me return. She knew it was better for me to keep moving. Plus, she knew how proud of me my mom was for getting into UCLA. My best friend from high school is named Veronica, but everyone calls her Ronnie. She's at UC Berkley now, and I miss her a lot. She freaked out when she saw the news. That's how I found out. She called me. I'm sorry I'm talking so much. I'm nervous."

"Please don't stop. I love hearing about your life. I'd like to hear more. Everything, really," Gennie said.

Sarah smiled. "Okay, well, I'll have to talk faster then."

Gennie laughed. "Would you like to stay the rest of the weekend? We can talk more." Gennie explained that Annie and Drake had a room for her. "And, I'd like to keep you here, at least for a couple days. We're safe here. The place is under lock and key."

"Sure, okay," Sarah said.

The doorbell rang, announcing the arrival of other guests. She'd been so wrapped up in the moment, she'd forgotten it was Thanksgiving. Her friends. How kind they were last night. *No matter what happens, no matter what the haters do, they can't take this from me. My tribe.* She glanced at her mother and daughter as they continued to chat, bouncing from one topic to the next. *My family. My rich and full life.*

The voices of Linus, John, Ellen, and Verle came from the foyer as they stomped snow from boots and hung jackets in the closet. She closed her eyes, absorbing the sounds and scents of the moment. The crackle of the wood-burning fireplace. Her mom's soft chatter, and Sarah's husky laugh. Linus already launching into a story of his heroic survival of John's driving during the icy ride over. Scents of roasting turkey and baked apple pie mingled and drifted in from the kitchen. She brought her fingers to her nose, breathing in the faint scent of Stefan's cologne from when he'd held her hands.

This is where I belong. Right here. Right now.

CHAPTER SEVEN

THE TRIBE GATHERED in the dining room of Drake and Annie's house, searching for their names on place cards written by eleven-year-old Alder in uneven handwriting. He'd spelled out her full name, *Genevieve*, but had run out of room on the small card, so the last three letters were squished together like sardines in a can. Below her name, he'd added a smiling face and a "sorry."

An open concept, the front room was both sitting and dining areas. Tall windows gave view to the yard and river below. Standing near the window, Gennie basked in the rays of the sun, letting them warm her as she absorbed the view like a painter released from a dark dungeon. Snow-covered mountains stretched out across the landscape, displayed against the brilliant blue sky in jagged peaks. Below, the swollen river, a ribbon of green, wound with winter fury through the gully. Just beyond the patio, a sparrow hopped from icy branch to icy branch, as if unsure where to land during this unexpected freeze.

When it was time to gather around the table, Gennie took her place between Stefan and Sarah. Her mom sat on the other side of Sarah. Stefan squeezed her knee under the table. Alder, Annie's son, sat directly across from Gennie, sneaking covert glances at Sarah. Tommy and Lee sat with their toddler, Ellie-Rose, who banged a plastic-coated spoon against her sippy cup. Linus, dressed in a perfectly draped silk shirt the color of a pink sunset, had his arm draped around John. Verle, sitting next to Ellen, mentioned how beautiful the table looked as he tucked his napkin into his shirt. Like newlywed bookends, Bella and Ben sat on one end of the long table, with Drake and Annie on the other. Bella's diamond wedding ring flashed under the lights as she pointed to the mound of mashed potatoes near her plate. Annie's blond curls bounced as she draped a napkin over her pregnant belly.

Drake clinked a fork against his wine glass to get everyone's attention. "Mrs. Banks and Sarah, welcome. We're so glad you could join us. We've been blessed to have many celebrations and meals at this table with our friends, and have developed a habit of long toasts before our meal. Normally, it's Tommy and Linus who carry on, but tonight I'm moving out of my comfort zone to give a small speech."

"Hail to the king," Linus said.

"Quiet as a church mouse here." Tommy made a zipping motion over his mouth.

"Annie, thank you for cooking during your day off, especially given your condition. We all know how lucky we are to have this meal made by the best chef in the world."

"Totally," Alder said, beaming with pride.

Annie blew them both a kiss.

Drake continued, "Words could never express how thankful I am for my wife and son, and the baby that will soon make us a family of four. Annie, I love you more every day. Alder, you're just the best son a man could ask for, no matter that we got a late start together."

"I'm adopted too," Alder said to Sarah, giving her a shy smile.

"All the cool kids are adopted." Sarah winked at him. Alder's expression transformed from shy to ecstatic.

"As I look around this table, I can't help but remember how lonely, and frankly devastated, I was during my first Thanksgiving here. I'd lost my wife and little girl." Drake choked up, his eyes glassy. "I thought my life was over."

Linus seemed to be looking for something in the bottom of his glass. Tommy bowed his head and closed his eyes, as if in prayer. Bella stared into her wine glass, her bottom lip quivering.

"Then, Annie and Alder appeared in my life. And with my new family, came all of you. So *many* of you."

Everyone laughed. Lee wiped under her nose with a tissue. Annie's cheeks glistened with tears. Stefan moved his hand from his knee and wrapped it around Gennie's shoulders.

Drake looked around the table. "There isn't a moment I don't miss my little girl, but I believe one day we will be reunited in Heaven. She would have wanted me to move on, to live life, and to love without fear, which is the hardest thing to do after a loss." Drake picked up his napkin and wiped under his eyes. "I'm just so thankful for this second chance. I don't take it for granted. Not one minute do I take it for granted. Don't know what's gotten into me today."

It's his new baby coming soon. That would make anyone who'd lost a child emotional.

"It's a day for reflection," Ellen said with her characteristic sniff. "Life's not rainbows and sunshine all the time. After I lost my son, it was like I had the plague, like my tragedy and grief might be contagious. But it's true. There is life again. Granddaughters. Great-granddaughters." She tweaked Ellie-Rose's strawberry blond hair. "And old coots to fall in love with."

Verle grinned. "Who you calling an old coot?"

Drake took in a deep breath and smiled. "Linus, take this over before I get us all crying again."

Linus raised his glass. "Join me in a toast. To the abundance presented on this table. To Drake for reminding us what this day is all about. And to second chances."

They all toasted. When the noise around the table decreased, Linus shook his head in mock bewilderment. "Seriously, though, Drake, I've never heard you say that many words in a row. You must be exhausted."

"Well, don't get used to it," said Drake. "Now let's eat before everything goes stone cold."

"Wait, we need to say grace first," Tommy said. Groans erupted around the table. "Sorry, as a fallen Catholic, but grateful Christian, I have to keep us on the straight and narrow."

"Please, do," said Annie. "The sinners around this table obviously need it."

"Why are you looking at me?" Bella asked.

Ben raised his eyebrows. "Everyone knows why, baby."

"I'm so misunderstood." Bella grinned and slapped her husband's hand.

They all bowed their heads.

"Dear Lord," Tommy said, "thank you for the friendships around this table, and for our families, and for new babies, and especially for friends who become family. And for those unexpected blessings that arrive to remind us of your deep love. Amen."

Sarah, my unexpected blessing.

They passed food, chatting and laughing. While Gennie waited for the platter of turkey, she watched Lee cut Ellie-Rose's food into small pieces. Next to her, Sarah spooned a stack of potatoes onto her plate. *Had she been a chubby toddler? When had she started to talk? What was her first word? What kind of food had she liked? At the park, did she like swings or the slide? I may never know the answers. I missed so much. No matter how many stories we shared, there would always be blanks, details lost. I gave birth to this beautiful girl, but I'm not her mother. Yet, here she is next to me. A miracle. A second chance.*

* *

After the dishes were done and leftovers packaged up for all to take home, John and Linus left, concerned about the icy roads after dark. Tommy and Lee announced they were leaving shortly thereafter.

"Little one needs a nap." Tommy held Ellie-Rose on his hip and kissed the top of her head. She snuggled against his neck, holding her blanket and sucking her thumb.

"Me too," Verle said.

Ellen rolled her eyes. "No nap for me. Fit as a fiddle."

"So she says," Verle said. "She falls asleep in her big chair with a book on her chest."

"I'm simply resting my eyes. But we have to go too." Ellen pulled Gennie into an embrace. "You hang tough, you hear me?"

"Yes, ma'am," Gennie said.

Lee squeezed her hand and hugged her, whispering in her ear. "Lean on those around you. You'll get through this."

After the goodbyes, Annie asked Alder to show Sarah to her room. Alder squared his shoulders and offered his arm. "Right this way, my lady."

"Thank you, kind sir." Sarah slipped her arm through his as they crossed the room.

"We have a pool room. Would you like to play?" Alder asked.

"Totally," Sarah said. "I can't believe you have your own pool table."

"I'm a bit of a shark," he said. "Just so you know."

Annie joined Gennie's mother at the table to put together a complex puzzle. The men headed downstairs to look at Drake's wine cellar.

Bella, wearing a jacket, sidled up beside Gennie. "I'm going out to the patio for some fresh air. Join me?"

"It's cold out there."

Bella reached into the pockets of her jacket and pulled out two airplane bottles of cinnamon whiskey. "This'll keep us warm."

Gennie chuckled. "Are you ever going to grow up?"

"I certainly hope not."

"Fine." Gennie grabbed her jacket and slipped on her hat and gloves. Bella was already on the deck, sitting in one of the chairs arranged around the fire pit. Drake had cleared the deck of snow, but a layer of ice remained. "Careful, it's slippery," Bella said.

Walking like a duck, Gennie made her way to the fire pit. "If I break my leg, it's on you."

The late afternoon sun hung low in the sky, shedding golden rays through the firs and pines. Bella switched on the gas coals as Gennie settled into one of the wooden chairs, her down jacket acting as a cushion against the cold. Bella handed her one of the tiny bottles.

Gennie sipped her drink. "Wow, that's good."

Bella grinned as she popped the top off her bottle. "See? You don't want me to change."

"I really don't."

Bella leaned over the coals, warming her hands. "You know I can't stand it when I don't know absolutely everything going on with you."

"Yes, I am aware of that." Gennie laughed.

"Tell me about Sarah," Bella said.

"I told her everything."

"Everything?"

"Yes. And she wants me to come forward."

"Holy shit. She's brave."

"She is." *Braver than I am.*

Bella took another sip of her drink. "I want the scoop on you and Stefan. Here's what I know so far." She clicked each item off on her fingers. "Fact one, he didn't go home to Canada. Fact two, you're staying together in the guest house. Fact three, there's one bed in the guesthouse."

"Technically, there's a fold-out couch." Gennie put her feet up on the rim of the circular pit. "If you want to know the truth, I'm head over heels in love with him."

"No way. Really?"

"Really."

"What about sex? Is it like with Moody?" Bella flushed and looked uncharacteristically abashed. "I'm sorry. Don't answer if you don't want to. I know how complicated all this is for you."

"We haven't. He's patient and understanding. We've kissed and he stayed with me last night in my room, but he knows I'm not ready."

"After what that piece of shit did to you, do you think you'll ever be ready?"

"I don't know."

Bella scrunched up her face, obviously thinking. "I've never seen you happier than when you're with him. He brings out your playful side."

"I guess he does." *I've been in a dormant state for a long time, like a bulb in the ground and Stefan's the warm spring, coaxing me out of the dark earth.*

"You know how much I want this for you," Bella said.

"Yeah, I know."

They sipped their whiskeys in silence. Snow slid from a tree branch ten or so feet from the porch.

"So, it's game on." Bella grinned as she reached into her jacket pocket and pulled out a bar of chocolate.

"How can you be hungry?" Gennie asked.

"I'm not hungry, exactly, but I remembered I had this chocolate hidden in my pocket, so I may as well eat it with my cinnamon drink."

Gennie made a face, then laughed.

"What? They're awesome together," Bella said.

Bella was a hundred and fifteen pounds of pure muscle. Apparently, muscles needed a lot of calories because the woman never stopped eating.

Gennie reached over and squeezed Bella's gloved hand. "Thanks for being my best friend."

"You're welcome." Bella tore the wrapper from the chocolate bar and took a bite, chewing for a moment before speaking. "I gotta tell you, I'm scared out of my mind about the company. Not because of what's happening with you, but because of me. What if I blow this thing?"

"You're not going to," Gennie said.

"It's so much money. So, so much money. Your money."

"I'm not worried. Worst case, if I don't get my investment back, I'm fine. You know I'm smart with my finances. If I never worked again, I'd be fine."

"You have way too much money," Bella said.

"And you eat a ridiculous amount and never gain weight, so the way I see it, we're pretty much even."

Bella popped up, stretching her arms over her head. "It's cold out here. Let's go in and have some pie."

"You really are a freak of nature."

CHAPTER EIGHT

THE NEXT MORNING, Gennie sat under a bright light in Annie's dining room while Bella did her makeup for the interview. Bella had just finished her eyes and was about to move on to her hair when the doorbell rang. Annie popped out from the kitchen, holding a dish towel. "I've got it, Bella. Just keep doing what you're doing."

A couple minutes later, Annie came back with Trix. "Sorry I'm so late." Trix wore knee high boots with four-inch heels and a long leather jacket, which she shrugged out of to reveal a skin-tight sweater dress. "I had no idea there were no cabs here."

"It's fine," Gennie said. *I told you last night on the phone I didn't need you here.* "We're just finishing up my makeup while Raquel's producers get everything ready."

"You look gorg, as always." Trix tossed her bag on the table and greeted Bella with a peck on the cheek. "Yo, B, what's up?"

"Getting our girl ready for her close-up," Bella said.

"How you holding up? Still want to go through with this?" Trix asked.

"Yes. It's the right thing to do," Gennie said.

"The buzz on this is going to break Twitter," Trix said. "Seriously, people's heads are going to explode."

"How did you get in the gate? It's not open, is it?" Gennie asked. *Please tell me the gate's not open.*

"No, that Linus from the inn brought me over," Trix said. "I think he thought I was either amusing or odd. He stared at me with this weird smile, like I was an exotic creature from outer space. I *did* throw a tiny tantrum about the no cab situation. But I mean, for God's sake, what kind of town doesn't have cabs?"

"River Valley," Bella said.

"You could've rented a car." Gennie stifled a sigh, imagining Trix's interaction with Linus. *The last thing I need is Trix here. I'm already nervous enough.*

"I'm not about to drive around in this forest by myself. I might get lost and get eaten by a bear." She tugged on her right earlobe. "All that would be left of me is my diamond earrings."

"You're hardly more than a snack for a bear," Bella said.

Trix lowered her voice, glancing out the windows. "Have there been any Sasquatch sightings here?"

"No, just Yetis," Bella said. "And they're mean bastards, so you've got to be careful."

"What's a Yeti?" Trix asked. "Are they for real?"

"Bella, stop," said Annie. "There are no Yetis here, Trix. Bella's just teasing you."

"As far as we know," Bella said. "But these woods are thick. And there's a guy in town who claims he saw Sasquatch in 1987."

Annie laughed. "That's crazy Bill Hignight. One night during a full moon he consumed a fifth of tequila, including the worm, and wandered out into the woods. He came back the next morning with stories of a Sasquatch sighting. Highly unreliable source."

"Sorry you came, Trix?" Gennie asked.

"Of course not. I know Bella's just trying to scare me. I'm not a total idiot," Trix said.

"Would you care for coffee, Trix?" Annie asked.

"Dying for some. Oh, yeah, and there's no Starbucks. I mean, wow. Just wow."

"Don't you worry, I've got coffee," Annie said. "Are you hungry? I just whipped up some muffins."

"Oh, no, thank you. I'm on a diet," Trix said as they passed through the kitchen door.

"How do you trust a woman who never eats?" Bella whispered. "Did you see her hipbones in that dress? There's no flesh to her, just skin and bones."

"She's very loyal."

"Loyal to her paycheck." Bella wrapped a chunk of Gennie's hair around a flat iron for a couple of seconds. When she released it, a perfect wave fell into place.

"Bella, you know it's more than that for her."

"Is it?"

"What are you saying?"

Bella picked up another bunch of hair, repeating the same movement. "I'm not saying anything. I just don't like her."

"Stefan doesn't either. How come you never told me that before?"

"I didn't fully realize it until just now. It's River Valley. Everything's clearer here."

* *

A few minutes later, Gennie was ready for filming. The crew had set lights and moved two chairs over by the window to take advantage of the view and were now nibbling on Annie's homemade muffins. Raquel sat on the couch, chatting with Stefan. Long-legged and pretty, with hair the color of a copper penny that complemented her big brown eyes, Raquel had a wide, full smile that often had a beguiling effect on her interviewees. Over the years, she'd earned a reputation of someone who pulled deeply personal stories from the celebrities and politicians she interviewed. They'd met years before when Raquel had worked on the local Los Angeles morning show and Gennie was doing publicity for her first movie. They had been friends ever since. They greeted each other with a hug. "Thanks for giving me this exclusive," Raquel said. "It means a lot."

"You're the only one I would give it to. But before we start, we need to talk. Privately."

They crossed the room to Drake's study. Gennie shut the door behind them. Raquel perched on the side of the desk, crossing her arms over her chest. "What's up?"

"This interview's going to be more than my story about a teenage pregnancy," Gennie said.

Raquel's eyebrows raised. "Okay?"

"Twenty years ago, Rick Murphy raped me. I was fifteen years old."

"Oh, shit."

* *

They sat in the chairs by the window as the crew clipped microphones to their blouses. Raquel spoke into Gennie's ear. "Sarah just approached me. She wants to do an interview. You okay with that?"

"Yes. Just go easy on her."

"I will, don't worry. As far as this goes, I'll write a lead-in about what happened. I'll use excerpts from Bentley's interviews, then we'll cut to us," said Rachel.

"This isn't my first rodeo."

"Yeah. Right. Of course. This isn't even your first rodeo with me." Raquel picked up a small notepad and settled back in her chair. "I'm a nervous wreck. If it gets too rough, we'll shut the cameras off for a few minutes and let you get your composure."

"Don't be afraid to cry," Trix called out to them from behind one of the cameras. "People need to see you suffering."

Raquel shot Trix a withering look. *Did everyone dislike Trix?*

Once the camera guys were ready, they started filming.

"Can you tell me what happened twenty years ago?" asked Raquel.

She'd perfected the story by this time, telling it succinctly but with the necessary details to give it authenticity. After she was done, she paused, waiting for the next question. *The room's so quiet. I've stunned the crew.*

Raquel took her through a series of questions where Gennie explained how she'd picked the Bentleys and how they'd agreed to a closed adoption.

"And you never told your mother it was Rick Murphy who'd assaulted you?" asked Raquel.

"He threatened to kill us if I said anything to anyone. So, I didn't." *Had one of the crew gasped?*

"Why now?"

"Obviously, I want to defend myself. I've been portrayed in the press as a baby killer, which couldn't be further from the truth. I believe George Bentley's in trouble financially, which motivated his breach of our closed adoption agreement. Also, I met Sarah Bentley.

She encouraged me to come forward with the truth, as did my mother. We all feel strongly that a rapist should not be a candidate for the President of the United States."

"Are you still afraid of Rick Murphy?"

"Very much so."

"Do you believe there are others?"

"I hope not. I sincerely hope not."

"But you have your doubts?" Raquel asked.

"I do."

"If there are others, what would you say to them?"

"Come forward. You are not alone."

"Let's assume Rick Murphy is not going to admit to guilt. What are you prepared to do to prove his guilt?"

"It's pretty simple. We've filed a motion with the courts for a paternity test. A DNA test will prove that Sarah is his biological child. There's no denying science. I was fifteen. It is statutory rape."

"You met Sarah yesterday. How was that?"

Gennie swallowed hard as her eyes filled with tears. Using the tissue one of the assistant producers had given her, she wiped the corners of her eyes. "Very emotional for both of us. Terribly gratifying to know what a graceful and intelligent young woman she is."

"Will you have a relationship going forward?" asked Rachel.

She glanced over at Sarah, who stood behind the cameras, next to Stefan and Annie. "I certainly hope so. It's up to her, of course. This has all come as a major shock to her."

"Can you share with us why you chose to have her? Fifteen. Raped. Not a typical choice."

Gennie hesitated. She must choose her words carefully. Her father's voice came to her. *Tell the truth. Your own truth. Don't worry about anyone else.*

"I was so naïve I didn't realize you could get pregnant that way. I thought you had to be in love." She smiled through her tears. "It sounds so dumb, but that's how young and sheltered I was. But when I figured it out, there was never any other choice but to have her. I'm not here to tell anyone what to do. These choices are very personal, and frankly, none of my business. I'm not here to push a platform. That's the last thing I want. I can only say what I felt in my heart. This was a baby that was meant for the world. That's all."

"After meeting her, do you feel you made the right choice?"
"The day I had her. Last year. Last month. Today. Always."

* *

After Gennie finished, Raquel took a break before starting the interview with Sarah. Meanwhile, Bella had fixed Sarah's hair and makeup. "You look beautiful," Bella said to her.

"I feel beautiful. It's kind of like magic what Bella does, isn't it?" Sarah asked.

"You don't have to tell me," Gennie said. "I enter the set in the morning looking like death. An hour later I look like a completely different person."

Raquel joined them by the window. "Sarah, do you have any questions before we start?"

"Not really. Gennie said I should just answer as honestly as I can."

"That's good advice. Also, if you need a break, just tell me and we can stop. There's no reason we can't do that since it's not live. Okay?"

"Okay."

Sarah and Rachel settled into the chairs as the crew made last minute adjustments. Gennie left them and went to sit with Stefan. When the camera rolled, Gennie reached for Stefan's hand. He squeezed it as they watched on the teleprompters.

"How did you discover that Genevieve Banks was your birth mother?" asked Rachel.

"Like everyone else. On television."

"That must have been hard for you."

"It was weird. Surreal, I guess I'd say."

"When I spoke to Genevieve, she told me you were instrumental in her deciding to go forward with the entire truth of what happened twenty years ago. Tell us why you felt it was important to tell the truth."

"Gennie told me it was my choice whether we discussed the rape. We talked about how it will change my life if people knew about what happened and who my biological father is." Her voice wavered. She glanced over at Gennie and seemed to gather strength because she continued, "I decided I wanted the truth out there, regardless of the personal cost. We can't let someone like him become president."

"This is going to sound blunt, but I have to ask," Raquel said. "What does it feel like knowing you were conceived by a violent crime?"

"Not great. It's also not great that the father who raised me is using Gennie's story to get himself out of a gambling debt. But they are who they are. I am who I am. Gennie's who she is. We must be stronger than the men who caused this. My adopted father's a weak man. My biological father is an evil man. Gennie and I couldn't sit by and not speak out for all victims of violent crime. We are here to say: enough. Men should not get away with sexual assault simply because they're rich."

Gennie watched, amazed at this poised and articulate young woman.

"She's impressive," Stefan whispered.

"Yes, she is," Gennie said. *My girl.*

"How do you think this will affect your life going forward?" Raquel asked.

"I don't know. I can only think about today."

"If there are other victims out there, what would you say to them?"

"I would tell them not to be afraid, and that Gennie and I are here for them."

"What's next for you, Sarah?" Raquel asked.

A ghost of a smile crossed Sarah's young features. "I guess getting to know Gennie better. Going back to school. Being normal."

"Do you think that's possible, given everything?"

"Life is what you make it. My mother always told me that growing up. I'm still me, no matter what people say or think."

* *

After Raquel and the camera crew had left for the lodge to edit and prepare the piece for an evening broadcast, Gennie stood near the window, looking out into the yard. A massive snowball fight was under way between Stefan, Drake, and the kids. Sarah and Alder shouted and shrieked with laughter as they ducked an attack. Gennie yawned. Her eyes itched and muscles ached like she had the flu. How nice it would be to get into bed and take a nap.

Unfortunately, Trix didn't seem inclined to leave anytime soon. She'd settled into one of the cozy chairs with her gaze glued to her phone. When Gennie turned from the window, Trix set her aside her phone and crossed her legs. "Well, that went about as well as can be expected," Trix said. "The girl's good in front of a camera. Comes off very sympathetic, but strong. You were surprisingly authentic."

"Surprisingly?"

"Don't take this the wrong way, but in the past, I've always thought you interviewed on the fake side. Like a little too Pollyanna. No one can be that nice or well-balanced for real."

Gennie plopped onto the couch. *Sometimes I kind of hate Trix.*

Trix picked up her phone again and looked at the screen. "Holy shit, you're trending on Twitter and the interview hasn't even aired. The amount of press we're going to get will be unprecedented. Everyone and their mother's going to be tuned in for this interview."

"Well, thank God for that," Gennie said. She looked at her watch. It was nearly two. *Should I tell Trix to leave?*

"Your sarcasm is not appreciated, Gennie. We've got to get you out of Hicksville. Your sense of reality is becoming more warped by the day."

"I'm glad you're excited about the ratings, Trix, but I don't think you have any idea what we're dealing with here. Murphy can crush all of us with the flick of a pen over a big, fat check."

"You're about to announce it on national television. He's not going to come after you now. If something happened to you, it would be obvious who did it. He's not stupid."

"No, he's not stupid. That's what I'm worried about."

Trix's phone vibrated. "Gotta run. Linus is here to take me back to the inn."

"Linus is not your personal chauffeur. He has a business to run."

"Don't be such a grouch. He's happy to do it," Trix said. "I'll call you later. I'm in your old room at the inn by the way."

"You really don't need to stay in River Valley. I can handle this without you," Gennie said, following Trix to the door.

"It's best if I'm here," she said. They stepped outside to the stone walkway. "Good God, it's cold. And is there really not a Starbucks within a fifty-mile radius?"

"River Valley doesn't need a Starbucks. The inn has great coffee. Order room service." *And stay in your room for the rest of the day.*

"All right. Kisses." Trix, in her high heel boots, wobbled over the stone walkway until she reached the cement drive, which had been cleared of snow but appeared slick.

"Careful," Gennie called out to Trix. "It's really slippery."

Trix's gait slowed as she headed toward Linus who was driving a sturdy-looking SUV. When she reached her destination, she called back to Gennie. "I'm risking my life for you, Banks. I hope you appreciate it."

Gennie waved to Linus and turned to go back inside, cold without a jacket. Stefan, Drake, and the kids were no longer in the yard, but she could hear voices coming from the back patio.

She wandered into the kitchen. Annie was just coming out of the pantry, carrying a loaf of bread. "Hey. You all right?" she asked Gennie.

"Fine. Tired. I can't thank you enough for letting us invade your house."

"There's no need to thank me. I like a full house. Anyway, it's my pleasure. I know what it's like to be hunted by a dangerous man."

Bella had told Gennie the story of Annie's ex being released from prison and coming after her. Gennie shivered.

Annie gingerly lowered herself onto a chair at the kitchen table. "This baby's supposed to come in two weeks, but I swear, it feels like she's coming any day now."

"She? I thought you didn't know the sex?"

"Call it intuition, but I'm pretty sure it's a girl." Annie rubbed her eyes. "I think I will take a rest. You should too. This had to be a trying day for you."

She followed Annie's advice and crossed the driveway to the guesthouse, the smell of grilled meat wafting up from the back patio. Once inside, she switched on a lamp and the gas fireplace. The front room's décor mimicked the big house, rustic but cozy. A bookshelf held several rows of paperbacks. Wanting to stay away from television and her phone, she grabbed a romance from the shelf. She collapsed onto the sofa, pulling a throw over her legs, and reclined on a pillow. After reading several pages, her eyes grew heavy. Before she knew it, she fell asleep.

*   *

That night, they all gathered in the front room of the big house and watched the telecast together. Trix slipped in right before the show started, with her phone planted on her ear.

The fire blazed, but Gennie shivered as the show started. Raquel did a lead-in, summarizing the events of the past several days, and finished by saying this was Gennie's official response and only interview about the subject.

The interview with Gennie ran first. Sitting next to Gennie, her Mom cried for much of the interview. *I'm detached from it. It's almost like I'm watching someone else.* The emotional roller coaster of the past few days had taken its toll. *I don't have any tears left.* Trix paced, much of her attention on her phone. "People are going crazy on social media."

Next, Sarah's interview started. "Oh, my goodness. Is that how I look?" she asked during the first commercial. "I look giant next to Raquel."

"She's a very small woman," Stefan said. "You look great."

"I think so too," Alder said.

Sarah patted his head. "Thanks, buddy."

"Twitter feed is very favorable. You're both coming off great," Trix said.

"This isn't a popularity contest," Stefan said.

"Well, excuse me for trying to salvage this mess," Trix said.

Stefan didn't say anything. He went to the bar and poured a whiskey. "Anyone else?"

Drake asked for a glass of wine, but everyone else declined. *Must keep my head clear for whatever's coming.*

Raquel closed the show by saying they'd contacted Murphy's team for comment but had received no response. The program went to commercial. Stefan turned the television off and started to pace in front of the window with his drink in hand.

Gennie's phone buzzed. *Unknown number.* Stefan looked at her. "Do you want me to get it?"

It's him. I know it's him. "Hello," she said.

"I warned you."

Before she could answer, the line went dead. She started to shake and dropped the phone on the table.

"Who was it?" her mom asked.

"It was him."

"Dammit," Stefan said.

"Could I have a glass of wine, please?" she asked. *Keep control of yourself. It's going to be okay. Don't let Sarah see you freaking out. Don't scare her.*

"Now what?" Sarah asked.

"Now we wait to see what he'll do," Gennie said.

"And for the court ordered paternity test," Stefan said.

"But what about us?" Sarah asked. "Do we stay here? Will I be able to go back to school on Monday?"

"I don't know." Gennie pulled her into a hug. "I just don't know."

* *

Later, after everyone went to bed and she was alone with Stefan in the guesthouse, they talked about the phone call.

"How did he get your number," Stefan asked.

"I don't know. How does he always know where I am? He has ways." She realized she still had her makeup on from the interview. "I'm going to take a shower. I feel dirty."

"Yeah, okay." He was sitting by the window, staring into the bottom of another glass of whiskey and didn't look her way.

When the water was hot, she got in and washed her body and face, then stood under the spray for several minutes. *We are safe here, but for how long? Eventually, we will have to go back into the world. I will hire each of them a bodyguard. I will protect them all, no matter how much money it takes. He will not hurt the people I love.*

After she was out of the shower, she wrapped her hair in the towel and put on pajamas. Stefan had moved from the window to the fireplace. "What's going on, Stefan?"

"I'm feeling helpless, and I don't like it. I should be able to protect you from all this and I can't. I hate it."

"I know the feeling. I mean, how am I going to keep Sarah safe if she goes back to school?"

He rubbed his eyes, then downed his drink. "One day at a time. Let's see what the bastard does tomorrow."

She sat beside him on the couch and took his hand. "Thank you, Stefan. I couldn't do this without you."

"You don't have to. You'll never have to do anything without me again, if I have anything to do with it."

CHAPTER NINE

THE DAY STARTED with her phone buzzing. Gennie rolled over to get it. Next to her, Stefan mumbled something and turned over onto his side.

It was a text from Trix: *Turn on the television. He's about to be on the Today Show.*

She reached over Stefan for the remote and switched on the television that hung over the dresser. It was an interview with Matt Lauer and Rick Murphy.

"Last night, actress Genevieve Banks accused you of raping her when she was fifteen. The child from that alleged incident was also interviewed. It's our understanding you want to address these allegations."

"Well, first, thank you for giving me the opportunity to set the record straight. Of course, none of this is true. Complete and utter lies."

"What would be Ms. Banks's motivation for telling such heinous lies?" Matt asked.

"Well, clearly her career is washed up, and she's desperate to be back in the public eye. It's a heck of a way to do it, but that's what these girls seem to enjoy doing for attention."

"Have you complied with the court order to take the paternity test?"

"I can assure you I'm not the father. I refuse to play into these antics. I have more important things to do in preparing to lead this great nation of ours. I've served the public all my life, and I'm not about to let some second-rate actress distract me from what's important."

"Wouldn't a paternity test just clear all this up? Doesn't that seem like the fastest solution?"

"Well, Matt, that allows this to become even bigger than it is. I will not waste my time on something so ridiculous. Ms. Banks is in trouble with the court of public opinion and hatched up this sad story to get out of the fact that she left a baby in the snow twenty years ago. What's even sadder is that she has the kid believing it's all true."

"Is it true that she met you twenty years ago at your office?"

"I met a lot of kids over the years. It's certainly possible. Doesn't mean I assaulted her. As far as the young woman's concerned, given the gambling problems of her father, it seems clear she's after money. Genevieve Banks, for that matter, could quite possibly be broke. We don't really know. All we know is that she's made up a ridiculous story to derail my candidacy. I don't think it's too much of a stretch to believe that perhaps this is sponsored by one of my opponents."

"Are you saying you think one of the other candidates is paying her to make up this story?" Matt asked.

"I wouldn't put it past any of them," he said. "I intend to launch a full investigation."

The interview wrapped up then.

Stefan's hair stuck up in every direction, and his eyes were bloodshot. "Get on the phone with Grant. Find out the status of the paternity petition," Stefan said. "That asshole isn't getting away with this."

Her phone buzzed with a call from Trix. With reluctance, Gennie answered. "What's up?"

"I just got off the phone with the studio heads of your next two films. They're dropping you."

"What? Why?"

"They said they want someone younger and cheaper," Trix said.

"Both of them?"

"Yeah, apparently, they all took the same course on how to be an asshole."

"It's Murphy. I told you his tentacles are far-reaching."

"Oh crap," Trix said. "One of the cable networks is doing a joint interview with people who've worked with you. They're saying you're unstable. Channel 46."

By this time, Stefan had made coffee and put a cup on the bedside table before climbing back into bed. She handed him the remote, her hands shaking too violently to hit the right buttons.

The television screen showed three people streamed in from various locations, with a hairspray laden interviewer asking them questions. She recognized two of the interviewees from a horror film she'd done when she was twenty. She hadn't seen either of them in anything for years. They hadn't aged well, either. Will Morton had lost all his hair and looked like he'd been in more than a few bar brawls. Fifty extra pounds had attached themselves to Beth Crowley. She'd been anorexic thin when they'd worked together. The third woman she didn't recognize. *Was it someone from acting school? Yes, that was it. What was her name? She was older than us. Ramona something. She wanted to be a standup comic. Yes, that's right. I went to one of her gigs and she was terrible. Not funny, but mean.*

The man was answering a question about Gennie's stability at the time he worked with her. "Oh, yeah, she was like really out there, you know. Didn't talk to people much. Just kind of kept to herself most of the time, except when she was yelling and screaming at the crew."

"Screaming?" the interviewer asked.

"You know, like diva stuff. She wanted coconut water in her dressing room. Threw a fit when she didn't get it. Things like that."

Coconut water? There was no coconut water back then. A liar. They're all liars.

Beth spoke next. "All I know is she was a fibber. Lied about things that didn't even matter. I swear she used to take things from my trailer. Hair brushes. Lipsticks. I confronted her once and she denied it, of course."

The failed comedienne spoke next. "I remember this one time she came to one of my standup gigs and got drunk. Started heckling me. That kind of thing. Very disconcerting, of course, when you're on stage."

"After commercial, we'll be back with a man who knew Ms. Banks and her mother before fame. It promises to be very illuminating."

Stefan muted the sound.

How had he found them so quickly?

"None of it's true, Stefan. Not a bit."

"He's paid them. None of them are doing well in the business. It wouldn't have cost him much."

Gennie picked up her coffee, but her stomach churned. She set it back on the table, her hands shaking.

The news program started again. This time an older man, wearing a suit and glasses, was the lone guest. A comb-over did nothing to disguise his near baldness. *I think I know him. Who is it? Where do I know him from?*

"We have Harry Pettus with us now. He claims to have worked with Genevieve Bank's mother years ago at a bank in Wisconsin. Mr. Pettus, did you know Joan Banks well?"

Harry. Mom's boss at the bank. He used to give me lollipops. Why would he do something like this? He loved Mom.

"Yep. Sure did. She was a teller for me from 1989 until the late nineties."

"Did you know the Banks family well?"

"Sure. I guess. Joan wasn't my sort of woman. I'm a church-going kind of guy, and Joan was one who enjoyed the nightlife, so to speak. There was a little bar around the corner from the bank, and she used to go there a lot with coworkers after work. No wonder her daughter turned up pregnant."

Gennie gasped, then put her hand over her mouth. "He's gotten to Harry. There isn't one ounce of truth to anything he just said. My mother never touched a drop of liquor when I was young. She always came straight home and made dinner and helped me with homework. That's just ridiculous."

"This story Gennie's concocted is a doozy," continued Harry. "A real doozy. Falsely accusing Rick Murphy who's served this great state of Wisconsin all his life. Well, that's just wrong."

"Turn it off. I can't hear any more," Gennie said.

The front door opened and slammed. Her mother, still wearing pajamas and a sleep mark across her cheek, appeared in the doorway of the bedroom. "Did you see that idiot, Harry?" She glanced at Stefan and blushed. "Sorry to barge in like this."

"It's all right. These are special circumstances," Stefan said. "I'll make us some coffee."

Her mother sank into the chair in the corner. "I can't believe Harry would do this to us."

"I always thought he was in love with you back then," Gennie said.

"He was. He made a pass at me one time during a Christmas party. Too much eggnog, but I just made a joke of it and sent him off to find his wife."

"He's a man scorned," called Stefan from the other room.

"Or, Murphy paid him off," Gennie said. "I'm sorry, Mom. Did you see the three clowns they had on before him?"

"All lies, but people won't know that. I don't want anyone thinking these things about you, Gennie girl."

Stefan came back in the room with two steaming mugs of coffee and handed one to her mom. He set the other on the bedside table next to Gennie.

"Thank you, dear. I'm flabbergasted by Harry. We worked together for years and years. He knew me well, and Stefan, I can assure you I've spent almost no time in bars, and I certainly would never have neglected my daughter any more than I had to by working thirty miles away from our home." She sipped her coffee and sighed. "This is maddening."

She looks so defeated. I hate him. I will kill you, Rick Murphy, before I allow you to hurt the people I love any more than you already have.

"Harry knew you interviewed with Murphy when you were fifteen. I bragged about it night and day for a month. He knows the truth, and yet he's lying."

"For money," Stefan said. "Murphy's behind all of this."

"Gennie, I think I should go on one of the talk shows and explain how it really was. I don't care what they say about me, but painting you as some hussy who ended up pregnant is just too much."

"But you hate being on camera," Gennie said. "I can do another interview. The Today Show has reached out several times. Trix could arrange it easily."

"No. I want to do it. Even if no one believes the truth, I'll feel better having said my piece. Call Trix, sweetie, and see if she can get me on one of the morning shows. Tell her I'll fly wherever the interview is."

After her mother left, Gennie took a deep breath and turned to Stefan. "I hope Grant gets that paternity test court mandated sooner rather than later."

"He will. Don't worry. You'll have your chance to show the world what a liar Rick Murphy is."

* *

Later, Gennie went outside for a walk. The weather remained clear and cold. She lifted her face to the sky, the sunlight warm on her face despite the freezing temperatures. Thin branches, bare of leaves, dipped low under the weight of ice. Snow crunched under her boots as she walked toward the path down to the river. At the beginning of the trail, she stopped, surprised to see trampled grass, flat and frozen, leading down to the river. Someone had cleared the path.

She trekked down the mountain with care. After a few minutes, she reached the river. During the summer months, a sandy beach and a deep pool made the perfect spot for swimming. Now, shrubs bowed under the weight of snow and cloaked the sand in white. A layer of ice coated the shallow edges of the water. Swift current, sparkling under the sun, carried bits of logs and twigs. She knelt, touching the icy edges of the river with her gloved fingers. Thin, it cracked under her fingers, broke apart, and floated into deeper water. She sat on her haunches, gazing across the river. A winter sparrow hopped between reedy branches.

What was she to do? How should she maneuver through these curves of unexpected turmoil? Dropped from two films. Murphy's doing. Regardless, it hurt to hear the studio head's excuses. *Younger and cheaper.* Telling the truth had sealed her fate. She could be finished. There would be someone in her twenties, prettier and less expensive, to take her place. In no time at all, she would be forgotten.

She'd built her career on ingénue roles, but she was approaching an age where she would no longer be suited for the pretty love interest. Although not terribly interesting, those films were lucrative, giving her the opportunity to do an independent film when she wanted. It was the smaller films, like the one they'd just wrapped with Richard, that had earned her two Oscar nominations and one win. None of which counted to the big studio executives. They wanted her for romantic comedy roles and to look pretty. She was guaranteed to bring in big money. People loved these films, and they loved her in them.

She sat on a rock. The sun warmed the back of her head. All her adult life, she'd focused on work, knowing that actresses were like football players. The public loved you when you were twenty but were done with you by the time you turned forty. She'd done films back to back, hardly taking a break since she got her first big role at twenty-one. Perhaps it was time to pull back, only do projects that touched her soul.

I am not just my work. And yet, aside from her mom and Bella, there hadn't been much else to her life. The work had saved her. She escaped inside each story so she didn't have to face the pain. Art had redeemed her. Commercial films had made her rich. *Who am I if I don't work?*

Luck had played a large factor in her acting career, along with physical attributes that people found appealing. These were simply good fortunes, not the essence of who she really was. What had she done that mattered to others? Making Sarah, giving her life, when it could have been easier to make the other choice. Who did she want to be for the remainder of her life? Just an actress? Just her work? No, she wanted a richer life, one filled with people she loved. This was what made a life, not the work, the money, the fame. It was the quality of relationships that delivered joy. *The small moments with people I love. This is what I'll remember at the end.*

Sarah's journey was just starting. She had the right to be happy and free. Whatever the cost, Gennie had to pay it. *I will fight for the people I love. Love is stronger than hate. The darkest of nights still become morning. The sun comes back around with hot rebellion.*

Firs rustled in the wind. The river gurgled. She plunged her gloved hands into the fallen snow and formed a ball. She hurled the snowball into the river and, surviving in the icy water, it bobbed in the vigorous current, drifting farther and farther away until she could no longer see it. The snap of a tree branch from across the river diverted her attention. An elk, with enormous antlers, stood between two trees, staring at her. She rose to her feet, reaching out her hand as if the river were not between them. *Daddy, is it you?*

A vision, as swift as the river's current, seized her. Like Venus rising, a little girl, naked and shivering, emerged from the snow, covering her chest and private parts with her arms. Gennie knew the big brown eyes and nose dotted with freckles. *She's me. I'm eight years old. The year Daddy died.*

The girl's voice was sad, but urgent. *You gave him all our power. You allowed him to ruin us.*

"No, *he* did this. *He* ruined us," Gennie said. "*He* stole our innocence."

Don't let him steal your future. What happened was not our fault, but if you continue to shun life, he continues to win. You must let go of the past, accept the pain, but live without fear. Do not let him win. Fight for us, Gennie. Fight for Stefan. Choose us. Choose to live. Choose love.

"Yes," she whispered. As quickly as it had come, the image disappeared. She looked back to the elk, but he, too, had vanished.

She knelt in the snow, wrapping her arms around her knees until she was round like a bulb. For only a moment more, she allowed herself to be confined in dormancy as she wept for the years he stole from her. She mourned every moment of those wasted days and did not turn away from the sadness or agony or regret, but let it seep into her and through her. The horror of what happened would always be there, but it was not the sum of her. *I am not fear, hate's companion. I am love. I am rising.* When her sobs ceased, she dried her eyes, and like a tulip inching out of the soil to seek the sun, she rose, little by little, reaching upward to the merciful sky, all the while tilting her face to bask in the light.

CHAPTER TEN

TRIX ARRANGED FOR GENNIE'S MOTHER to appear on the Today Show for the following day. Blair had arranged a late afternoon flight and hired a bodyguard to accompany her on the trip, along with a retired NYC police officer to guard her hotel room. There was no way Gennie was letting her go out there without protection. Gennie knocked on her mother's bedroom door.

"Can I come in?"

"Yes, come in, honey. I'm trying to figure out what to wear tomorrow."

This guestroom, smaller than Sarah's, was decorated in soft blues with black furniture. A long shag rug covered the hardwood floor. An open suitcase was on the end of the bed, with several pieces of clothing haphazardly packed. Gennie sat on the hardback chair in the corner of the room.

Her mom held up a red dress. "How about this one? Red's a power color, right? Will it wash me out? I'm too old to go on television."

"The red one's fine. They'll have a makeup person who will make sure you look good under the lights. Plus, you look great."

Her mother threw a pair of boots into the suitcase. "Boots are good, right?"

"Sure. Mom, stop for a moment. I want to tell you something."

Her mother halted near the bed. "What's up?"

"I wanted to thank you for everything. All the sacrifices you made for me, how you took care of me when everything happened. I don't know if I've ever thanked you enough."

"Oh, Gennie girl, you've done so much for me. How could you say that? I'm spoiled rotten."

"I love being able to do things for you, Mom. That's been the greatest part of all the success."

"You've always been the sweetest girl in the world." Her mother crossed the room, putting her hands on the sides of Gennie's face. "I love you so much."

"I love you too. I'm worried about sending you to New York. If anything happened to you...I can't even think about it."

Her mother perched on the edge of the bed. "Do you remember what I was like right after your dad died?"

"Kind of. I've blanked a lot of it out."

"I was grieving, of course, but I was also really, really mad. At God. At the drunk driver. I was even angry at your father, like he chose to die and leave me alone. My first reaction to something traumatic is anger. I don't know why. And, right now I'm angry as heck, which means I should channel it and go after Murphy. He hurt my little girl, and I'm telling you right now, he will pay for it. I will not rest until he does."

"Mom, I'm scared for you," Gennie said.

She jumped from the bed and started putting more items into the suitcase. "I need to take this trip and set the record straight, or I'll go crazy. I'm so filled with anger, I don't know what to do with myself. I want to kill him with my bare hands."

"You might have to fight Stefan for that privilege."

"Stefan Spencer is a fine, fine man." She tossed another pair of pants into the suitcase. "You're more yourself with him than when you were with Moody. Moody wasn't suited for you."

"Why do you say that?"

"Well, you're a little bit country, and he's all rock and roll."

Gennie laughed. "A little bit country? Really?"

Her mom tossed a pair of tights into her bag. "You're a small-town girl at heart."

"I am?"

"For sure. No one knows a person like her mother."

"What do you think about buying some land here? We could build a house. I could live here, at least part of the time. We could keep the beach house too."

"I think that's a wonderful idea. And for the record, I also think Stefan's the catch of the century, and he's suited to you. He's a little bit country, just like you."

"I'm so crazy about him, but I'm afraid I won't be able to give him what he needs. Look at what happened with Moody."

"Honey, being intimate is more than just sex. Being vulnerable to someone, telling them about your dark places, is as close as one can get to another person."

"We *do* have that together."

"It is *definitely* true that sleeping next to a person is intimate. You have to worry about morning breath and bedhead."

They laughed as her mom crossed the room and took Gennie's face in her hands. "All I've ever wanted was for you to be happy."

"The work has made me enormously gratified."

Her mom sighed, looking away with a sad expression. "Yes, but it isn't all there is to life. It would be nice to share it with someone you love. I know it's not easy to be alone."

"Why haven't *you* ever remarried?"

"It's impossible to expect to find the kind of love I had with your father twice in a lifetime."

"But you're lonely. I know you are, especially when I'm gone for such long periods."

"No, I'm fine. I have yoga and my work at the hospital." She volunteered several times a week to hold sick babies, usually because their mothers were addicted to crack when they were born, or to do special things for the kids in the children's wings. "And, I have my book club. I love those ladies. Do you know last week we stayed up until midnight talking and laughing?"

Her mom went back to packing. Movement outside the window caught Gennie's attention. A branch swayed, dumping snow. It was a squirrel, hopping trees.

"And now, my love, I have a plane to catch. Operation take down Rick Murphy's in full swing."

"The bodyguard I've hired will stay by your side the entire time. I've also hired a retired NYC police officer to guard your hotel door tomorrow night."

"I hope it won't be necessary, but it will help me sleep at night to know he's out there." A knock on the bedroom door drew their attention away from each other. "Come in."

Sarah came inside the room, wearing a button-down jean shirt and sweatpants. "Hey, Tommy's here to take you to the airport." Sarah grabbed the luggage, and they all went out to the yard where Tommy was waiting, chatting with Stefan.

"You all set, Joan?" Tommy asked

"As ready as I'll ever be." She gave a quick hug to Sarah and then a longer one to Gennie. "Pray for me."

"We will," Sarah said.

"Just be careful, Mom."

"I won't leave her side until she's with the bodyguard," Tommy said.

* *

They stood in the driveway, watching the car disappear around the corner. Sarah squinted in the sunlight. "Gennie, how do you know if the bodyguard can be trusted?"

"He's from an agency I've used for years," Gennie said.

"But you don't know him?"

"Most likely, no."

"Murphy's gotten to a lot of people," Sarah said.

"I didn't even think about it," Gennie said. "Stefan?"

Stefan glanced down the driveway, then stomped his feet. "Come inside. It's cold out here. It'll be fine." *He hesitated. He's worried too.*

After fretting for a few more minutes, she texted Tommy. *Please make sure the guard seems legit. I'm worried Murphy may have gotten to him.*

No reply. *He's driving. They're fine.*

Stefan reassured her with a tap on her arm. "Tommy will make sure she's safe."

Sarah shuffled into the main house, while Gennie and Stefan walked hand in hand toward the guest cottage. When they were inside, her phone buzzed with a text from Blair. *Call me ASAP.*

She called right away, bracing herself. *What else has happened?*

"Gennie, you're not going to believe this. In the last hour, two women left messages here at your office number, asking if they could speak with your assistant. They said they had urgent messages regarding Rick Murphy. I called them both back and they had the same story. They were raped by Rick Murphy too. They're going public this afternoon, but they wanted you to know first. I have their numbers if you want to talk to them."

Legs shaking, she sat at the desk in the sitting room. "Yes, please text me their names and numbers. I'll call them now."

Her phone buzzed almost immediately. She clicked on the first woman's number: Beverly Tuttle with a Wisconsin area code. A woman answered on the second ring, sounding breathless. After thanking Gennie for calling, she launched into her story. "I know you're busy and I don't want to keep you, so I'll keep it short." *A nice Wisconsin girl, always polite, never wanting to make a fuss.*

"When I was a sophomore in college, I accepted an internship with his campaign. We worked out of his home office. I worked in this little office with one other intern, Dirk. The day it happened, Dirk had a dentist appointment and left early. Otherwise, we usually walked out to our cars together." Beverly paused and cleared her throat before continuing. "Murphy must have waited for the day when Dirk went home early. As soon as he left, Murphy trapped me in my office. That's where it happened."

This poor girl. We have to get this monster behind bars. He must pay for what he's done.

"He threatened to kill my brother and my mother if I told anyone. Then, he took a wad of cash out of his pants pocket and threw it on the table and said, 'Buy yourself some new panties. Don't bother coming back tomorrow. I'll tell everyone you quit.' I can still see his face when he said it—all red and blotchy."

Gennie murmured how sorry she was. "Are you sure you want to do this?"

"When you went public, I knew I had to do it too. There's power in numbers."

"I agree. How many years ago did this happen?" Gennie asked.

"Five. My statute of limitations hasn't run out yet."

"Do you have an attorney?" *I'll pay whatever for it if she needs one.*

"Yes, we're announcing it in a press conference this afternoon," said Beverly. "I'm formally pressing charges."

"What about your family? Are they safe? What about you?"

"I have to take the risk. It's time to take back my life. I've let him ruin it. I'm afraid all the time. Any time a man wants to get close, I freak out. I've accepted that I'll never feel normal again, but I will no longer let him win. Even if he kills me, I'm telling the truth."

"Please be safe."

"My attorney's going to petition for police protection." There was silence on the other end of the phone for a second or two, before she spoke again. "What you did yesterday was one of the bravest things I've ever seen. Thank you."

After they hung up, Gennie wept tears of regret. *If only I had come out sooner, I could have saved Beverly.*

A few minutes later, she called the next number. Susan Roma was sixteen when she came by his house one afternoon to visit his daughter.

"Murphy said Kate wasn't there, but that she'd return soon. Did I want to wait for her? I thought nothing of it. Friends' dads were always inviting us inside to wait. He then asked if I wanted to see his office. He was a senator, and I thought how cool it would be to see where he worked. When we got to his office, he offered me a piece of chocolate from a box on his desk, which I gladly took. Then, he asked me if I wanted a drink, which shocked me. I said no, that my mother didn't allow me to drink. He poured a whiskey for himself, downed it, then shut the door—they were double doors with solid metal handles—and pulled a key from his pocket and locked the door. An old-fashioned key. I remember exactly what it looked like. He put the key in his pocket. That's when I noticed how his pants were tented. He pushed me to the floor." She hesitated. "You know the rest."

"Yes, I do." Gennie walked to the window and looked over to the main house. Sarah and Alder were sitting on the porch swing, drinking something from mugs. Sarah laughed at something he said, her cheeks pink from either cold or exercise. "Did he threaten you if you told anyone?"

"He told me he would kill my parents and my little sister if I ever said a word to anyone. I went to private school with his daughter, which was torture for me, thinking he might show up at school at any moment. I was there on a scholarship. My family was poor, but I begged my mother to let me go back to public school. I made up some story about mean girls bullying me."

"I'm sorry, Susan."

"Other than my husband I've never told anyone that I was raped, let alone by whom. I felt like it was my fault."

"I felt the same way," Gennie said.

"When I heard your interview last night, I thought if Genevieve Banks can do it, I can do it. I'm an attorney. I often represent rape victims. Not too hard to figure out why I chose that for a profession, right?"

"Right," Gennie said. *She helps others because she couldn't help herself.* "I'm assuming, with your contacts, you have a good attorney?"

"Yes. Liz Teeny has agreed to represent me."

"I've seen her on the news." Liz Teeny was a shark disguised in a designer suit who had represented victims in several high-profile rape trials. Recently, she'd secured a guilty verdict against a college basketball player accused of raping a young woman at a fraternity party. Liz Teeny was tiny in stature and name, but not in personality. Deceptively cute, like a fuzzy, small animal that could tear a person apart limb by limb, she appeared unafraid of anything or anyone.

Susan continued, "She's a killer, and she understands how frightened I am of Murphy because she's dealt with his kind before."

"And gotten guilty verdicts."

"Exactly. We're going public this afternoon, hoping to add momentum to what you started. We both believe there are many more victims. Liz would love to talk to you if you have time today."

"Yes, absolutely." Before they hung up, Susan gave her Liz's phone number. It was a Los Angeles area code. *Figures she lives in Los Angeles. No shortage of work for a shark in tinsel town.*

Liz's secretary put her through right away. She wasted no time with pleasantries. "Ms. Banks, would you tell me the details of the day it happened?" asked Liz. "I know it's hard, but it will help Susan's case if I know his modus operandi."

Taking a deep breath, she told Liz every detail she could remember, keeping it factual and managing not to cry. She ended with the roses and the phone call after the interview.

"My God. This guy's a monster. He sends Susan chocolates every year. Do you have good representation?"

"Yes. Grant Perry's an old friend of Stefan's. He's done this kind of thing before."

"Right. Sure. I know Grant. Good attorney." Had Liz's tone become softer, more feminine at the mention of Grant's name? *Do they have a history?* She made a mental note to ask Stefan about it. "Have Grant call me, if you would? I'd like to compare notes. Talk strategy."

She agreed and encouraged Liz to call her anytime if she had further questions.

"We're doing a press conference in an hour, so I need to go," said Liz. "I'll be in touch."

* *

When Stefan returned thirty minutes later, his hair was damp from his workout. "You won't believe what's happened." She told him about the phone calls with all three women.

When she finished, he paced in front of the window. "Jesus, this guy should be shot, but not before a little torture." He wiped his face with the towel around his neck. "I swear to God, I would kill him with my bare hands if I could."

Their conversation was interrupted when Gennie's cell phone rang again. "It's Grant."

Grant didn't bother with hello. "We got him. Court ordered him to take the paternity test today. We'll get the results no later than tomorrow."

"That's great news. Thank you." She filled him in on the other women.

"Holy shit. That means there *are* more. If Liz Teeny's involved, this could get interesting," Grant said.

"She knew who you were. Do you know her personally?" Gennie asked.

"Yeah, kinda."

"What does that mean?"

"It means we used to have a thing. Back in law school. It didn't end well," Grant said. "Mostly because I was an ass."

"Are you able to work with her?" Gennie asked.

"Heck yeah. We're professionals."

"I wondered why she sounded weird when I said your name."

"She probably still has the hots for me."

She chuckled. "Yeah, I don't think that was it. Anyway, she wants you to call her to talk strategy."

"What time's the news conference?" he asked.

"In about an hour from now."

"Okay, I'll check in with you later."

After promising to say hello to Stefan for him, she hung up the phone. "Did you know about Grant and Liz?" she asked.

Stefan nodded. "Those two were the biggest disaster known to mankind. Epic fail on Grant's part. He was way too immature to handle a relationship and cheated on her with one of my actress friends. This was forever ago, before any of us had anything even remotely close to success, but I swear Grant still regrets it to this day. She's his *one that got away*."

"Wait? Isn't Grant married?"

Stefan shuddered. "To the meanest woman ever born."

Gennie laughed. "She can't be the meanest."

"She is. I'm not kidding. The worst." He came toward her, smelling of sweat and aftershave. A shot of desire roared through her. She wanted to touch him, to press her body against him. *What is happening to me?* Her body was awakening after a long slumber. What did it mean for her and Stefan? *Can I be normal? Don't jinx it by overthinking. Be in the moment.*

Stefan was looking at her with a bemused expression. "What're you thinking in that little head of yours?"

"I was thinking about you. About kissing you."

"Why didn't you say so?" He approached her, leaning close and giving her a quick peck on the mouth. "I have to shower. I'm too disgusting to even be in the same room with you." He waggled a finger at her. "However, I'm happy to oblige with a longer kiss when I no longer smell like a locker room."

She watched him walk into the bathroom. *Could his butt be any tighter?* Her phone buzzed again. It was Tommy. *Had something happened?* "Hey, Tommy."

"Gennie, I have a bad feeling about this bodyguard guy. He seems nervous. Sweating profusely. I think they may have gotten to him."

"Crap. Okay. What do we do?"

"I'll go with her," he said.

"But what about your family?"

"Lee will be all right for a day or two. She has Ellen to help. I'll fly with your mom and not let her out of my sight. They still have seats available in first class so I can sit next to her. Can you have Blair book me a room in the hotel?"

"Yes, sure. And I'll pay for the flight. How do we get rid of the other guy?"

"I'll tell him you changed your mind."

"I'll have Blair call the agency and tell them I wasn't feeling secure sending her off with a stranger. That will send a message to Murphy if you're right." What about the hotel? Did Murphy know where they were staying? "I'll have Blair book you guys in a different hotel. He knows where you're staying. Crap, what about the retired officer I hired?"

"Cancel him. I'll guard her myself. We can't trust anyone but our inner circle from now on."

"Yeah, okay."

"Book rooms that are adjoining. I don't want your mom alone at night. I'll touch base when we land. It'll be around two a.m. New York time. Don't worry. I'll stay next to her every moment."

*   *

The shower shut off just as the press conference was scheduled to begin. Gennie settled on the bed to watch, searching the covers for the remote. Neither of them had bothered to make the bed that morning. They'd been spoiled in a hotel for too long. On Stefan's side of the bed, the sheets and blankets were tangled. The remote was probably stuck in one of the folds. She patted the blanket searching for it as Stefan came out of the bathroom, wearing nothing but a towel around his waist. Her breath caught at the sight of him. When they filmed a love scene for the movie, he'd been without his shirt, but she'd been so nervous she hadn't fully absorbed how muscular his shoulders and chest were. Six-pack abs. Her eyes traveled lower to the muscles above the towel line. Heat surged through her. *Look away. Pretend you don't notice how hot he is.* "Your side of the bed is so messy I can't find the remote."

"That's because it's on the bedside table." He pulled a pair of jeans and a shirt from the closet. "And look, I even hung my clothes." *Too bad he feels the need to dress. He can run around naked for all I care.*

"Progress." She laughed as she grabbed the remote. As she searched the channels, Stefan disappeared into the bathroom, coming out minutes later wearing faded jeans and a long t-shirt. His hair, wet and uncombed, pointed every which way in divine dishevelment.

He plopped onto the bed, pulling on thick socks, and leaned over to peck her cheek.

Liz and Susan were in a conference room with at least a dozen microphones on the table in front of them. Susan, slim, with long auburn hair and a striking face, stared into the camera with a look of steely reserve. Liz was in front of the row of microphones, obviously quite comfortable before the cameras. With a heart-shaped face and enormous brown eyes, accentuated by flawless makeup and chestnut-brown hair styled in a layered, chin-length bob, she was as slick and pretty as a Hollywood starlet. "She looks more like a model than an attorney," Gennie said.

"She's tiny and adorable. I could fit her in my pocket," Stefan said.

In his pocket? Why would he want to put her in his pocket? She looked over at him. *Is he interested in Liz?* His face was impassive, revealing nothing. *I'm ridiculous. He's allowed to think other women are pretty. Focus on what's happening on television, not petty jealousy.* She couldn't stop herself. The question bubbled out of her. "Did you date her?"

"What? No. We were friends. She only had eyes for Grant, trust me." Smiling, he reached for her hand. "But I like that you're jealous."

She pulled her hand away. "I'm not jealous."

"Whatever you say." He scooted closer to her and kissed her neck. *Why did he have to smell so good all the time?*

"You think way too much of yourself," she said.

Laughing, he tugged on the collar of her sweater. "That's what my mother always says."

"Shush now. It's starting." This time she reached for his hand. He held it in his lap as the press conference started.

Liz thanked the reporters for joining, then began to speak. "Nineteen years ago, my client, Susan Roma, was raped by Rick Murphy. She was sixteen at the time. His then-teenage daughter, Kate Murphy, was her best friend at school." She shared the account of that day piece by piece. "We will be suing him in a civil case for damages as well as pursuing criminal charges."

The reporters shouted questions. "We have nothing more at this time," said Liz. "We'll keep you informed as things develop."

The feed went to the newscaster, who said they would now be showing a live feed from the press conference of Beverly Tuttle. "Given the timing, we can only assume it's further accusations against Rick Murphy," the white-haired host said.

The event was a similar setup to Susan's. Beverly's attorney spoke for her as well. "Six years ago, when she was twenty years old, Beverly Tuttle accepted an internship with Rick Murphy's office." She continued, giving a detailed accounting of the incident. "We are filing a civil suit against Mr. Murphy."

After it ended, the feed went back to the news desk. They'd added another commentator. "While this was happening, we were informed that two other women have come forward, announcing that they were also raped by Rick Murphy. They claim to have been raped in the mid-2000s while working in his office. Their attorneys have announced they will also file charges against Senator Murphy."

Two more. That's five of us total. Strength in numbers. "We may actually get this guy. I can't believe this is happening."

"You did this, baby. You," Stefan said.

"I couldn't have done it without you by my side." The doorbell rang.

"I'll get it." She hopped from the bed to answer. "It's probably Drake."

"I'm going to shave," he said. "I'll be right out."

Trix stood in the doorway with an ecstatic expression on her gaunt face. "Can you believe this? It's the best news ever. Now he can't possibly call you a liar and have anyone believe him."

Other women experiencing the trauma of rape isn't exactly something to celebrate. Trix is Trix. Subtle points of humanity are lost on her.

Trix held a paper cup between her leather-gloved hands. "I found decent coffee at that diner. They even had real cream, which is a plus."

Cream must be her only source of calories. The woman grew skinnier by the day. *She's starting to look like a cue ball on a toothpick.* "Are you taking back what you said about River Valley yet?"

Trix smiled and walked past her into the house, shedding her leather gloves. "It's still Podunk, but I have to admit, people are super nice. It's a little weird, if you want to know the truth. It's like, what are they hiding behind all that 'gee whiz, what can I do for you next?' act."

"I don't think it's an act and no one here says *gee whiz*," Gennie said.

"It's the essence, if not the actual words." Trix set the coffee and gloves on the mantle above the fireplace. "I have to pee, though. Can I use your bathroom?"

"You'll have to use the one attached to the bedroom. It's the only one." Gennie gestured toward it. "But you have to wait a minute. Stefan's in there shaving."

"I don't mind," Trix said, grinning.

"Trix, really?"

She stopped in front of the closed door of the bedroom. "I know you two are sleeping together. There's no reason to pretend with me. I'm your manager, not your priest. But listen, if you two think you're going to keep this a secret much longer, you've got another thing coming. TMZ will figure out where you guys are soon and then they'll be all over this romance. You're so hot right now. I'll start the hashtag *Steffi* the minute it's out."

"How would they? Unless someone leaks it?"

"They find out things, Gennie. Don't be naïve."

"They can't find us here. Drake has this place wired like Fort Knox," Gennie said.

Stefan came out of the bedroom. He'd combed his hair and shaved. Her legs weakened at the sight of him.

"Hey, Trix," Stefan said, his voice cold.

"Hello, Stefan. You're looking delicious, as always." Trix glanced at her phone. "Oh shit, this is insane. The news channels and social media are in a frenzy with this Murphy stuff." She looked up at Gennie. "Why does Drake have this place locked up so tight anyway?"

"I don't know the details, but his first wife and child were murdered," Gennie said.

"That's horrendous. No wonder he's such a freak," Trix said.

"He's not a freak," Stefan said. "He's a genius who invented some kind algorithm or something and made a billion dollars."

"Why is everyone super rich but me? Anyway, I really need to use your bathroom. I may be awhile. Coffee does things to my intestines." With that, she disappeared into the bedroom, shutting the door behind her.

"I really can't stand that woman," Stefan whispered.

Gennie put her finger to her lips. "She'll hear you."

"I couldn't care less." He reached for her, pulling her into his arms, and tucking her hair behind her ears. "You know what I do care about?"

She smiled, tilting her head to the right and looking into his eyes. "Me?"

"Bingo." He kissed her.

Trix interrupted them when she returned from the bathroom. "Okay, you two lovebirds. I have to run."

Stefan stepped away from Gennie, crossing his arms. "Trix, are you flying home anytime soon?"

"Yes, I'm on a flight this evening. I'll have to manage things from there. I can't stand this cold. Terrible for my skin."

"I'll miss you, but we'll just have to, somehow, go on without you," Stefan said. *Even Trix could hear the sarcasm in that sentence.*

CHAPTER ELEVEN

THAT NIGHT, AFTER SAYING GOODNIGHT to their hosts and the kids, Gennie and Stefan grabbed a bottle of wine and went out to the guesthouse.

Stefan shrugged out of his coat, then threw it on the couch. "Do you ever hang anything up?" she asked.

"You sound like my mother." He grabbed her in his arms, pulling her body against him. "Fortunately, I still think you're sexy."

She grinned up at him. "Maybe I should nag you more often."

"You're beautiful even when you nag." He leaned down, capturing her bottom lip between his, and tightening his grip around her waist. She wrapped her arms around his neck, burying her fingers in his thick hair, and kissed him back, darting her tongue against his. His warm mouth tasted of red wine. "Stefan," she whispered, pressing her aching nipples against his hard chest. She imagined him tossing her onto the bed, undressing her slowly, releasing her body from its frozen jail. "I don't know what to do here."

He withdrew, looking into her eyes. "What do you want?"

"I don't know how to say it." This was a lie. *I know the words, but I can't say them. I want you.* To speak them out loud would sound ridiculous, like a scene from a melodrama. Regardless, it was the truth. Her skin ached for the touch of his calloused fingers. Every inch of her body craved the caresses of his hands, his mouth, his tongue. The deep need for his hard body stripped away all fear, leaving only desire. She closed her eyes, pressing her mouth to his strong neck where his rapid pulse beat a furious rhythm. "Stefan." His name, a moan, stirred him.

He tightened his grip, pressing his hips against her, his desire evident. "If you want me to stop, I will." The tone of his voice, as rough as the edges of a serrated knife, made her shudder. "I might have to take a walk outside, though."

"I don't want you to stop."

"Are you sure?"

"Please, Stefan. Don't let me think."

He picked her up and kicked open the door to the bedroom, kissing her as they moved to the bed. After setting her down gently, he switched on the bedside lamp. She lay back against the pillows, her legs curled under her, watching him.

He sat on the edge of the bed, wrapping one hand around her thigh. The spot between her legs twitched. Her pulse raced.

"Gennie, I would rather die than hurt you, and I'm afraid. More afraid than I've ever been in my life."

She gazed at him, imbibing every inch of his beauty in the dim light. Shadows obscured his face, except for his eyes which glittered like a wild animal at the edge of a forest just before it ventured into the unknown territory of civilization. Her chest ached; his vulnerability was contagious. *I love him so much it hurts.* She reached for him, cupping his face in her hands, feeling naked and raw. "I'm afraid, too, but I'm ready to let go."

"What's changed, Gennie?" He trailed his fingers along the length of her arm.

"Everything." She placed his hand over her heart. "Can you feel my heart pounding?"

He smiled. "I feel it. The first time I ever met you my heart was pounding so hard I thought you could see it through my shirt. You smiled up at me with those shy eyes, and I thought you were the most beautiful woman I'd ever seen. I had no idea what would happen between us, but I knew I would do anything to make you happy."

She remembered his tender, sensitive eyes had seemed to see into her soul. She hadn't liked it, and yet she couldn't turn from him. "You make me happy, Stefan. More than I've ever been."

"I want you to do this because you want to, not because you think it's what I want," he said.

"This is for me. Rest assured, I'm thinking of my own needs right now, not yours." She smiled, as a lone tear traveled down her cheek.

He swept the tear away with his fingertip. "I'll stop talking."

"Good idea."

He flipped off the lamp. The room went dark. As her eyes adjusted, Stefan went from a shadow to an outline. She scooted into the middle of the bed and turned on her side, feet together and her right cheek resting on a pillow. The bed vibrated as he joined her. On his side, inches from her, he traced her jawline with his fingers. "There's no rush. I'll go slowly, but you tell me the word, and I'll stop."

She let him kiss her, then push her gently back on the bed, covering her with his body. The hard contours of his torso were glorious under her hands. He trailed kisses down her neck, then nibbled her ear. She sighed, arching toward his touch. He sat up and took off his shirt.

She touched his chest with her fingertips. Not much hair. Hard muscles. She moved down, exploring his abdomen.

He kissed the length of her arm before moving up to capture her bottom lip between his, then darted his tongue into her mouth. Her nipples ached for his touch. She arched her back, and he took the hint, sliding her shirt off before moving down her neck and chest until he reached her breasts. He caressed one breast over her bra. It wasn't good enough. She wanted more. "Take my bra off."

With a quick snap of his fingers, he had it unfastened. She laughed. "You *have* done this before." She held up her arms as he slid her bra from her. He made a groaning sound at the back of his throat, then moved down, flicking one nipple and then the other with his tongue, until she moaned. She tugged at the button on her jeans. "Get these off me."

"Let me," he whispered. He unzipped her pants and then slid them over her hips, jerking at the end to pull them past her feet. Kissing her arches, he then moved up her legs, flicking with his tongue, until he reached the spot between her legs. She whimpered. He slid his fingers under her panties. She was wet and hot. "Don't stop," she said as he slid off her panties. "Don't give me time to remember."

He scooted out of his pants, tossing them across the room, then got on top of her, his erection hot against her thigh. "Are you sure?" he asked.

"Yes," she murmured. "So sure."

He pushed inside her, gently. She gasped, but it didn't hurt. "Just say stop if it gets to be too much."

She answered by grabbing him by the hips and pushing him deeper inside her, wrapping her legs around him. He moved in and out in a slow rhythm, hovering over her.

She met his thrusts, the feeling growing more intense. He flicked his tongue against one nipple then the other. She cried out, arching her back as waves of pleasure overtook her.

When the orgasm subsided, she loosened her grip and tried to catch her breath. Shuddering, he groaned and pushed deeper inside her as he climaxed. It took him a moment afterward to roll off her, his breath coming fast. A second later, he took her in his arms, holding her against his chest.

"You still okay?" he asked.

"Yes," she murmured.

"Damn, that wasn't bad for a first time."

"It's been so long since I've let anyone even close to what happened there," she said. "Moody tried, but it was a disaster. He stopped trying after a while."

"All these years? You've never been with anyone?" he asked, gently.

"No."

"I'm sorry, baby." He stroked her hair.

"I didn't know it could be this way."

"This is just the beginning. The longer we're together, the more trust we'll build."

"We have a lot to look forward to then," she said.

He kissed her forehead. "Yes, we do. Now, you must get some rest. Big day tomorrow."

She was already drifting off, relaxed in his embrace. "Goodnight, Stefan."

"Night, baby."

* *

Around 2 a.m., she woke. Stefan, having moved to the far side of the bed while they slept, snored softly, no louder than a cat's purr. She rolled onto her back and stared up at the ceiling, wide awake and cold. The room was icy, the comforter no match for the frigid weather and her nakedness. In all her adult years, she had never slept in the nude. There were so many firsts the past several days, most of them the result of Stefan. She turned on her side, attempting to make out his features in the darkness. He slept on his side, with the covers pulled over his head. She shivered and searched with her feet for Stefan's warmth, but found only cold sheets. They might have to get a smaller bed. A king was not made for lovers, but old married couples tired of one another's touch. It seemed impossible that she would ever tire of Stefan's caresses or his warm, hard body. *What will the years bring?* There was no way to know. *Whatever my future brings, it must contain Stefan.* When she thought of life without him, it was like a fog she could not see through. In every aspiration, every imagined moment, he was there by her side. She had given herself to him in a way she never thought she could. There was no longer a choice of life without him.

Sliding from the bed, she padded over to the bureau to find a pair of flannel pajamas, the area between her legs pleasantly sore. After she had slipped into her pajamas, she wrapped a throw blanket around her shoulders and went to the window, pulling up the shade. A three-quarter moon, high in the sky, nestled amid the stars. Perhaps it was time to forge a new life. What would it be like to live here? Could she have a normal, everyday existence? She could build a home down some country road that only the locals knew existed. There could be a pool on the property for Sarah and a guest house for her mother. She could do one movie a year for money and spend the rest of the time finding scripts that she cared about making. Or, maybe she would just give it all up and become a recluse here in Oregon. Bella's company and all the other investments she had would continue to make money.

She gazed at the front entrance of the big house. The porch light remained on, making the driveway and yard visible. Other than the plowed drive, several feet of snow remained. Benches and ceramic containers with shrubs framed the wide front doors. She was about to turn away when a movement at the far end of the driveway caught her attention. A pair of elk, male and female, walked daintily through the snow, despite their enormous girth. She held her breath as they approached the guest house. When they reached her window, they stopped. The male's horns were wide and tall, the symbols of his strength and power. His female companion had a sweet face and gentle eyes, more like a deer, yet she was proud and strong.

An image, as clear as a photograph in front of her eyes, appeared. Stefan, smiling gently, held a baby wearing a pink hat. Gennie, standing next to him, held the hand of a little boy. She blinked, and the image disappeared. Had she really seen it?

She dropped the shade and turned around, letting her eyes adjust to the darkness before heading across the room and getting back into bed. Stefan turned over and wrapped his arm around her waist, snuggling her close. "You're cold," he mumbled. "Stay in bed."

"Stefan?"

He murmured something.

"I saw elk." she said.

He kissed the top of her head. "I don't think so. Drake said there are only deer and wolves on the property."

"I know what I saw."

"Okay, baby, whatever you say."

She closed her eyes and drifted to sleep.

CHAPTER TWELVE

THE NEXT MORNING, Gennie woke to a text from Trix in all capital letters: TURN ON CNN.

Rick Murphy, with his wife beside him, was holding a press conference. "I categorically deny all the allegations brought forth by these desperate women clearly vying for their fifteen minutes of fame. Unfortunately, the last few days have taken a toll on my family, and we've decided it is best to withdraw my candidacy for president." He smiled, showing his perfect, white teeth. "I assure you, after all this is cleared up, we will revisit the idea."

A reporter stood up in the crowd. "Our sources tell us that you have indeed been proven to be the father of Sarah Bentley. Do you have a comment?"

How did the press know about the results before they did? There were no secrets from the vultures. Good or bad, this was the world they lived in now.

"Clearly something's been rigged. I'm not the father of that unfortunate girl. I plan on orchestrating a full investigation to get to the bottom of this obvious conspiracy." At that point, the campaign manager stepped forward and announced the end of the event.

"We got him," Stefan said.

Yes, yes, yes. It's happening. We're going to win this fight. Now that it was public knowledge about the paternity, everyone would know that he was at the very least a statutory rapist. He would go to jail.

* *

The interview with Matt Lauer and her mother aired shortly thereafter. "Welcome to the show, Mrs. Banks."

"Thanks for having me."

"What a crazy time it's been for your family. How's your daughter holding up?"

"These last few days have been hard on her. Although, it's nothing compared to what she went through twenty years ago. Regardless, she's determined to fight for justice. Rick Murphy has ruined too many lives."

Matt crossed his legs, displaying a sympathetic smile. "It must've been quite a shock to hear her accusations about Senator Murphy."

"It was. Thinking back, I realize that her behavior after her visit to the senator's house was odd. For months afterward, she had trouble sleeping and would often come into my room at night and slip into bed with me. She'd never done that before. In hindsight, I realize her behavior was a result of the assault. I had no idea it was Senator Murphy until recently. She was afraid for our safety. All these years, and I had no idea."

"She's a good actress," Matt said.

Her mother smiled. "Yes, she is. She's also kind, which anyone who's ever worked with her or for her knows. These people who've come out of the woodwork to spread lies about her are, simply put, liars. We believe Senator Murphy's behind all of it, paying people to say bad things about her in the press."

"What evidence do you have?"

"We don't. I only know that Gennie was in fear for my life for twenty years because of that man. He's dangerous and he's rich. We all know what the Murphy family can accomplish when they want to hide something."

"Are you referring to the incident with Minnie Stevens?" Matt asked.

"I am. And if Minnie Stevens's murder could be covered up, there's no telling what else this family has done."

"Is there any truth to the statements by your former boss about the lack of care your daughter received when she was young?" Matt asked.

"Of course not. I worked for Harry for almost a decade. I was a dutiful and competent employee, never late for work and infrequently missing days. I am not, and never have been, a drinker. My husband died when Genevieve was young, killed by a drunk driver. We both take drinking and driving extremely seriously since it robbed us of the husband and father we adored. If I'm guilty of anything, it's that I worked full-time to support us in a job thirty miles from our home. They were long days, especially in the winter months, but my daughter was always well cared for. Nothing she did caused this to happen. Nothing I did caused this to happen. One man is responsible. Rick Murphy. And we're going to make sure he goes to jail." Her eyes shone with tears, but her voice remained steady.

"Since your daughter came forward, four other women have filed charges. Do you think there are more?"

"I believe there are. If any of them are listening, come forward. You are not alone. Gennie's prepared to help in any way she can. You do not have to be afraid any longer."

Matt thanked her, and the broadcast went to commercial.

"She did well," Gennie said, picking up her phone to text her mom.

"She did extremely well. Poised and calm," Stefan said.

Mom, you did great and looked very pretty.

Her mother responded almost immediately. *Thanks, honey. Tommy and I are going to breakfast now and then heading to the airport. We'll be home by this afternoon. Love you.*

Love you back.

She put down her phone and turned to give Stefan her full attention. "For the first time since it happened, I feel hope and some relief. It's going to be a hard couple of months, but it'll be worth it. I hope my mom feels better now, having said her piece."

"I hope so too. How about you? You good?" Stefan asked. *He can't hide the worry in his voice. Sweet, sweet man.*

She took his hand and brought it to her mouth. "I feel amazing. You are amazing."

He smiled and took her into his arms. "Say the word and we can do it again."

"Word."

Just then, both their phones started buzzing with texts and calls. She grabbed hers from the bed. Stefan crossed the room to where his was charging on the dresser.

Trix. She can always ruin a good moment without even trying.

"Good morning, Trix," Gennie said. "Didn't my mom do great?"

"She was fine. Listen, I've got crazy news. TMZ leaked photographs of you and Stefan this morning."

Photographs? "What are you talking about?"

"Photos of you guys having freaking hot sex. I mean, I'd love to be sad about it, but it's the most amazing publicity you two could ever get for your film. And *so* tender and sweet. Not like some of the ones people leak with their asses in every shot."

Oh crap, oh crap, oh crap. It made no sense. How would photos leak from inside their room?

She looked over at Stefan. He had his ear to his phone, nodding, a grim expression on his face. *He's getting the same news.*

"How did this happen?" he asked into the phone.

Trix continued to babble, but Gennie wasn't listening. She disconnected. Sweaty and trembling, she sank into the chair. *Think. Think. How could this have happened?* There must be a hidden camera somewhere inside this room. *Where was it?* She leaped from the bed, scanning the space. Her gaze stopped at the bedside lamp. A white object was clipped to the lampshade. Stefan's lamp had the same. They were tiny cameras, pointing directly at the bed. She snatched them from the shades and tossed them to the floor. Stefan stared at her with a dazed expression. *Who had done this?* A housekeeper? No, there hadn't been one in the guest house yet this week. They came tomorrow. Annie had told her that yesterday.

"Did you do this?" she screamed.

"Gennie, of course I didn't. I would never do something like this."

"How else did they get in here? No one's been here but us."

"I don't know."

She was so enraged she couldn't think. *It had to be Stefan. No one else has been in here.* "Is it that important to you for the world to know about us?" Angry sobs hurt her chest, but she talked through them. "You know how hard it was for me. And to spread it around the world? What's the matter with you?"

His hands were in front of him like she might physically attack him. "Sweetheart, I would never do this to you. Think about it a second. What do I have to gain? I'm famous enough. I don't need money. Think of how long I waited for you. If I cared about any of that, I would not even be here."

All this was true. *Stefan wouldn't do this to do you. Don't be an idiot.* Then, she knew. *Trix. Trix was here yesterday.* She was in the bathroom long enough to slip these on the shades. "It was Trix."

"Oh, shit. Right. She was here with her fucking coffee. I knew she was a conniving bitch, but this is beyond anything I would have expected from her."

Everything was clear now. Murphy had paid her off—exchanged money for betrayal. Trix was always about the money. She would have been an easy target.

"It's Murphy," Stefan said, echoing her thoughts. "I'm going to kill him."

"This is payback. I knew if we went after him, he'd come back hard. Especially since we've ruined his chances for the presidency." She looked at Stefan. He was ashen. Ashamed, she reached out to him. "I'm sorry, Stefan. I don't know what I was thinking. I went crazy for a moment."

He held her tightly against his chest. "It's okay. I know."

"I have to call Trix," she said.

"Yeah. Right now."

Her cell phone. What had she done with it? Was she still connected to Trix? She found the phone under the blanket. She punched in Trix's number.

"Hey, what happened to you?" Trix asked. "I wasn't finished telling you. It's gone viral. I mean, everyone and their mother are looking at it."

"How in the world do you think this is a good thing? I was raped and almost killed when I was fifteen years old. I was a *child* and Rick Murphy took my innocence. You violated the most sacred act anyone can do and made it public. My God, Trix, how could you do this?"

"Wait a minute," Trix said. "You've got this all wrong."

"I know it was you. After all the years together. After all the money you've made from my work. To betray me for money from the devil? If it's the last thing I do, I'll ruin you. Do you hear me? I hope whatever he paid you was worth it because you're going to jail."

She didn't wait to hear Trix's response. Her hands itched to throw the phone, but instead, she picked up the paperback book on the bedside table and hurled it at the wall. *Damn you to hell, Trix.* She turned to Stefan. "Again, I'm sorry. I don't know what happened to me. I wasn't thinking right. I know you'd never do something this heinous."

He took her in his arms. "Sweetie, I forgive you. You were upset. It's awful." He sighed into her hair. "Never forget that we're on the same team. I would never hurt you. After everything you've gone through. I can't believe this is happening. I'm sorry, baby."

She was too angry to cry. Later, maybe, but right now she was seeking revenge. She would make Trix pay if it was the last thing she ever did.

"I'm calling Grant. I'm pressing charges against her for invasion of privacy." The world will know it was her. Even if she didn't go to jail, she would never work again. She dialed Grant's number. He picked up right away.

"I wish I didn't know why you're calling," he said.

"How bad is it?" she asked. "I mean, how explicit?"

"I haven't looked at them, out of courtesy to you and Stefan, but my assistant says they're fuzzy and it's not even completely obvious it's you. Stefan's face is clear, though, so I don't think they're fakes."

"We know how it happened." She told him about Trix.

"Son of a bitch. Isn't she supposed to be on your side?"

"I want to press charges."

"I'm on it."

"Could she face jail time?" Gennie asked.

"Yes. Photographing without consent. Invasion of privacy. Voyeurism. We can get her on all of it. If we can prove it was her."

"She's the only one who's been in this room, except for us. Murphy's people paid her off. I'm certain of it."

"I'll get started on everything. I'll call you later. And Gennie, it's going to be all right. Both these assholes are going to jail. It's just a matter of time."

After she hung up, still filled with rage, she turned to Stefan. He stood at the end of the bed, staring at the floor. *What's wrong with me? I'm not the only one hurt over this.* She'd lashed out at the one person who understood exactly what it felt like. "Stefan, are you okay?"

His face crumpled as he collapsed onto the bed. "This is not how I wanted to tell my mother about you. It's going to be on every entertainment program and site. Jesus, Gennie, you were right about Murphy. He's everywhere."

"I knew we were in for a fight, but this is too much." She sat next to him on the bed, resting her head on his shoulder. "I feel like I've been violated all over again."

"I'm going to kill Murphy with my bare hands," Stefan said.

His eyes, dark and angry, scared her. "Stefan, please, don't even think about something like that. I don't want you going to jail. He's not worth it."

"We have to fight back somehow. He has to be stopped."

Her phone rang again. "It's my mother."

"Hi, honey. Just wanted to tell you we're on the way to the airport. We'll be home soon."

She hasn't seen the news. She doesn't know yet. "You did great, Mom."

"Tommy said so too. I'm just glad it's over."

"Me too. Just come home. I miss you."

"Tommy's been so supportive. He's calling himself my wing man."

"That's funny." Gennie hesitated. "I take it you haven't been on social media or your phone this morning?"

"No, Tommy told me to stay off my phone. He said trolls might say mean things about us," said Mom.

"He's right." She looked over at Stefan. He remained on the bed, looking down at his phone. "Trix did something, Mom. Something awful. I'll tell you about it when you get home, but stay off the internet."

After she hung up, she turned back to Stefan. "Do you want some coffee?"

"I don't think my stomach can handle it right now." He squeezed her hand. "I think I may have had enough."

Not of me? Please don't say of me. "Enough of me?"

He put his hands on her shoulders. "Gennie, no. I'll never get enough of you. But I think I may be done with this whole ridiculous world we live in. This fake Hollywood world. It's not who I am, Gennie. Press junkets and people who sell sex photographs and stupid action films I have to make to stay on top, to be bankable, to earn money for people who care nothing about art or film. I look at Tommy, you know, the way he lives his life on his own terms. No one owns him. He doesn't have to answer to a big record label or Hollywood production company. He gets to live here and have a normal life. He swims in the river and attends church and goes to the grocery store without someone trying to take his photo. We're trapped like animals, Gennie, in our own homes. It'll be worse now that people know we're together. They'll be dying to get photos of us together. It's embarrassing, really, that *this* is the world we live in. I made a hundred million dollars last year because of that blockbuster I starred in — a movie so bad I was embarrassed for my mother to see it. I don't want to live like this anymore."

"What about the work? Tommy can write his songs and play in bars, but what would we do? Can you imagine never acting again?"

"What if we did it on our own terms? Only scripts we wanted, only the stories we felt compelled to tell? I could start my own production company."

She stayed in devil's advocate mode, curious to see how closely his thought process mirrored her own. "Our money runs out fast if we're funding films."

"Then we just accept roles that truly speak to us. Maybe we do a film a year. I don't know. Maybe we move to River Valley and have lots of babies and raise them here so they become awesome kids like Alder."

Babies? With me? The vision I saw last night? Could it really happen? "I don't want to be trapped anymore either. I want to swim at the beach without being worried someone will take my photograph in my bikini and plaster it everywhere, and all the haters on social media will comment about how flabby my butt looks. I'm tired. I shouldn't be this tired at thirty-five. Even before all this with Murphy and finding Sarah, I was tired." She moved from the bed over to the window, opening the shades. "You know the elk that came to me that night?"

"Yes, of course I do."

She looked out the window. No sign of elk tracks. She had seen them. They were real. They had to be. "Last night I woke up around two a.m. I was cold, so I got up to put pajamas on and stood by the window, looking out to the yard. Two elk appeared, a male and female. They just stood there looking at me, powerful and peaceful. Then, I had this vison of you and me, with babies, standing in front of the house. A toddler boy and a little baby girl."

"A boy and a girl?" His voice softened. "Do you want that? A family? With me?"

"I want to be with you. With or without the work. With or without children. Here or anywhere. If you're with me, I'm good."

"But you saw babies? A boy and a girl?" He grinned. "Were they cute?"

"The cutest." She crossed to him, planting herself between his legs and wrapping her arms around his neck.

"Then they must've looked like you," he said. "Baby, I'm sorry this happened with the photographs, but I'm not sorry about last night. No matter what she did, we have that special night to remember. You fought so hard to go there with me."

"You fought so hard to get me there."

"Don't let all this bullshit take that memory from you. From us."

She ran her fingers through his hair. "They'll be more nights like that one, Stefan. More and more memories until we have a lifetime of them."

"I never believed in soulmates." He held her tightly, her chin resting on the top of his head.

"Me either," she said.

"I've changed my mind."

"Me too."

"You tell me when you're ready again, Gennie. I know this may have caused a setback. I can be as patient as you need."

"I'm ready now," she said. "Let's forget the world and make a new memory."

* *

They fell asleep afterward. She woke an hour later to someone pounding on their door. She sat up, heart hammering. *That's an urgent knock. Something's wrong.* They moved quickly to the front room. It was Drake, looking as if he just ran a mile uphill.

"Gennie, Lee just called. She couldn't get you, so she called me. The car"—his voice broke—"the car taking Tommy and your mom to the airport crashed."

"Oh my God." Gennie reached for Stefan, her legs weak. "How bad is it?"

"We don't know. They were both taken by ambulance to the hospital in critical condition," Drake said.

She turned to Stefan, panicked. "I have to go out there."

"Lee wants to as well," Drake said. "There's a flight out in two hours. If we leave now, we can make it."

"I'm going with you," Stefan said. "There's no way you're going without me."

"Grab a few things," Drake said. "I'll meet you in the driveway in fifteen minutes."

CHAPTER THIRTEEN

THREE HOURS LATER, they were on a commercial flight to New York City. Luckily, there had been first class seats available for the three of them. Gennie and Stefan sat together, with Lee across the aisle, sitting upright and gripping her cell phone, like Tommy might call her at any moment even though her phone was on airplane mode. She hadn't said much since they'd boarded the plane, her face pale and drawn. Next to Lee, a young man in a business suit worked on his laptop, seemingly oblivious to his surroundings. *Good, maybe he won't notice us.*

On the way to the airport, they had called the hospital and were told that both Tommy and her mother were being prepped for surgery. Both were bleeding internally. Surgery would determine how serious the injuries were. Along with the internal bleeding, both of her mother's legs were broken. The hospital had no details about the accident itself, only that the ambulance brought them into the emergency room around eleven a.m.

"It's going to be fine." Stefan reached across the aisle to squeeze Lee's hand. "They're alive. The surgeons are probably some of the best in the world."

"Tommy's tough. He'll be okay. He has to be." Lee dropped her phone into the pocket on the back of the seat in front of her. "I can't lose him. He's everything to Ellie-Rose and me."

Normally Lee appeared reserved and in complete control of the restaurant and everything around her. Lee's fear flustered Gennie. *I'm responsible. I should never have let Tommy or Mom go, knowing the risks as I did. It was selfish. I should have gone myself.*

"I just wish we knew more," Gennie said.

"I wish we could get there faster," Lee said.

The first class cabin smelled of coffee. Next to her, Stefan sipped a whiskey. She looked across to the seats behind Lee. A man, sitting alone and dressed in a black sweater and jeans, stared at her. She averted her eyes. *Great.* He probably recognized her despite the cap, sunglasses, and long jacket with a high collar. Usually this type of disguise worked when she traveled on commercial flights, but when they'd sat, she'd taken off her sunglasses for a moment. He must have seen her face. Hopefully he would not try to talk to them—or point them out to anyone. The less fuss around them the better. They needed to stay off the radar. She hoped Murphy would assume they were still at Drake's. Without Trix giving him information, maybe it would take him longer to catch on to their whereabouts. *I just want to get us all back to River Valley in one piece.*

Oh, crap. Black Sweater Guy's staring at me because of the photographs. She went instantly hot. He was probably blowing up social media at this very moment. Since she'd heard the news about her mother and Tommy, she hadn't thought once about the photos; but the reality of them came rushing back to her. Gennie raged with a reignited fury. *Dammit, Trix. I hate you.*

"What're you looking at?" Stefan growled, more beast than man.

The guy flinched and turned away, suddenly interested in peering out the window.

"Hey, asshole, I'm talking to you." Stefan snapped his fingers. "Have a little decency, man."

Everyone in first class had twisted around to stare at them. *So much for incognito.*

Black Sweater Guy turned back to address them. "Sorry, man. I didn't mean to bother you. It's just you don't see two huge stars every day. My wife and I love your work. She's going to be so mad she wasn't with me."

He sounds so innocent. Was it possible he didn't know about the photos? Maybe not everyone evaluated the world by the traffic on social media. Or, maybe he didn't care. Maybe there were still decent people in the world, not just in River Valley.

The flight attendant arrived with another whiskey for Stefan. "Is everything okay here?"

"Yeah. We're good." Stefan poured from the tiny liquor bottle it into his glass. "Other than I'm acting like an ass. Can I buy all the coach passengers a drink to make up for it?"

She smiled. "I think that would be excellent penance."

After the flight attendant walked away, Stefan turned to Black Sweater Guy. "Hey, I'm sorry I snapped at you. Not to make excuses, but I'm having a rough day."

"It's probably a pain in the ass to be bothered all the time. Everyone deserves a little privacy. My wife's going to chastise me for being an idiot."

"No. You tell her it was my fault." Stefan reached out his hand. "If you give me your cell phone, I'll send her a selfie and tell her how sorry I am for being an ass to her perfectly nice husband."

Black Sweater Guy grinned and handed Stefan his phone.

"What's her name?" Stefan asked.

"Corie."

Stefan snapped a selfie, then typed a few lines into the phone. He handed it back to Black Sweater Guy, and then shook his hand. "Again, my apologies."

"This totally makes up for it. She's going to freak out."

"Have a good rest of your flight, man."

"You too. And I hope things get better for you."

Stefan shifted in his seat to face the front, stretching out his legs. "Sorry, baby," he whispered in her ear.

"It's okay. I understand." Gennie rested her hand on his knee. *He can admit when he's wrong, even under all this stress. I love this man.*

* *

A couple of hours into the flight, the cabin was quiet. Despite the fact they'd risen at five, Gennie was wide awake, worry gnawing at her stomach. None of them seemed capable of concentrating on a movie or a book. Maybe they should talk. As if he'd read her mind, Stefan started asking Lee questions. Lee told them about how she had met Tommy when she first came to River Valley. "I was reluctant to get involved with him because of my personal situation. I was literally

in hiding and here was this amazing man who liked me just the way
I was." She smiled. "I was prickly back then. I mean, more so than
now. I'm shy, actually, but I know I come off kind of snooty."

"Not snooty. Reserved," Gennie said.

"I wasn't exactly my best self at the time. I was devastated over
my husband's suicide and to find out I had all this debt and I was
pregnant. You can't imagine how distraught I was. Tommy loved me
through all of it. He's such a generous person and so brave with his
heart. He was out there from the very beginning, vulnerable. It was
amazing to me."

Like Stefan. He's so vulnerable and willing to love me just as I am.
How was that possible given all of her problems? Now, these
photographs were out there for the world to see. It was her worst
nightmare. How would she be able to walk around in the world
knowing everyone had seen her having sex? She hoped Grant hadn't
been lying to her when he'd said you couldn't see much.

The flight attendant brought them lunch, which Gennie forced
herself to eat, knowing she needed her strength for what was on the
other end of this long flight. She encouraged Lee to do the same. "It
tastes like sand," Lee said.

"I know, but you have to eat. Tommy's going to need you."

Finally, they arrived at LaGuardia. They immediately turned their
phones on, but there were no messages from the hospital. Was it
possible they were both still in surgery? Drake had arranged for a car
to pick them up, and thankfully, it was waiting when they exited the
airport. Stefan instructed the driver to take them to Bellevue Hospital
on First Avenue. They were quiet on the way there, the silence
punctuated with horns and the rumble of engines outside the car.

At the hospital, the woman at the information desk confirmed
that Tommy and her mother were still in surgery. She advised them
to head up to the eighth-floor waiting room. The surgeons would be
out to talk to them after the operations were complete.

The waiting room was sparse, both in décor and staff. The
woman at reception had no information for them other than to wait.
Time passed in slow increments. Lee paced. Stefan sat slumped in a
chair. Gennie stood at the window, looking out to the busy street
below. Compared to River Valley, the number of pedestrians on the

sidewalks was almost overwhelming. *How do all these people live here and remain sane?*

Her thoughts turned to Moody. She'd thought of him earlier, but had put him out of her mind when worry over her mother and Tommy had squelched all other concerns. He would be hurt and bewildered over the photographs. He would wonder why it was Stefan and not him. *I should call him and explain about Stefan and the pictures. I owe him that much after everything that went down.*

She told Stefan and Lee that she needed to make a phone call. "I'll be back in a few minutes." Stefan looked confused but didn't press for details.

In the hallway, she asked a nurse if there was somewhere she could make a private call. She was directed to a small room, not much bigger than a phone booth, with a small desk, chair, and outlets to plug in phones and computers. She plopped into the chair, weary, and pulled up Moody's contact information on her phone. He answered after the second ring.

"Halo, Gennie." She smiled. His clipped British accent hadn't changed.

"Hi, Moody."

"You all right, love?" Moody sounded raspy like he'd been up all night. He was on a European tour for his new record. She remembered he often sounded like this the day after a concert. They'd talked over the phone from locations all over the world when they were married.

"I'm fine. I wanted to call and explain things. I'm sorry it wasn't sooner. It's been a crazy few days."

"Yes indeed. Sounds like a kerfuffle of the highest magnitude." He chuckled, softly. *He's sad even though he's trying to hide it, pretending everything's fine.*

"Where are you?" she asked.

"London. In a hotel room. Having a cocktail. Just finished a show." The sound of ice clinking in a glass came through the phone. "I had no idea, love, about what happened to you. Although, I suspected. It makes things clearer, but I'm terribly sorry for all of it. Bloody awful."

What can I say to make this better? "I'm sorry I never told you about my past. I was afraid he'd hurt you." She went on to tell him about her mother's accident. "So, I'm in New York. At the hospital."

"It was Murphy's doing, I gather?" Moody asked.

"Has to be. He's not messing around," Gennie said.

"How's your mum? Any news?"

"Still in surgery."

"She'll be okay, Gennie."

"I hope so."

"She's tougher than she looks. Like you," he said.

Sweating, she moved to the next subject. "I suppose you saw the photo scandal?"

"I heard. I didn't look at them. It might break my unrelenting self-confidence."

"You weren't to blame for my problems. You did everything right. Maybe it was bad timing for us. I wasn't ready. Now, with everything out in the open, it's freed me somehow. And Stefan is...I don't know what to say. I'm sorry. That's all."

"Love, you don't have to apologize. We're not married any longer. You can be with whomever you darn well please. I want you to be happy. If he makes you happy, then I'm happy." More clinking of ice.

"Moody, I loved you very much. I'm sorry you were the one blamed in the press. You didn't deserve that."

"It was my rap to take. I cheated, not you. I made a promise and didn't keep it. The world's right about who the scoundrel is here." His voice remained soft, gentle. "And, don't be sorry. It goes with my bad-boy image. Record sales have never been so high."

"If they only knew the truth," she said.

"You mustn't ever tell anyone how boring I am."

"I wouldn't dare." She smiled, remembering his nighttime ritual of a cup of tea before bed. *So charmingly English.*

All teasing gone from his tone, he continued, "Love, I was just as much to blame for what happened between us. I don't mean just the cheating. I chose the road over us. This bloody music's never let me go, and I don't know that it ever will. It's all I've ever known. This touring life didn't make me a good husband. Two people can't build a life together when you're never together. It wasn't just your problems. But listen, you get that fucker. Whatever you do, don't stop until he's locked away for the rest of his miserable life. Do it for you, and for all those other women."

"I will." She leaned back in the chair and gazed at the ceiling. "You seeing anyone?"

A few seconds ticked by before he answered. "I've been seeing someone, yes. Nothing serious. She'd like it to be, but I'm uncertain."

"Who is she?"

"Our new backup singer. Enormously talented. Beautiful. The whole package, I suppose."

"What's the holdup, then?"

"Me. Perhaps bad timing. I don't know, really."

"Don't pass up a chance for love just because of past hurts, Moody."

"Our voices do blend together rather nicely."

"And music's her life too?"

"I suppose it is."

"Don't be a stranger, okay?" she said.

"Thanks, love. Now you should go. Prayers for your mum."

"Thanks, Moody. Bye for now."

"Thanks for calling, Gennie. You didn't have to, but I appreciate it nevertheless. Goodbye then."

Gennie set the phone down and bowed her head, letting tears fall as they wanted, mourning the lost love and the damage she'd done to a good man's heart. *Please, God, heal his heart so that he finds the love he deserves.*

* *

Fifteen minutes later, she was back in the waiting room when a doctor came out with news of Tommy. He spoke in a hushed voice without inflection. "He's out of surgery and did remarkably well. We found significant bleeding in the tissues surrounding both his liver and heart, but we successfully repaired those areas. He suffered no other damage that we can see. Amazingly, no bones were broken, and he has no head trauma, which is what we worry about the most."

"Can I see him?" Lee asked.

"He's in recovery, so you won't be able to see him until the morning."

"Not before?" Lee looked like she might burst into tears.

"I'm sorry, no. He wouldn't know you were there anyway. He's still heavily sedated. By morning, he'll be strong enough to see you."

"Will he have to be here long?" Lee asked. "We live in Oregon."

"He's in good shape and very strong. If he recovers quickly, which I believe he will, my guess is he'll be able to travel home in about a week's time; then it will be your job to keep him from pushing too hard."

For the first time that day, Lee smiled. "You obviously don't know my husband."

The doctor patted Lee's shoulder. "I know his type."

After that, it was another waiting game. *Mom's condition must be worse than Tommy's. Please, God, let her be okay.*

Finally, a doctor came out and asked for her. "I'm the surgeon assigned to your mother. She had multiple fractures in both legs and several cracked ribs. We repaired everything, but she'll be in traction for a few weeks."

"But she'll be okay?" Gennie asked. "Eventually?"

"She'll need physical therapy, especially given her age, but a full recovery is expected. We'll monitor pain management while she's recovering."

"When can I see her?"

"It'll be a couple of hours before she's awake, and with the pain medicine, she'll be pretty out of it until morning. My suggestion would be to go home and come back in the morning."

Stefan and Lee had been by Gennie's side while the doctor talked. After the doctor had excused himself, Stefan put his arm around her, pulling her close. "Ladies, I had my assistant book us hotel rooms over by Rockefeller Center where I usually stay when I'm here. I've known the manager for a long time and he's able to keep the paparazzi away from the front of the building. The security is exceptional, so we should be able to rest easy. Let's get checked in, have some dinner, and try to get a good night's sleep. I have a car ready to take us whenever we're ready."

Gennie nodded, too tired to argue with him, not that she would have. A hotel room and a shower sounded like heaven.

"Now that I know he's okay, I'm starving. Can we have room service?" Lee asked. "I haven't had room service in forever."

"Yes, we can have room service," Stefan said, smiling. "Whatever you want."

* *

At the hotel, Gennie and Stefan walked Lee to her room. Stefan had rented and paid for two suites, ignoring Lee's protests. "You're going to be here at least a week, and we want you to have the best situation possible," Stefan said.

After agreeing that Lee would come over for dinner after she'd called home to check in on Ellie-Rose, Gennie and Stefan walked down the hall to their suite. The view looked out over Manhattan. It was dark, nearing ten o'clock east coast time. Holiday lights twinkled from buildings, and the Christmas tree at Rockefeller Center glowed brightly. Gennie paced in front of the window, feeling restless. "This was a way to lure us out of River Valley. Now that we're here, we're not safe."

"We're safe in this hotel. You can relax for now." Stefan was at the fully stocked bar, pouring a whiskey. "You want wine, baby?"

She nodded, turning back to look out the window. Behind her, she heard a cork pop. A few seconds later, Stefan appeared by her side and handed her a glass of white wine. "This has to go down as one of the weirdest days in history," he said.

"This morning seems like a million years ago." She took a sip of her wine, set it on the coffee table, and plopped on the couch.

Stefan kneeled on the floor, placing his hands on her knees. "Are you okay?"

Her bottom lip trembled. "I'm scared. He sent a message loud and clear. He will hurt the people I love if I don't back off."

"You can't back off."

She looked into his eyes. "I've been scared for twenty years. Maybe now it's time to play by his rules. Fire with fire."

Stefan sat on the coffee table and took a sip from his drink. "What do you mean?"

"That's just it. I don't know. But we have to play dirty."

"We could have him killed," Stefan said. "Or, I could do it myself." He finished his whiskey and went to the bar, pouring another. She'd never seen him drink as much as he had today. *It isn't every day naked sex pictures are leaked to the world.*

When he returned, he sat next to her with his drink in hand.

She placed her hand on his thigh. "That's a large glass of whiskey."

"Forgive me just this once. It's the only thing keeping me from doing something stupid right now." He took a sip. "I'm so full of rage I don't know what to do with myself. I want to kill him. I want to throw Trix in jail for a thousand years. And I can't do a damn thing. I can't do anything to keep this bastard from hurting you, and it's killing me."

She rested her cheek against his shoulder. "You've already done more to rescue me than he did to hurt me. You've won. You taught me how to feel again, to love again."

"But I can't keep you safe. That's all I want. For you and your mother and Sarah to be safe, and I can't do a thing about it. It's a man's worst nightmare."

Her phone buzzed. "It's Raquel." She answered the phone and put it on speaker mode.

"Hey, Gennie," Raquel said.

"Hi. Stefan's here with me. We have you on speaker," Gennie said.

"Hi, Stefan. I just heard a news report that your mother was in an accident. Is she okay?"

"She's going to be, but they broke both her legs and a couple ribs."

"You think it's Murphy?"

"I know it is. She and a friend were on their way back to the airport after the interview. A car came out of nowhere, smashed into them, and then sped away. They found the car abandoned later, but no trace of a driver. The car was unregistered."

"Son of a bitch," Raquel said.

"Did you see the photographs?" Stefan asked.

"I didn't see them," Raquel said. "But I know about them."

"It was Trix," Gennie said. "She planted the cameras in our room."

"Wow. I'm sorry, you guys," Raquel said. "For the record, I always thought she was a twit."

"Join the club," Stefan said.

"Do you want to do another interview?" Raquel asked. "I think it needs to be out there that he did this, just like he said he would. I suspect he'll be arrested soon for the statutory rape charges, but from jail he can continue to hurt you and the other women. We've got to bring attention to it."

Gennie thought for a moment. The court of public opinion was the only thing she had going for her. He could control the police, but not Raquel. "Yes. Let's do it. Tomorrow after I visit my mother."

"Come to the studio around ten. We'll tape it here. I can have it ready for the evening show."

Gennie agreed, then hung up the phone.

"I've come this far. There's no way to prove any of this is him, but I want it out there. In case anything happens to me," she said.

"Gennie, please don't say it. I can't stand the thought." He put his face in his hands. "If anything happens to you, I will kill him. I can promise you that."

She crawled onto his lap, cradling his head against her chest. "One night at a time. We're safe for now."

His arms tightened around her waist. "I think I'm a little drunk."

She giggled just as they heard a knock on the door. "I told you to take it easy." She kissed the top of his head, then disentangled herself from his arms and rose to her feet. "I bet that's Lee. I'll let her in and order you a cheeseburger."

"Good idea."

CHAPTER FOURTEEN

HER MOTHER WAS AWAKE when Gennie arrived with a large bouquet of lilies. Her face was bleached of color, magnifying the dark smudges under her eyes. Both her legs were in traction and suspended several feet in the air. A young nurse stood next to the bed, writing into a chart.

"Good morning, Mom." Gennie set the lilies on the bedside table, fighting tears. *She seems so small and fragile and pinched.*

"Hi, sweetie." Her mom lifted her arm from under the sheet and reached for her. "The flowers are wonderful. Thank you."

"Are you hurting?" Gennie held her cold hand and kissed her on the cheek. She smelled of antiseptic, not her usual floral perfume.

"Not too much. They have me on some good drugs."

Gennie's lip trembled. *Do not cry. You will scare her.*

"I'm so sorry, sweetie. I shouldn't have come. It was too risky."

"Don't be sorry, Mom. You were fighting for me. I'm proud of you."

"All this fuss. And I can't leave here until forever." Her eyes leaked tears. Gennie grabbed a tissue and patted her cheeks.

"Please, don't cry. It's no fuss. I'm going to be with you the whole time. You're strong. You'll heal quickly. Then, we'll go home, and you can sit on our deck and look at the ocean. You'll be back to normal in no time."

"I'm an old lady. The doctor said it will be a long road to recovery."

"Well, he doesn't know how tough you are." The nurse caught Gennie's eye and gestured toward the hallway. "Mom, I'm going to talk to the nurse for a moment."

"Yes, okay."

Gennie placed a fresh tissue into her mom's hand. "Just two seconds and I'll be back."

Out in the hallway, the nurse, a tall blond with Nordic features and a slight Danish accent, held her mother's chart against her chest. "I'm Gwen. I'm on duty all day and will monitor your mother carefully. She's doing fine, but the pain meds will make her more emotional than usual. Don't take the tears too seriously."

"Okay." A painful lump formed at the back of Gennie's throat. "She's normally quite stoic."

"The best thing for her is to sleep and recover. Your job is just to listen to her and reassure her that everything's going to be fine."

"All right. I can do that."

"And *my* job is to reassure *you* that everything will be just fine. It will take some time for her bones to heal, but they will." Gwen patted her arm. "She had the very best surgeons. With some therapy, she'll be walking the beach once again."

Gennie smiled. *Mom loves to walk the beach.* "She doesn't look like herself. It scared me."

"Perfectly understandable. But she's going to take cues from you, so keep up the positive talk, yes?"

"Yes."

"Good."

She followed Gwen back into the room. Her mom stared blankly at the ceiling. "Hey, Mom. You doing okay?"

"I'm a little fuzzy."

"It's the drugs. Totally normal," Gennie said.

"The lilies smell delicious. I had lilies at my wedding. Did I ever tell you that?"

"You've mentioned that, yes. But you can tell me again."

"Is my hair a mess? I can't imagine what a fright I look."

"Would you like me to brush it?" Gennie asked.

"Yes, please. My makeup bag's in my purse. Would you fix my face? I want to look nice for the doctor."

The doctor? Gennie took a brush from her purse and used it on her mother's hair. "I'm no Bella, but I'll do my best."

Her mom closed her eyes. "That feels nice."

Gwen gave Gennie a reassuring smile. "The doctor will make his rounds in the next hour. I have another patient to look in on, but I'll stop back here later." She indicated the call button on the side of the hospital bed. "You just push this if she needs anything." She smoothed the sheets. "Mrs. Banks, you let either your daughter or I know if you need more pain medication. We want you comfortable."

"Yes, ma'am."

After Gwen had left, Gennie grabbed her mom's makeup bag. "Do you want foundation?"

"Yes, the works, please. I want to look nice for the doctor."

The doctor again? What kind of drugs did they have her on?

"Did I mention that the doctor's a very attractive man?"

"No, I don't believe so," Gennie said. *What's gotten into her?*

"He came by earlier. Swoon-worthy."

Swoon-worthy? Gennie smoothed her mother's bangs off her forehead. Using a sponge, she dotted foundation on her cheeks and forehead.

"And age appropriate." Her mother smiled and looked dreamily at the ceiling. "For me, that is. Not you. He's much too old for you."

"Mom, are you interested in the doctor?"

"Well, no, of course not. I simply noticed how attractive he was and that he wasn't wearing a ring. Maybe he's a widower."

"Close your eyes." She spread shadow over her mom's eyelids. "It would be all right, you know, to be interested in a man."

"I'm much too old."

"That's not true. You have a lot of good years left. Any man would be lucky to have you."

"Have I held you back Gennie girl?"

Where is she going with this? The drugs had her all over the place. "Held me back? From what?"

"It's been the two of us against the world for a long time now. Perhaps I've held on too tightly. You were all I had after your dad died. Have I been a burden to you? Have I kept you from having a family of your own because I didn't want things to change between us?"

Gennie swept blush over her cheeks. "Mom, my failed marriage was not because of anything you did. You've been everything and more that a mother should be."

"I don't want you to worry about me any longer. You go on and make plans with Stefan."

"Mom, you'll always be part of my life. My best friend."

"I would've given anything to have been the one. Anything."

"I know."

After mascara and lipstick, Gennie declared her ready for her close-up. *Or, your visit from the cute doctor.* From her own purse, she took out a bottle of hand lotion and squirted some into her hand. "Here, let's put some lotion on your hands."

Her mother giggled. "I can't feel a thing. You have two heads. Two beautiful heads."

Gennie smiled as she rubbed her mother's hands and forearms with the lotion. "It's weird to see you so stoned."

"Did you tell me something about Trix? What did she do?"

"Yes, that. Two nights ago, Stefan and I were intimate for the first time."

"Oh, honey. Was it terrible?" asked Mom.

"No, no, nothing like that. It was wonderful." She rubbed her own hands together, slick from the lotion. "Trix planted cameras in our room and took photographs of us. And they're all over the internet."

"That bitch. That awful bitch. She's always been all about the money."

"I'm sure Murphy bought her off. The photos are fuzzy, according to Grant. They're mostly of Stefan, but still, it's horrifying."

"She should go to jail."

"She will. Now, let's not talk about it any further. Your job is to rest. I don't want you upset."

A knock interrupted whatever her mother was about to say next. Stefan stood in the doorway, carrying an enormous bouquet of flowers. Much bigger than the bouquet Gennie had brought. How had he managed to do that?

Her mom smiled and clapped her hands. "Stefan, you came. And you brought flowers. How lovely."

"Of course, I came." He set them on the table near her bed. "Are you managing all right?"

"She's a little out of it," whispered Gennie.

Her mom giggled, gazing up at Stefan with adoring eyes. "My goodness, he's so handsome, Gennie. Where are you two staying?"

"Over by Rockefeller Center. It's all lit up for the holiday," Stefan said.

"I've been there," her mom said. "Gennie takes me all over the world. Did you know that?"

"I didn't," Stefan said, glancing over at Gennie, obviously amused. "Where have you been together?"

Her mom listed some of the places they'd traveled together. "But you know what I've wanted more than the travel and houses and beautiful clothes? I've wanted her to find a nice man and have a baby. But that fucking Murphy ruined everything."

"Mom." Gennie almost laughed. A curse word out of her mother's mouth sounded foreign, like she had shouted out a word in Latin with no idea of its meaning.

"But now you're here." Her mom waggled a finger at Stefan. "And I'm so very happy. Tell me, do you want to have children?"

"I think so." He grinned at Gennie. "Maybe two. A boy and a girl."

A knock on the door distracted them from further discussion. *Thank goodness. This line of questioning is dangerous.*

"Hello. I'm Doctor Revere. I'm the doctor on rotation this morning. Your mother and I met earlier this morning. She's doing very well."

Mom called this one. Doctor Revere is most certainly swoon-worthy. Of average height, but in obvious good physical condition given his wide shoulders and narrow hips, he strode into the room like a man headed to battle. Bald, with bright blue eyes and a strong jawline, he possessed an authoritative air that shouted confidence. Gennie threw back her shoulders, suddenly aware she'd been slouching.

The doctor held out his hand to Gennie. "You must be Mrs. Banks's daughter?"

"Yes, pleased to meet you." She gestured toward Stefan. "This is my boyfriend, Stefan Spencer." *Did I just say boyfriend?*

After they shook hands, the doctor turned his attention to her mother. "Mrs. Banks, you're looking excellent this morning."

"Gennie put some makeup on me. I was feeling dowdy."

"We mustn't have you feeling dowdy." He smiled at her. "Your chart indicates everything's going as well as we can hope for, given how many bones you broke yesterday."

"Thank you, doctor. However, I'm quite high from these drugs. I haven't felt like this since 1967 when I went to a Grateful Dead concert."

A Grateful Dead concert?

A deep, throaty laugh erupted from Doctor Revere. "Ah, yes, I was high at a few of those myself, but don't tell the medical board. We don't want you in pain. You'll heal faster if you're comfortable."

"How long do you think she'll be here?" Gennie asked. "When can we take her home to L.A.?"

"I'd say a couple of weeks. With legs in traction like this, we have to give them a decent amount of time to heal. Just long enough for us to get to know each other," said Doctor Revere. "Mrs. Banks, you'll be sick of me by the time they let you go."

"Call me Joan, please. And I doubt I could grow sick of you."

They smiled at one another like a couple of kids. *What was happening here?*

"We also have an excellent rehab facility if you're interested in rehabbing here in New York," said Doctor Revere.

"Well, maybe I would."

"I can give you an excellent referral," the doctor said. He turned back to Gennie. "I have other patients to visit, but I'll be back to check on her later. I know you want to visit, but it's probably best to let her rest. Her body's been through a lot. I'll take good care of her."

I bet you will. The doctor has the hots for my mom. Traction and all.

After the doctor left, her mother smiled up at her with glazed eyes. "Didn't I tell you he was handsome?"

"He is handsome. No question."

"I think he likes you, Joan," Stefan said.

"We had the most amazing chat this morning about books and our children. He has two. They're grown and live in Connecticut. Three grandchildren." Her eyelids drooped. "I'm so sleepy."

Gennie kissed her cheek. "You sleep, Mom. We'll be back to see you this afternoon."

But she was asleep already. Gennie looked over at Stefan. "What the heck? She and the doctor were acting like a couple of lovesick kids."

"They obviously had a connection," Stefan said.

"You think?"

"Kind of like us." He grabbed her and kissed her.

Gwen entered, holding a large bouquet of red roses. Gennie's heart started pounding. *Roses. Murphy. They had to be from him.*

"These came for your mother. She's very popular." Gwen set them on the bedside table.

Gennie snatched the card from the plastic holder sticking out of the vase. *It's him. I knew it. The bastard.* She dropped the card on the floor. It landed face up, the large handwriting displaying the message.

You'll be sorry.

*   *

Several hours later, in the news studio, the makeup artist powdered Gennie's face as the crew adjusted lights and cameras. Raquel sat across from her, reading through notes scribbled on a legal pad. Stefan stood behind one of the cameras with his arms folded over his chest, his expression tense.

The cameras rolled.

"Can you tell us what happened yesterday morning?" Raquel asked.

Gennie launched into her story, leaving nothing out, ending with Trix and the photographs.

Raquel followed up on Trix with further questions. "She's been your manager for many years. How does it feel to have been betrayed by her in this way?"

"It hurts. This is a difficult business, and we spend years surrounding ourselves with people we think we can trust." She looked down at her hands. *Do not cry. Do not cry.* She drew in a shaky breath. "Because of what happened to me, physical intimacy has been challenging. For her to have violated my personal space simply because Murphy offered her money is incomprehensible to me. This was a woman I trusted with my most sacred personal secrets."

"Do you intend to press charges?"

"I do. Not only did she violate her confidentiality agreement, but what she did is illegal. I understand that because of my job, I am in the public eye and with that comes scrutiny. However, that doesn't mean I don't have the same right to privacy in my home, in my own bedroom, as anyone else. I understand people are curious about famous people's lives. I am too. But we owe it to ourselves and our society to stop focusing on what some celebrity had for dinner and address the problems of education or poverty. If we focused our energy on causes we cared about rather than gossip—essentially mind-candy with extra corn syrup—the world would certainly be in a better place."

"In the past, you've asked the press to refrain from questions about your former husband, but today you want to talk about it. What would you like to say about your marriage and ultimate divorce?"

"When news of Moody's affair was revealed, he took a lot of heat." Gennie cleared her throat. "I kept quiet because it's a very personal subject and the demise of marriages are always complicated. It is never one person's fault, and in this case, a very good man made a choice that unfortunately went public. But that's not the whole story. Moody's a great person. He loved me, as I did him. He was good to me and understanding about my problems, even though I never told him about what happened because I was afraid of Rick Murphy. Moody's affair was the result of my inabilities to participate in an intimate relationship. It was because of me. Despite his bad-boy image, he's one of the sweetest men on the planet. I'm sorry I didn't come forward with the truth then, but again, I was afraid. And, I was right. Given what's happened, Murphy's threats were not just threats."

"Are you saying you never consummated your marriage with Moody?" Raquel asked.

"That's correct. And the fact that Moody never said anything publicly about my problems should tell us all what kind of man he is and the kind of character he possesses."

"You're in a new relationship now?"

"Yes. With Stefan Spencer. Which, thanks to the photographs, everyone now knows about."

"What do you want people to know about you and Stefan Spencer?"

"Because of Murphy's propaganda, it's been conveyed to the press that I was seeking attention and publicity by leaking the photos. None of that could be further from the truth. Stefan and I are like hunted animals with the way we're followed around. We wanted to keep our relationship quiet because we knew it would cause the paparazzi to pursue us with even more vigor."

"Has the release of the photos brought a lot of the old feelings back?"

"Sure. It would be impossible for it not to."

"What evidence do you have that Rick Murphy is responsible for all this?"

Gennie held up the card from the flowers. "This was delivered to my mother's hospital room. There's no way to prove it's from him. But it is. He's responsible for her accident. For the photographs. For anything that may happen to me in the future. It's Rick Murphy."

"Are you stating this for the record?"

"If you mean because I'm afraid for my life, then yes. I have no doubt that somehow, somewhere, he will get me. He has many people and organizations under his control, all willing to do his bidding for the right amount of cash. That's what's kept me from coming forward all these years. And now, since I told the truth, it prompted other women to come forward. He's angry. He wants revenge. He'll come for me, whether it's today or next week. I am not safe. And, neither are the people I love."

CHAPTER FIFTEEN

AFTER THE INTERVIEW HAD FINISHED, they headed to the hospital to check on Gennie's mom and Tommy. Lee was with Tommy, feeding him chicken broth from a spoon. He looked remarkably good for a man who had been in surgery for internal bleeding just the day before.

Gennie went to his bedside, apologizing and expressing her relief that he was recuperating. "I feel responsible for this whole mess."

"Stop that. I'm going to be fine," Tommy said. "I'm glad Joan's all right. The last thing I remember was her face right before the car plowed into us." His brown eyes shone from his wan face. "This has been a reminder that we have to live every day like it could be our last."

"Thank God it wasn't," Lee said.

"The police came by earlier," Lee said. "They had a lot of questions for Tommy."

"Unfortunately, I didn't have much to tell them," he said. "I didn't get a good look at the driver of the other car."

"Did they ask anything about Murphy?" Stefan asked.

"Not a word," Tommy said. "I brought it up, and they said they were following up on all leads."

"Very unconvincingly, I might add," Lee said.

"Meaning, they dismissed it?" Gennie asked.

"That was the feeling I got," Lee said.

They said their goodbyes and left to check on her mother. Gennie was happy to learn she'd had lunch and was now, once again, sleeping comfortably. Gwen had gone home and been replaced with a nurse named Jessica.

"When she wakes, we'll try to get some dinner into her and then give her something to help her sleep through the night," Jessica said.

"Should we stay?" Gennie asked.

"I think it would make your mom feel better if you two were to go back to your hotel, have a nice meal, and get some rest. She told me how little sleep either of you've gotten the past few nights."

"Only my mom would be worried about us when she's stuck in a hospital bed," Gennie said.

"She's a special lady," said Jessica.

"I think so too," Gennie said.

* *

It was already dark when the car dropped them at the entrance of the hotel. A crowd of paparazzi lingered on either side of the hotel. Gennie's breath caught as the crowd surged toward them. Two security guards, employees of the hotel, rushed over to them, shuffling them inside while shouting verbal threats to the pariahs. Once the doors shut, one of the guards, looking like a linebacker in a black suit, apologized. "Frederick has us all on high alert, Mr. Spencer. We'll make sure none of these idiots get into the hotel. Unfortunately, we can't do much about them snapping pictures between your car and the lobby." He ushered them away from the windows and into the middle of the lobby.

"You did well getting us in here like you did." Stefan thrust cash into each of the guards' hands.

"Not necessary, sir," said the other guard. If possible, he was bigger than his partner. His shoulder span was twice that of Stefan's. His bald head shone with perspiration under the lobby lights.

"I insist," Stefan said. "It's a cold night, and we appreciate you looking after us."

"Thank you, sir. Goodnight, then." The guards left them, disappearing into the dark night.

"Who's Frederick?" she whispered.

"My buddy who manages the hotel. I told you about him. We go way back. School chums in Canada. We played hockey together for years."

"Right. I forgot."

Stefan pointed to the entryway of the hotel's bar. "I always meet him for a drink in the bar. It's very old school in there, like something out of the 1950s."

Gennie, having been distraught since they arrived, hadn't taken the time to look at the lobby until now. A boutique hotel, it had the ambiance of an exclusive European inn: dim lights, vintage furniture, a white marble floor, and a large fireplace as the centerpiece. It soothed Gennie's frayed nerves. The hotel was surprisingly quiet, other than a clerk checking in a new arrival and a young couple sitting in front of the fireplace sipping champagne. The woman was blond and pretty, wearing a pink sweater and skinny jeans. The man was muscular and clean-cut, with a military haircut. They looked over and grew silent as Gennie and Stefan walked by. Gennie averted her gaze and put her head down. *Please do not stop us. Just leave us be.*

A bellboy, seemingly coming out of nowhere, appeared before them. "May I get anything for you?" he asked.

"No, thank you," Stefan said. "We're on our way up to our room."

"Of course, sir." The bellboy escorted them to the elevator, punching the button before stepping aside with a nod of his cap.

The young man from the fireplace sidled up next to them, holding a small notepad. "Excuse me. I'm sorry to bother you. I'm Don." He pointed to the girl by the fireplace. "And that's my bride. We're on our honeymoon. We could only afford one night in this place, but it's so worth it to see you two here. We're from Kansas, and my wife is your biggest fan, Ms. Banks." He held out the notepad. "Would you be so kind as to give us an autograph?"

"Certainly. What's her name?"

"Star," he said. "If you met her mother, you'd know why."

Gennie smiled as she wrote on the napkin. *Dear Star, Congratulations on your marriage. Wishing you many happy years together. Thanks for your support. Love, Genevieve Banks.*

"Thanks so much, Ms. Banks. I can't wait to tell my mama." He turned to Stefan. "Love your movies, man. They're my absolute favorite."

"Do you want his autograph?" Gennie asked, smiling.

"Nah, men don't ask for autographs from other bros," Don said.

Stefan laughed and slapped his shoulder. "I think that's a good rule of thumb. I'm going to buy you guys dinner tonight instead. There's a restaurant down the block called Nico's. Best Italian you'll ever have. I'll call ahead. Reservation around seven, sound good?"

"Dude, that's too generous. It's not necessary," Don said.

"Let him," Gennie said. "It makes him feel good."

Stefan grinned. "She's right. I'll tell the maître d' over at Nico's to take good care of you guys. Happy honeymoon."

After thanking them again, Don went back to his wife. From her delighted scream, Don must have told her the good news.

"I'm exhausted," Gennie said. "But that was so sweet."

Stefan put his arm around her shoulder. "We'll get you into pajamas and order some dinner."

While they waited for the elevator to arrive, a young man in a blue suit and purple tie approached. "Stefan Spencer, you old goat, is that you?"

"Hell, if it isn't Frederick Shore." Grinning, Stefan held out his arms, and the two men embraced.

"Your neck's gotten bigger," said Frederick.

"You're as scrawny as ever."

Frederick rolled his eyes and winked at Gennie. "Trim. We call it trim. And the ladies love it."

"Gennie, this is Frederick. It's surprising they'd give this old bum a job, but it turns out he runs this hotel."

Frederick raised an eyebrow and smiled. "Don't listen to a word he says. Especially any stories from our misspent youth. He's known for exaggeration."

"Is he now?" She laughed, shaking his hand. "It's nice to meet you." Manicured nails and slim wrists. Not a callous or scar on his white hands. "Thank you for taking such good care of us. Your guards just managed to keep the paparazzi from mauling us."

"It's an honor, Ms. Banks." Frederick *was* slim, with thick, black hair slicked back with gel and small, almost pretty features. "Please don't hesitate to let me know if you need anything."

"There *is* something," Stefan said. "You see that young couple over there? They're on their honeymoon. For one night. That's all they could afford. I want to pay for them to stay here a week, meals in the restaurant included. Can you arrange that?"

"You're just as soft as ever, Spencer," Frederick said. "He's like a girl the way he thinks of these things."

"I know. Isn't he wonderful?" Gennie asked.

"You've got her snowed, Spencer," Frederick said. "If you get sick of him, you know where to find me."

They were all laughing when the elevator arrived. Several people stepped off, staring at Gennie and Stefan, but politely passing by without a comment. They bade farewell to Frederick and punched the top floor button. Gennie sighed with relief that no one else got on the elevator. They reached their floor without incident.

Once in the room, Gennie took off her coat and plopped onto the couch with her feet on the coffee table, too bushed to speak or take off her boots. Stefan tossed his coat onto the chair, handed the room service menu to Gennie, and flipped on the fireplace.

His cell phone buzzed from his pocket. "Hello. Oh sure, I didn't think of it. It's no problem What's that, eh?" Stefan walked to the window, his phone held up to his ear. "Sure, yes, I'll certainly ask her." He shoved his phone into the back pocket of his jeans. "That was Frederick. I need to go down to his office to give him my card for our honeymooners. I usually have a drink and a cigar with him when I stay here. Would you mind if I went down for an hour? We could have dinner when I get back."

"Sure, that's fine. I'll take a bath and have a glass of wine."

His eyes twinkled. "Now you're making me want to stay."

"I'll be here when you return. You deserve to blow off a little steam."

"I'll smell terrible when I get back. Like cigar."

"The shower will be here too," she said, smiling.

"Will you order a steak for me off the menu? Medium rare."

"Baked potato or fries?" she asked.

"Baked. With everything on it."

She rolled her eyes. "Your diet is atrocious."

"You'll save me from myself one of these days." He leaned over, pecking her on the mouth. "I won't be long."

"Have fun." She looked up at him, wishing he wasn't going, even for a short time. Was this what is was like to be madly in love? She didn't want to be away from him even for a minute. It didn't matter, though. She must let him go and have a little fun. The poor man deserved it. She tugged on his arm, planting a kiss in the middle of his palm. "I love you."

He knelt by the couch and cradled her face in his hands. "I love you. So damn much."

"I think we should get married," she said.

He laughed. "Well, that *is* good news. But you need to wait until I can ask you properly. And it's going to be a surprise. A grand gesture like in the movies."

"If you insist."

"And a ring so big it's embarrassing."

She rolled her eyes. "It's not the size that counts."

"Said no woman ever." A shiver went down her spine as he kissed her on the mouth. "I'll see you in a few."

Seconds later, the door clicked shut behind him. She checked to make sure the door was locked. Using the phone in the bar, she ordered food next: grilled chicken for her, steak for him. She poured a glass of wine and snuggled onto the couch. Without much enthusiasm, she flipped through television channels with the remote. Nothing held her interest. Her eyes felt heavy. She yawned as she pulled a blanket over her and lay lengthwise on the couch.

She dozed. A knock on the door woke her. Room service already? She forced herself off the couch, padding across the suite. She would need a tip. *Where did I put my purse?* On the bar? Yes, there it was. She grabbed a five-dollar bill from her wallet and trudged to the door as she stifled a yawn. The second she opened the door, she knew she'd made a mistake. An enormous man with a barrel chest and no neck shoved a revolver into her sternum. She screamed, but he clapped his hand over her mouth and thrust her against the wall, the gun aimed at her throat. "Be quiet or you die."

In two swift movements, he gagged her with a thick cloth and tied her hands behind her back. A muslin bag was thrust over her head. The gun poked into the middle of her back as he grabbed her wrists in his fat, hot hands and steered her forward.

The door squeaked, and she almost tripped as *No-Neck* pushed her into the hallway. *Remain calm.* She conjured an image of the elk. *Be strong.* Somehow, she would get out of this. *I have to. I have so many reasons to live.*

They walked no more than ten steps. "Stop here," he said. She heard a keycard slipping into a slot, and then the swing of a door. *We're down the hall from our suite.* No-Neck shoved her, and she stumbled forward.

He untied the string around her neck and yanked off the bag. She blinked, her eyes adjusting. The suite was similar to theirs but smaller. Rick Murphy sat in a chair by the window. He'd gained at least forty pounds since she'd last seen him in person. A comb-over had replaced his once thick hair. He glared at her with deep set, beady eyes. He held an amber drink in his hand—the only thing about him that hadn't changed in twenty years.

"Leave us, Marvin," he said.

"Yes sir."

She struggled against the tie that bound her hands. It would not budge. Behind her, the door opened and closed.

Murphy set his drink aside and crossed the room with surprising, catlike stealth for a man his size. When he reached her, he pulled a switchblade from his pocket. He pushed a button; the blade sprung open. He rubbed his thumb along the sharp edge. "Dull. Dull knives always hurt the most. Did you know that?" He encased the knife in its cover and slipped it back in his pocket. "You're probably not interested in knives." He spoke in a pleasant tone like they were friends meeting for a drink. "It's been too long. You're lovely, as always. I've seen all your movies."

She stared up at him, helpless. Bile rose to the back of her throat.

He dragged her by the arm over to the window and shoved her onto a hardback chair. Her hands were still tied together at the wrist, but he further immobilized her by tying them to the back of the chair.

"First things first. You're wondering how I got here, what, with the entire world watching your interview tonight. It aired an hour ago, and you really outdid yourself. I snuck up here wearing jeans and a baseball cap. No one looked twice at me. The working man's invisible, Gennie, which is who I've been fighting for my entire career. Health care. Working wages. Good schools. I've done so much good, but none of that will be remembered, thanks to you." He sat in the other chair, picking up his drink and downing it. "I need another drink." Keeping his eyes on her, he walked over to the bar and poured another three fingers into his glass. He studied her from there, with his head cocked to the side. "I don't know what to do with you, Gennie. I tried to work with you all these years. What I asked of you was so simple, and yet, you couldn't do it. And now, I have all kinds of problems. They're stacking up one by one. By the time this is through, I'll have nothing left." He sat back in the chair, crossing his legs. His socks were a plaid—blue and red. "These women will not shut up. All my life, women just keep talking and talking. All day, every day. I just want you all to shut your mouths." His words were starting to slur.

Good. Get nice and drunk.

"I've brought you here to see if we might work out an arrangement. One that involves your silence. I've been watching your interviews, and they've given me a lot of information. For one, I know who you love." He waggled a finger at her, then sipped from his drink. "In my experience, Gennie, when I figure out what a person loves and what they're willing to sacrifice to have it, I have them right where I want them. I can get what I want, by threatening to destroy what they love. It's all so simple, really."

He stood unsteadily, holding on to the back of his chair for support. "You've been clever; I have to admit that. I've always appreciated a clever adversary. Locking the girl and your mother away behind your millionaire friend's gates was smart. It all went wrong when your mother felt the need to defend herself, which I knew she would. Nice Wisconsin girls take motherhood seriously. She couldn't stand for the world to think she was a bad mother because you see, deep down, that's her greatest fear. I knew when we got that idiot she worked with to make up stories, we'd get her out of that compound." He returned to the bar, pouring more whiskey into his tumbler. "Your mother's not dead on purpose. The driver angled it just right to ensure he didn't kill them, just maim them, therefore pulling you out of your haven.

"The problem became what to do with you. How to best hurt you? Death? Burning your beautiful face? What would cause the most pain? I've debated, made a list of pros and cons. Death for Genevieve Banks or death for Stefan Spencer?"

She flinched. Straining against the gag in her mouth, she tried to speak; it was no use. Nothing came out but a muffled scream that proved how right he was. *Not Stefan. Please, not Stefan.*

"Ah, see there. That's what you love. Stefan Spencer. However, now they'll link it to me if he suddenly ends up dead in the Hudson. It certainly adds to my list of troubles if I have your boyfriend murdered. So, I'm in a conundrum." He snapped his fingers as he returned to his chair. "Something occurred to me, though. Something important. You're in love. You were reunited with this baby you gave up. You have a lot to live for. You probably want to live more than you ever have. Love does that to a person.

"You want to live. To punish you the most, I will take your life. But if I do that, it must be the end of the road for me too. There's no escaping. I'm going to jail. Even after all my sacrifice for the good of the American people, they'll hunt me down like an animal. And I unequivocally cannot go to jail. I'm as good as dead in jail. Hell, there's more girls too. Tomorrow more will start to come forward, like fucking sheep." He drank, smacking his lips as he swallowed. "Have you been out to the balcony in your suite? Probably not. The view from the twentieth floor is fantastic. It's high. High enough to kill a person if they jumped. Have you ever contemplated that in any of the hotels you've stayed in? I hadn't. But today, it came to me. A fall from this balcony would end in death for whomever fell or was pushed or jumped. This was my way out. Once a decision is made, there's great a sense of relief, almost a state of euphoria. So, I decided to get good and drunk, and then toss you off this balcony—right before I jump myself." His words slurred.

"Of all the girls, I've only had to kill one. I misjudged her. She wasn't the type to be quiet, even after I threatened to hurt her loved ones. Feisty and trashy, as it turns out. Wouldn't keep her trap shut, and I finally figured out why. She didn't love anything or anyone. Nothing mattered to her except survival. I can't work with a person like that. The little bitch threatened blackmail. Next day she was dead. They never found her body."

He finished his drink, staring at her with bleary eyes. "I never thought it would be nice-girl Genevieve Banks who took me down. My mother used to say, 'it's that which you worry over that never happens.' Your ultimate demise comes from the one thing that never occurred to you."

Use your head. He's drunk and unsteady. Tied to the chair, how could she move? If only she could wriggle free, she could lunge for him. *Use your legs. Rise up with the chair on your back and lunge for him.*

"Well, it's best we get on with it." He stood, swaying. "I don't feel a thing. Everything's numb."

He leaned over her, reaching behind the chair to untie the rope, his crotch in her face. She shuddered with repulsion. *Stay focused. You know what to do.* The years of her acting training, like an athlete with muscle memory, roared to life. *Do not succumb to fear. Practice 'as if.' This is an acting exercise. An improv.* She closed her eyes, growing imaginary muscles, imaginary strength of mind and spirit. *I am a soldier, all muscle and rage, fighting an evil enemy. A fearless warrior triumphing over evil. My body is strong, my mind quicker than my enemy.*

The minute the rope around her waist loosened, she shot up like the clown in a toy jack-in-a-box. She butted the top of her head into his crotch, causing him to cry out and stumble several feet. In the next second, she hurled herself into him. Because of his inebriation, it was enough to knock him backward and onto the floor. Like a bug on its back, Murphy tried to resurrect himself, but before he could get his bearings, she stomped the heel of her boot into his crotch. He screamed and struggled to rise. She moved her foot to his chest, pinning him to the floor. *You will die. I must live to love. I must save my village. A warrior would go for the jugular.* She gouged the heel of her boot against his windpipe. His face reddened, beady eyes blazing. Should she kill him this way? Suffocate him to death? No. *Make him suffer by sending him to spend the rest of his life in a prison.* Yes, that fate was worse than dying. He'd said so himself. She released his neck. *Knock him out. Use your Oregon boots to knock him out.* With the steel-toe of her boot, she kicked the side of his head, hard. He convulsed with an awful shudder. Then, nothing. Motionless, his eyes stared blankly up at the ceiling. Had he passed out? Or, had she killed him? *Oh, my God, what have I done?* Without the use of her hands, she couldn't feel his pulse. It didn't matter now. Whatever she'd done to him would have to be dealt with later. *I have to get out of this room. How can I open the door with my hands tied? Think.*

She looked around the room, frantic. She rushed to the door. It was not a doorknob, but a handle! If she turned around and tugged on it with her tied hands, perhaps it would open. She looked behind her. Murphy remained where he was, lifeless. With her back to the door, she lifted her arms as high as they would go and found the handle with her fingers. She pushed down on it, then pulled the door open as far as she could, and did a pirouette like a ballerina ninja, catching the door with her foot before it closed. She slipped out to the hallway. No one. Not a no-neck monster in sight.

She ran to the elevator, punching the button with her hip. How long would it take? Her heart pounded hard in her chest. Perspiration dripped into her eyes. Her legs shook, threatening to collapse. *Stay brave. Almost done. Please come. Please come. Please come.*

The hum of the elevator's approach almost made her cry with relief. When the doors opened, she stumbled inside, hitting the lobby button with her hip. Down she went, one floor after another, until they reached the eighth floor. She held her breath as the doors opened. *Please God, don't let it be the no-neck monster.*

The honeymoon couple, dressed for dinner, stumbled into the elevator. The wife gasped. *What was her name? Something odd. Star. That was it.* "Ms. Banks. Oh my God." The doors closed and the elevator plunged a floor. Gennie inhaled through her nose, trying to calm her rapid heart. A tiny squeak escaped from her chest.

"Don, get this thing off her mouth."

"Yes, yes, of course." Don moved closer. "I'll be gentle, okay?"

Gennie nodded. He went behind her, tugging until finally the gag came free. Her mouth felt raw and sore, and her throat was so dry she wasn't sure she would be able to speak. "Thank you."

"I have a pocket knife," Don said. "I'm going to cut the ties around your wrists. Please stay still."

"You poor thing. Were you kidnapped?" Her hands flew to her mouth. "Was it Rick Murphy? Did he do this to you? Don, call 911."

"Yes. A man with a gun showed up at my door and took me to one of the suites. Murphy was there. I think I may have killed him." She breathed in and out, fighting hysteria. "He was drunk, so I managed to knock him down, then I kicked him in the head and he stopped moving."

Don was talking into his phone. "Yes, we found Genevieve Banks in the elevator, gagged and tied. She says Rick Murphy kidnapped her. Send police to the Met Hotel immediately. What? No, she's okay. She escaped, and we found her in the elevator. She's shaken up, nearly hysterical, and she has rope burns on her wrists. Rick Murphy's unconscious in one of the suites on the twentieth floor." He stopped, looking over at Gennie. "Do you know which one?"

"P8," Gennie said.

He repeated this into the phone. "She's afraid he may be dead, but she's not sure. Ms. Banks, is he armed?"

"He has a knife. I didn't see a gun. But the man who grabbed me from my room has one. Tell them he's most likely somewhere in the hotel," Gennie said.

Don conveyed the message to the operator. Gennie trembled. Black spots danced before her eyes. She leaned against the side of the elevator as the spots grew bigger.

"Star, I think she's going to faint," Don said.

Star reached for her, steadying her with an arm around her waist. "It's all right, Ms. Banks, we've got you."

Don continued to talk into the phone. "Yeah, all right. I won't hang up." He tucked Gennie's arm into his. She leaned against his bulk.

"The operator wants you to know they're sending out dozens of officers as we speak. She wants me to keep her on the line," Don said.

The elevator stopped. They were at the first floor. Doors opened, and the three of them walked into the lobby, Don and Star on either side of her, holding her upright. She scanned the space, looking for No-Neck. Her pulse quickened when she found him, sitting by the fireplace. "He's right there," she whispered. "By the fireplace. The big guy. He's the one who took me from my room."

Don tightened his grip and spoke into the phone. "The guy who grabbed her is in the lobby. He's armed. What should we do? Find a guard? Okay." Don looked around the lobby. "Yes, I see one. By the entrance." He nodded, speaking quietly, as he turned them toward the front desk. "She says to walk to the reception desk and have them alert the guard as to what's happening. The police will be here any second." As if on cue, the faint sound of sirens penetrated the lobby.

No-Neck must have heard them, too, because he stood, looking around the lobby until his gaze landed on Gennie. Surprise, followed by comprehension, washed over his face. He knew. She was safe. His boss was not. He reached inside his jacket and pulled out a gun. With a quick flick of his hand, he fired a shot into the ceiling. "Everybody down. Nobody move." The lobby exploded with panicked screams as people hit the floor. The guard raised his gun, but it was too late. No-Neck shot him. He fell to the ground.

"Yes, he's fired a shot," Don said into the phone as all three of them fell to their knees. "Guard's been shot."

"Hang up the phone," No-Neck said, striding toward them.

At that same moment, on the other side of the lobby, Stefan and Frederick appeared in the entryway of the bar. They halted like a glass wall had suddenly fallen from the ceiling. She locked eyes with Stefan for a split second. He tipped his chin. A message. *Keep his attention on you.*

"The police are almost here," Gennie said.

No-Neck was upon them. He kicked Don's phone from his hand, keeping the gun pointed at Gennie. "You two, on your bellies."

Don and Star obeyed. Stefan and Frederick, as silent as cat burglars, inched around the wall toward them. Gennie put her hands in the air, still on her knees. "Take me," she said. "But let the rest of them go. I'm who you want. You can use me to get what you want. I killed your boss." She said all this as she slowly stood. "He won't be able to protect you."

No-Neck stared at her with glittering eyes. He hesitated. *I surprised him. He doesn't know what to do.* That indecision cost him because Stefan was behind him now, stealth as a cat. Stefan kicked him in the back of the knees. No-Neck's legs buckled, and he fell to the floor. The gun went off, its boom deafening amid more screams. The bullet landed in the wall behind the front desk. Before No-Neck could recover, Frederick kicked him in the ribs. No-Neck cried out as Don leaped to his feet and kicked the gun out of his hand. It slid several feet. Like they were in a hockey match, Stefan ran to the gun and passed it like it was a puck over the white marble floor to Frederick. Seamlessly, like they were playing a friendly afternoon game, Frederick caught it with his foot, then scooped it off the floor and pointed it at No-Neck.

"Don't move, asshole," Frederick said.

The entrance swarmed with officers, guns raised. Everything happened at once. At least a dozen of them headed up the stairs, while another half dozen took the elevator. Several advanced on No-Neck, cuffing him and dragging him across the lobby and out the door. Paramedics swooped in and put the guard onto a stretcher. Frederick, near the entrance of the hotel, spoke with two men in suits. Detectives. *They will want to talk to me. What should I tell them? That I killed a man out of sheer rage?*

Stefan pulled her into his arms, and she collapsed against him. "My God, what happened?"

"His henchman knocked on the door, and I wasn't thinking. I thought it was room service. He grabbed me." She told him the rest in a halting voice, finishing with her awful suspicion. "I think I may have killed him."

"You escaped, baby. That's all that matters."

"I thought I was going to die, and all I could think of was how much I wanted to live. I wanted to see you and my family one more time. If these two hadn't found me, I don't know where we'd all be."

Next to them, Don and Star clung to one another like ragdolls.

Gennie explained to Stefan how they'd found her in the elevator and quickly figured out what was happening. "Don had the presence of my mind to call 911 and get the police here. Thank you, both. I don't know what I would have done if you hadn't been in the elevator. You kept your head, Don. It was amazing. Truly."

"When he pulled out that gun, I thought he was going to start shooting," Star said.

"Me too," Don said. "Holy shit, this is not how I thought we'd spend our first night in the Big Apple."

"I was freaked," Star said. "Scared out of my mind. We're from Kansas. My mother didn't want us to come to New York— too dangerous. What will she think now?"

"You tell her that you and Don saved a lot of lives today and to stop worrying about you."

Star smiled. "I knew the minute I saw you that Murphy had gotten you. We'd just finished watching your interview. I'm a big fan." She blushed. "It was like my mind just turned super calm all of the sudden." She looked at her husband. "I'm usually afraid of everything."

"Not today, sweetie," Don said. "I'm so proud of you."

"I'm proud of you," Star said.

"From now on, don't be afraid of things," Gennie said. "It's just a waste of energy."

"And you're obviously able to handle yourself," Stefan said to Star. He brought Gennie closer. "As are you, baby. You don't have to be afraid of the monster any longer. You took care of him."

"My acting training came in handy today. I never thought all those classes would be good for anything except being skilled at my job. Turns out they were good for more."

He grinned. "And here we thought acting was vapid."

She turned to Don and Star. "I'm afraid the police will want to talk to you. It's not exactly what you had in mind for your honeymoon. I'm sorry about that."

Don snapped his fingers. "With all the excitement, I forgot to thank you for paying for us to stay. It's a dream come true for us."

"Yes, thank you," Star said.

They were interrupted by several detectives. They introduced themselves as Detectives Burns and Turner. Both men were dressed in dark suits. The taller of the two, with bloodshot eyes, did the talking. "We have some questions, Ms. Banks, as well as for you two. Can you follow us, please?"

"Can I come with her?" Stefan asked. "She's been through hell."

"I'm afraid not. We need to speak to each of them alone. Protocol," Detective Turner said.

Stefan kissed her cheek. "It's okay, sweetheart. I'll be right here waiting for you."

*   *

Later, Gennie sat in their room in front of the fire. Despite the warm blanket wrapped around her shoulders, she couldn't seem to get warm. The last few hours had passed in a blur of questions, followed by details from the police about Murphy's fate. When the officers arrived, they found him passed out on the floor, very much alive. He had a large bump on the side of his head, but the alcohol was more to blame for his incapacitation than Gennie's boot.

While she was being questioned, Stefan, worried that they might have seen the story on the news or social media, had called her mother and Lee, along with the crew back in River Valley, to reassure them that Gennie was safe and to tell them the details of what had transpired.

The minute she could, Gennie called her mother. "Mom, it's me. I'm okay."

"Thank God. Gennie, it's over. We're safe."

"We can finally move on," Gennie said.

"Thank God."

"How's your doctor?"

"He's fine. Very attentive."

I'll bet he is. "Mom, it's time for you to move on too. Dad's been gone a long time. You deserve to be happy again."

"Perhaps you're right."

"You say yes when that cute doctor asks you out," Gennie said.

"Do you think he will?"

"Well, maybe not for a while since you're in traction. But he has a good excuse to see you every day."

"Yes, he does that. I love you Gennie girl. I'm thankful you're okay. You're my brave girl. Always have been."

"I love you too, Mom."

After they hung up, she called Sarah.

"You must have been scared," Sarah said.

"I was. I wasn't sure I was going to get out of there alive."

"You don't have to be afraid anymore. You're free," Sarah said.

"I am. It feels good. I can finally move on."

"I have something to ask you. A favor," Sarah said. "I got a note from school today. My dad says he doesn't have money for next semester. I'll have drop out if I can't come up with the money."

"I'll pay it, sweetie. I'll set up an account for you too, so you have some living money."

"Are you sure?"

"More than sure. I'm happy to do it."

"I have to leave tomorrow, so I won't see you before you get back."

"I'm going to stay for another week here to help my mom, but I'll be in Malibu after that. We can see each other then, if you want? You could stay at the house for the weekend."

"I would love that," Sarah said.

"We have a lot of time to get to know each other, so don't worry about that."

"Do you think you'll come to River Valley ever again?" Sarah asked.

Gennie glanced at Stefan. He was gazing into the fire with his lids half-closed and his arms crossed over his chest. "I do. I'm going to buy a piece of land and have a house built. What do you think of that idea?"

She could hear the smile in Sarah's voice. "Really? That would be great. I'm going to apply for a teaching job here when I finish school. I belong here. I can't explain it, but I know it's true."

"I understand perfectly." Gennie stood and went to the window to look out at the lights of Manhattan. "When's your spring break?"

"Middle of March."

"Maybe we can take a little trip up to Oregon to look at property. Would you be up for that?"

"Totally."

"Good. Will you call me when you get home, so I know you're safe?" Gennie asked.

"I will. And, Gennie, I'm glad you're finally free."

"Me too."

EPILOGUE

STEFAN'S PHONE WOKE GENNIE on a morning in early January, its insistent ring impossible to ignore. He rolled over with a groan and answered in a sleep-soaked voice. "Hello. Oh, hey Martin." Gennie smiled to herself. An early morning call in January from his manager could only mean one thing. Stefan was nominated for an Oscar. She almost laughed as all traces of sleepiness vanished from his face.

What?" He sat upright, wiping his eyes. "You're kidding? Well, hell yeah, it's wonderful. I'm just shocked. Sure. Yeah, I'll call you later this morning." When he hung up, he looked over at Gennie. "You won't believe it."

She pushed the hair out of her eyes. "You got a nomination for *Vice*."

"Am I dreaming?"

"No, sir. This is as real as it gets. I knew it. You're the only one who doesn't know how enormously gifted you are."

He took her hand. "It's weird to think I filmed that movie before I met you. It seems a lifetime ago."

She sidled up next to him. "Well, I'm pretty sure you're here. And so am I…and we're already awake."

He grinned as he turned off his phone. "Let's put the phone on sleep mode, shall we?"

"Great idea."

* *

The night of the Oscars, Gennie wore a soft-gray gown made of sheer tulle and embellished with flowered embroidery and tiny beads down the bodice. Stefan was dashing in a black tuxedo and bowtie. She felt like a fairy princess as she and Stefan sat in their assigned seats in the Dolby Theatre. The show, always long, seemed interminable as the awards were given out one by one. The Best Actor category was one of the last awards of the night. *I'm a wreck. It's worse than when I was nominated.*

Finally, the Best Actor category arrived. Presenting the award was Matthew McConaughey and Kate Winslet, both of whom Gennie adored. When they had taken their seats earlier, Kate had stopped by to say hello and wish Stefan luck, which sounded twice as good with her British accent.

Matthew announced the nominees. It was an impressive group. For the first time, she started having doubts. Stefan hadn't participated in the usual campaigning that went on behind the scenes, saying he'd rather win on his own merits, not because he ran a good campaign.

Kate opened the envelope. She smiled.

Please let it be Stefan.

"The Academy Award goes to Stefan Spencer," said Kate.

Gennie jumped to her feet, clapping so hard her hands hurt. Around them, his friends and colleagues from *Vice* all stood, applauding and cheering. Stefan looked stunned for a moment but quickly gathered himself.

"Congratulations, baby," she said.

"I love you." He kissed Gennie before walking up the steps to the stage. *My heart's going to explode from happiness.* Finally, he had the recognition he deserved. On stage, Matthew handed him the statue. Kate hugged him before she and Matthew moved upstage to let Stefan have the podium.

Stefan appeared strangely calm. *The man has nerves of steel.* "Thank you to the Academy." He reached into his tuxedo jacket where he'd tucked his speech, but instead of the notecard she saw him prepare earlier, he pulled out a small box. *What is he doing?* It looked like a jewelry box of some kind. Her heart pounded. Sweat gathered on the end of her nose. *Oh no, he isn't doing it now? It can't be.*

He spoke into the microphone. "This award is the greatest honor of my life. Thank you to everyone involved in the film. As a little boy dreaming big dreams in the woods of British Columbia, I couldn't have predicted this incredible life God's granted me. However, I have one more dream, something that would outdo all other awards or achievements, and that is if the woman of my dreams, the love of my life, would agree to marry me. Genevieve Banks, will you be my wife?"

At the Oscars? Holy crap. It was a grand gesture all right. She nodded her head and mouthed yes. The crowd cheered so loudly it sounded like a football stadium rather than an award ceremony.

Next to her, Stefan's costar nudged her. "Get up there."

"I don't know. I shouldn't."

"Yes, go."

Behind her, the director of the film, Michael Conway, leaned forward. "Go, now. Before they start the music."

She stumbled on shaky legs up the aisle as he walked away from the podium. When he reached her, he set the Oscar on the floor next to him and dropped to one knee. Taking her hand, he placed the diamond ring on her wedding finger.

The princess cut diamond was enormous and sparkled under the stage lights. He'd accomplished his goal. *This ring is embarrassing, but I don't care. I love it.* The music had started by then. The director was probably having a fit in the booth, wanting them off stage. Kate and Matthew came forward, ushering them backstage.

"I cannot believe you did this," Gennie said. "I don't know whether I'm mad or glad," she joked.

He pulled her into his arms. "Go big or go home, baby."

"But it was your night. Your win."

"Nothing is as big a win as you," he said. "Don't you ever forget it."

*   *

After the show, their driver held the limo door open for them. Inside, a bottle of wine was on ice. "I hear there's some celebrating to be done," he said, handing them each a glass.

"Yes sir," Stefan said. "This beautiful woman is going to be my wife. Can you believe it?"

"You're one lucky SOB, young man," said the driver. "Which party will you be attending?"

"We'll be going back to Malibu," Gennie said. "We're having a party of our own."

"With our friends," Stefan said.

Our real friends. Their friends from their real home.

"Excellent. We should be in Malibu in about forty-five minutes. There are some appetizers laid out for you to enjoy. Just knock on the window if you need anything at all."

They traveled the city streets of Los Angeles at a slow pace. Traffic was terrible, as usual. Gennie thought of River Valley, longing for the peace and quiet, the brilliance of the stars, the clear water of the river. *Soon we will be home, and this will be the place we visit.*

They talked of nothing and everything during that ride to the beach house: the children they would have, trips they wanted to take together, Sarah's impending graduation and whether she would be able to get a teaching job in River Valley, and of her mother's surprise announcement that she would be staying in New York until the spring. Therapy, she had said, but Gennie knew it was the handsome doctor who kept her there.

"I want us to make a pact to never spend more than two weeks apart," he said.

"I agree. Which means we'll have to juggle projects." She'd already decided on that day months ago when she'd squatted in the snow beside the river that she would not sell her soul to the devil for money. "I'm only accepting projects that mean something to me."

"That goes for me too." He reached across the seat and picked up his Oscar. "I'm at peace now. Nothing left to prove, other than to you. I'll try and be a good husband, Gennie. I won't be perfect, but I hope to be worthy of a husband Oscar. I'll spend my life trying."

"Stefan, you've already proven all I need to know about you."

He set the Oscar next to him on the seat. "He'll look nice next to yours in our new house, don't you think?"

"Is it gauche to place them on the mantle?" She laughed. "Don't answer that. I know the answer's yes, but I don't care."

By this time, they were driving along the coastal highway, cresting waves illuminated in the moonlight. "What a night," he said.

She looked out the window, catching her reflection. The little girl she once was met her gaze. *You did it. You followed the light. You lived. You won.*

When they arrived back to the beach house, their River Valley crew was gathered on the patio. Gennie had arranged for a private plane to fly them all down at once, and everyone was there, even Annie, with tiny baby Beatrice. Everyone cheered as they walked up the steps. Bella was the first to reach her, throwing her arms around her. "I'm so happy for you, Gennie."

The men were gathered around Stefan, congratulating him on his win of both the statue and the girl, as servers passed around glasses of champagne and cider.

"Stefan, speech, speech," called Tommy, hitting his fork against a wine glass.

Stefan laughed. "I think the world has heard just about enough from me tonight."

Gennie raised her hand. "I'd like to."

Everyone gathered around her. She took a moment to take in the dear faces of the people she loved. *I'm the luckiest girl in the world.*

"First, thank you for being here not only for Stefan's win, but also to share this happy night with us. We fell in love in your town, where we felt safe and free for the first time in many years. The support you gave me during such an awful time—it is not something I will ever forget. Your friendships helped me heal and gave me the courage to face my fiercest foe, literally with the heel and toe of those badass boots you all gave me."

She stole a glance at Stefan, his eyes glassy. "We've purchased property in River Valley. A beautiful spot not far from Lee and Tommy's, with access to the river. We love our piece of land, as we love all of you. We break ground the minute the weather allows. I'm starting a foundation for women, victims of assault and abuse, headquartered in River Valley. Women like Annie and me, who endured the unspeakable, yet survived. I want to help others like us, who may not have the means or the power to fight back. We will help them fight. We will help them get their lives back." She glanced at Mike, letting her eyes twinkle at him. "A wise man once told me that you know who your friends are when times are hard. In times of fortune, having those same people there to share it with makes it all the sweeter. So, neighbors, God bless you. Thank you. Now, let us eat, drink, and be merry."

There were cheers, more toasts, and much clinking of glasses. They feasted on Mexican food as the Santa Ana winds blew smog and clouds away from the coast. The stars appeared, and the moon hung low over the sea. Tommy grabbed his guitar and began to play softly under the stars, the crashing waves his background singers.

And they danced.

*   *

Thank you for reading my latest book baby. I hope you enjoyed it! Please consider leaving a review on Amazon. Every review, no matter the length, helps spread the word about the book.

Also, I love to hear from you. Below are links to my social media pages. Stop by and say hello or follow me for all the latest news on releases, contests and my ongoing struggle with what to make for dinner.

Facebook
https://www.facebook.com/AuthorTessThompson/

Twitter
https://twitter.com/TessWrites

Pinterest
https://www.pinterest.com/tesswrites/

Instagram
https://www.instagram.com/tessielou44/

Amazon Author Page
https://www.amazon.com/-/e/B004W3WOTG

Made in the USA
Monee, IL
07 October 2021

79571702R00115